The Vengeance of Love

The Vengeance of Love

The Blood of Velho: Book 1

LoriO

THE VENGEANCE OF LOVE

First edition. July 29, 2025.

ISBN: 979-8998757518

Written by LoriO.

Cover Design by Andy Payne

DEDICATION

To the God above—thank you for the incredible blessing of this story and for constantly reminding me that you use imperfect people in your perfect plan.

To Gerta—thank you for forcing me to believe in myself. Chasing a dream is the scariest thing in the world, and I couldn't have done it without you by my side. Your encouragement and unwavering faith in me made all the difference. Te dua shumë.

To my sister, Marci—thank you for obsessing over every scene and character with me. I couldn't have done this without you, nor would I have wanted to. Your support and excitement turned this into an incredible—and slightly ridiculous—adventure. The mansion is just a tiny bit closer now.

Know thyself.

— Inscription at the Temple of Apollo at Delphi

Part I.
Trust.

Chapter 1

The prison had a specific unpleasant smell, a combination of sweat, blood, and stale piss, and Chello tried not to think about the things that went on behind closed doors as he and Greyson were led down the dimly lit hallway. The clanking sound of each steel-barred door the guard opened for them echoed in his head, and he didn't like being down here.

The guard led them to the end of the prison hall and pointed. "That's the one you want. But be warned, she's slippery and has a knack for cutting loose and escaping. If you've come to beat her, I suggest doing it inside the cell with the door locked."

"We're not here to *beat* her," Chello told him incredulously.

The guard shrugged and stepped away, leaning against the far wall disinterestedly.

Chello peered into the cell and got his first look at her, the prisoner they needed help from. She was in the corner, upside down, feet against the wall, doing vertical push-ups. Her arm muscles were well-defined, but he couldn't make out much more. Whoever she was, she was strong.

"We've come to have a little chat," Greyson told her.

Chello watched as she paused briefly, then continued her exercise.

Greyson let out an aggravated sigh. He wasn't known for his patience. He was older than most of the Praectors, his liege was the head of security, one of the most important people in the city.

Greyson was serious, rarely smiled, and had little patience. He was tall and broad-shouldered, with black hair showing flecks of gray. In contrast, Chello was of average height and stockier, had closely cropped blond hair, and had much more patience.

"Listen to me, *girl!* Come here!" Greyson barked.

Chello watched as the prisoner stopped and slowly let her feet fall from the wall and then stood up, her breath heavy in her chest. She was tall and lean, her mocha skin stretched over well-toned muscles. Her hair was a long, dark, tangled mass of unruliness, evidence of time spent in her cell. She slowly walked over to the bars that separated them, and he saw no fear in her sharp hazel eyes.

"What do you want...*boy?*" she retorted.

Chello had to fight back a smile. What a bold thing she was. She may not know who they were, but both he and Greyson were in full uniform, which must tell her this was something official. Yet, she didn't care as she bit back at Greyson.

"Are you the one who escaped the Greensk prison?" Greyson asked, and behind them, there was a shuffling noise.

Chello turned and looked at the cell across the corridor. A small, thin-framed man with spectacles, barely more than a boy, moved to his cell door to listen in.

"Why? They want me back?" the girl asked, turning away from them. She proceeded to stretch her sides, leaning from right to left.

"Face me when I'm talking to you, prisoner!" Greyson demanded.

She turned around and scoffed, yet didn't move back to the door. "What're you gonna do, big man? Come in here and get that fancy uniform dirty?"

Again, Chello was shocked at her mouth. He watched as she squinted, recognition washing over her face.

"I remember you," she told Greyson.

Chello furrowed his brow and looked at him. That would be unlikely, but he saw how Greyson shifted uncomfortably, his eyes flickering towards him.

"Just answer the question, will you? No sense making things worse for yourself," Greyson told her.

Behind them, the small man hit his hands against the bars of his cell, prompting the woman to look over.

She nodded at the other prisoner and then crossed her arms over her chest. "Yeah. I did," she admitted.

Greyson nodded. "How did you do it?"

The woman unfolded her arms and put them on her hips. "I don't kiss and tell. Sorry, big man," she taunted, and Greyson grimaced.

Chello could tell he was going to lose his patience, and that wouldn't help any of them. Like it or not, they needed this prisoner's help.

"If I may?" Chello asked politely.

The woman looked at him, his gentle tone throwing her off.

"It's Mina, right? I'm Chello, and this is Greyson. We're Praectors for the Peterman family, who run city security." He paused, but when she didn't speak, he continued: "Greensk prison is notoriously

3

impossible to penetrate, so what you did is rather extraordinary. We'd like to understand how you did so."

The woman let a sly grin spread over her face and took a measured step forward, looking from Chello to Greyson. "What is this, good cop, bad cop?"

Chello smiled. "More like handsome cop, ugly cop," he said, motioning to himself, then to Greyson, who glared at him. "But in any case, we need your help."

She smiled, and again the man in the cell across from her banged on his bars, and she looked over at him.

Chello turned and saw him make a few gestures with his hands, but the guard who brought them down took out his club and banged it on his cell bars, sending the small man scrambling back into its depths.

The woman glared at the guard but then turned her attention back to them. "Surely, you don't think I would help you out of the kindness of my heart, do you, boys? What's in it for me? Should I have any information you need?"

"Your shithole life is what's in it for you!" Greyson snapped.

Chello put up his hand, trying to calm him. "If you help us, we'll give you your freedom."

She stepped forward and moved in front of him, looking into his eyes. "My freedom?" she asked doubtfully.

"Yes. The head of security has given us the authority to offer such. Can you tell us what you know?"

Chello watched as her eyes briefly cut over to the prisoner behind them, and then she swallowed, pacing her small cell.

"There's no magic secret. It was luck, and a whole lot of help from the God," she told him. "But if you want to know what I did,

4

how I got out and through the deadly marshes surrounding it, I'll share that for my freedom."

Greyson laughed before Chello could respond. "I'm afraid we're going to need a lot more than that, girl," he told her with a sneer. He looked at the guard and said, "Cuff her, hands and feet, and get her out."

Greyson turned and began walking down the corridor, and Chello turned to do the same. He stopped when the woman called out:

"I'll need Yip with me." She motioned to the man in the other cell. "He did most of the calculating when we were in Greensk."

Chello looked at the man who had edged back out to the bars of his cell and nodded at the guard. "Both of them," Chello told him, and walked back down the corridor after Greyson.

***

It didn't take long for the guards to bring them forward, both the woman and the skimpy man-boy from the other cell. They were shackled hands and feet, and then together. Chello frowned, looking at the head guard who led them into the holding room.

"Are all these chains necessary?" he asked.

The guard scoffed. "I told you, this one likes to escape," he said, knocking his elbow into the back of Mina's head.

Greyson grunted a laugh.

Chello looked them up and down, the woman dark and strong, the man thin and frail, with white skin that looked like it hadn't seen the sun in a very long time. His head was a greasy mess of blondish-brown hair, and his thin face seemed too small for his wire-rimmed spectacles. They seemed an unlikely pairing.

"We have a team standing by on the topside. I think we can take them from here," Chello told the guards, and all of them snickered.

"You don't get it, do you? She's slippery, no matter how shackled you have her. You'll want us to take them up with you in the box," the guard told him, and Chello stared at him with hard eyes.

"We'll take our chances, friend. Greyson and I are highly trained and pretty slippery ourselves."

"Suit yourselves," the guard shrugged and handed the chain lead over to him.

Chello took it, and he and Greyson got into the elevator box with the two prisoners. He looked at the woman curiously, wondering how she was so skilled at escaping.

"Don't worry, I won't try anything," she told him with a smirk. "Not yet anyway. I'm interested to see if you keep your word. If you go back on it, then I'll disappear."

Chello couldn't help but smile back. "I appreciate that, thank you."

Greyson scowled at him, the pleasantries with a criminal seeming unnecessary to him. "Let's go!" he spat out, and they closed the gate and ascended out of the prison.

Chapter 2

Mina walked next to Yip, their shackles making it difficult to maneuver without stumbling into each other. When they had reached the top, which was ground level, they were brought through a series of corridors and then shoved through an open doorway. They stumbled as they entered, and Mina saw that the room was already full of people. Everyone was sitting at a large, polished table, and all heads turned, and conversations stopped as they entered.

Greyson pointed at two chairs, side by side. "Sit. Both of you," he ordered, and locked their chains to the floor bolt.

Mina let her eyes sweep the room, counting the numbers. Fourteen in total, a mix of men and women, all wearing the same deep green and gold uniform. Like the men who came and got her, most had the same strange eyes, the left pupil a bright green color.

She watched as the man called Greyson went to the other end of the table and sat next to someone who looked like he was in charge. His uniform was slightly different, a gold sash running across the chest with various medals pinned to it. He was older, with more gray hair than black on his cropped head and in his trimmed beard.

Greyson leaned in and whispered to him, and the man nodded, maintaining his hard and intense face. He had an air of superiority about him, and he looked around as if everything and everyone were a waste of his time. Mina sensed something when she looked at him. Not quite one of the visions she sometimes got when things were about to turn bad, but a certain uneasiness.

Her senses and instincts were always spot on, a magical gift from the God, her mother used to tell her. When she was in danger, she usually knew it moments before it happened. She had a knack for seeing the way out of impossible situations, warnings, and triggers going off inside of her. That wasn't happening now, but her insides clenched a bit at the sight of the man in charge.

Mina let her eyes fall on the nice one, Chello, who was also whispering, but to a woman, probably in her late twenties, like Mina, with dark chestnut hair pulled back into a bun. She looked important, uppity perhaps, but not completely indifferent as she looked at them with curious eyes. She didn't have the same strange eyes as the rest of them, both of hers a beautiful shade of blue.

"Well, here we are," the man in charge said out loud, and everyone stopped and paid attention to him. "I asked for one and got two. What a surprise."

"Director Peterman, sir," Chello called out. "She indicated that the man assisted her in her escape, so I thought it best to bring him as well."

The Director nodded and eyed them both. "I'm sure the two of you are curious as to why we have pulled you out of your cells." He stood out of his chair and began to pace in a tight circle, his hands behind his back. "Let me assure you, it's against my better judgment. And if I didn't think it would aid my daughter, you'd be back in the bowels of the prison where you belong."

The woman with the beautiful blue eyes frowned and looked at him, seeming displeased by what he was saying.

"Belong? I'm still waiting to hear the charges leveled at us and the cause of our arrest. We've been stuck in your shitty prison for months now without understanding why," Mina shot back, causing every face in the room to stare at her in disbelief. It was clear that no one spoke to this man in anything but a submissive tone.

The Director laughed, but it wasn't a humorous laugh; it was on the edge of sinister. "Your kind do damage to cities just by existing. Make no mistake about it," he told her. "And as sure as the two moons that rise every night, you can believe I'm not going to let you infect us. Fusia is a city at the forefront of the technological landscape, years ahead of any other in the habitable Sphere of this planet. While others cling to the relics of the past, fumbling with oil lamps and crude mechanics, we've transcended imagination itself. Our tech-no team has revolutionized medicine and devised weapons and devices that others can only dream of. Fusia isn't just at the forefront, we are the very summit of the Sphere. And I will not see the uncivilized taint our existence."

Mina frowned at him, his speech derogatory and self-serving. She let her eyes scan the room, where many stared at the table or their hands, no one appearing to revel in his declaration.

"But let's stay on track, shall we?" he continued. "I understand you've spent some time in the Greensk prison, am I right?"

Mina shifted in her seat. "I have. I give it one star. Terrible accommodations and unfriendly staff," she told him with a smirk. She wanted to make sure he knew she wasn't afraid of him.

Again, most of the people at the table looked at her incredulously, but she noticed Chello trying to hide a small smile.

The Director, however, did not smile. He glared at her and said, "This isn't a game, Mina." He seemed to take pleasure in the shock that was on her face at him knowing her name. "Oh yes, I know your name. I know more about you than I care to know about any criminal, so let's just cut through the crap, shall we? You're the only one, as far as anyone knows, to have escaped the Greensk prison. Not only that, but you also survived the deadly marshes that surround the back side of it. I need to know exactly how you did it."

His eyes, one green and one blue, were drilling into her, and she felt an uneasiness running through her. She scanned the others at the table. Some had parchment and pens at the ready, and some were casually eating from a bowl of fruit, looking on as if watching a play.

"That isn't an easy thing to explain," Mina told him. "There's no script, no plan, or sure-fire route I can share."

The Director nodded and smiled at her, but again, it felt sinister. "That's what I thought." He stood behind his chair and tapped his fingers on the top of it. "So, since you can't tell us how you did it, you're going to have to show us."

Mina felt Yip tense next to her, and his leg started rattling under the table. She slowly reached over and placed her hand on his arm, trying to calm him.

"I don't understand," she told the Director, furrowing her brow.

"The team you see sitting before you is set to embark on a mission into the Greensk prison to free one of our own. You are going to go with them and show them how to do it. Then, once we recover our man, you are to lead the team back out of the marshes safely."

Mina looked at him incredulously, an unbelieving smile spreading on her face. Was he serious? Did he really think such a thing could be accomplished?

"That's impossible," she told him.

"Oh, I think it is, for someone like you. You've done it before, you can do it again. And this time you'll have an elite team with you," he told her, and Mina shook her head.

"That isn't how it works," she told him, and she saw a flash of annoyance cross his face.

"Then why don't you tell us how it works?"

Mina swallowed and looked at Chello. She wasn't sure why she looked at him, but he was the nicest one, and she didn't know where else to turn her attention. He nodded at her as if encouraging her to go on.

"This many people won't make it alive," she said bluntly. "I made it out because I was alone...well, we were alone," she corrected, looking at Yip. "The more people, the more impossible it will be. Everyone will die before they reach the prison."

There was some mumbling around the table, and the Director seemed to think about what she said, and he turned to Greyson and nodded. Mina watched as Greyson stood and pushed some buttons on the wall, causing it to illuminate, a map coming to life. She recognized the city of Greensk immediately, and the prison tower and the marshes it backed up to.

"This is the Greensk prison on the southwest side of Greensk City," Greyson called out, and everyone fell silent. "As you can see, the city sprawls out before it, and the marshes encircle the back of it. What path did you take, girl?"

Mina looked at him, folding her arms across her chest, and then let her eyes move to the map. She had never seen anything like it before, completely projected, not on parchment or a scroll. It seemed to be illuminating from the wall, rather than projected onto it.

"Why would you go in through the marshes? Why not go in through the city and then out from the marshes?" Mina asked, and next to her, Yip tapped her on the shoulder. She looked at him, and he made a series of gestures, and she nodded.

"Is that an option?" someone at the table asked, and Greyson shook his head.

"We can't be seen going anywhere near the city. The team will enter through the marshes. We can't have a repeat of what happened with Jaxon." He looked back at Mina and asked, "How did you do it? Show us."

"Can you unchain us so I can approach the map?" she asked, and everyone looked at the Director.

"Director Peterman?" the man closest to her asked, and he nodded but said:

"If you try to get cute, you will be killed instantly. Do keep that in mind."

Mina smiled at him. "Luckily, cute isn't my thing," she told him, and he scowled at her. She rubbed her wrists once the cuffs were off and walked up to the front of the room, aware that all eyes were on her.

Mina looked at the map, the past coming back to her in memories she would rather not think about...she and Yip, wading through the marshes, every step a gamble between survival and death.

"We escaped through the main waste sewer tunnel, here," she said, pointing. "I'm not sure if they even know that. We replaced the grates as we went. The tunnel dumps out here, in a pool which surrounds the prison tower," she told them, and when she put her finger to the map, a circle illuminated.

"Wow, cool," she murmured, never having seen such technology.

"So, you swam?" Greyson asked.

Mina shook her head. "No, you can't stay in the water. There are dwellers there."

"What's a dweller?" A burly man with dark features asked, concern on his bearded face.

"Creatures that used to be human that lust for flesh and blood. They'll tear you apart with their teeth. They dwell in the water." Mina told him.

Yip banged on the table, and Mina looked at him, and he gestured a bit.

"Yip thinks they're prisoners who were experimented on, experiments that went bad."

"Why do you think that?" Greyson asked Yip, but he didn't speak. "Answer me, boy!"

"Easy, big guy. He can't talk," Mina told him, and he glared at her. She held his stare with her own. "Greensk prison is an experimental playground for those fecks. They use the prisoners as their test rats, doing all sorts of things to them. Yip thinks the dwellers were victims."

The woman with the striking blue eyes let out a concerned sigh, and Chello put his hand on her shoulder, trying to comfort her.

"What then?" Chello asked, seeming to want to move on from the topic of experimental torture of prisoners.

Mina looked at the map, trying to gauge how they came across. "If you can get out of the water without being eaten or drowned, the ledges here and here," she pointed, "will lead back out to the flats. But there are creatures we don't have names for, things you won't believe exist. They have venom and poison in their bite. And they lurk everywhere. And if you survive that, there's quicksand and poisonous gas fissures to get through," she told them, dragging her finger along the map and watching it illuminate.

"Feck's sake, does it ever end?" the burly man asked.

Mina smiled a humorless smile. "That's just half of it. If you can get past the flats, you can find momentary safety by climbing this ridge. There's nothing at the top. But when you come down the other side, the flats continue, and the gas fissures and vapors are deadly. The sky over the marshes is a deep purple, it never changes, never turns light or dark, just the purple haze. And that's because of the gas vapors in the flats. Past that is the vine forest. The vines are alive, they choke and strangle, and swarm once disturbed. Nearly impossible to pass unscathed."

"That all?" the Director asked, his arms folded over his chest, staring at her.

"No. Between all of this are the actual marshes. And those are filled with things that can't be described." Mina winced, thinking of the things that attacked them, the way they almost lost their lives. "We didn't even get a look at most of what tried to kill us. Things in the water with long tentacles, giant poisonous frogs, snakes, and strange, unnamed things." She thought for a moment and then looked over at Yip. "Am I missing anything?"

They all looked at Yip, who again made gestures with his hands and then his midsection.

"Ah, right. How could I forget the thorns? They almost killed you." Mina turned back to the Director and said: "Climbing the ridge, there's a section of thorny brambles. The thorns shoot out at you if you get too close."

Mina looked around at the people at the table, who stared back at her with shocked expressions, none of them understanding how someone could make it out alive. She nodded and folded her arms across her chest.

"There is no set path, so what I've said may change based on the route you take."

"How did you survive all that?" the large, burly man asked.

She wasn't sure, but she thought she detected a hint of awe in his tone. Mina shrugged.

"Sir, if I may, perhaps there's another way…" someone started.

"There is no other way," the Director said coldly.

"You all won't make it. You need to send as few people as possible," Mina told him, and he frowned and motioned for her to go back to her seat.

"What do you suggest?" Greyson asked the Director.

Director Peterman shook his head, looking at the woman. "Aria, maybe this isn't the task for your Vanguard Ascension," he told her, and she frowned.

"Father, I have to do this. We need to get Jaxon back."

The Director frowned. "Jaxon failed his attempt, and now he's reaping the consequences. I can't have you doing the same. It's bad enough to have one child fail, I can't risk two. There are plenty of other options to consider with a lower fail rate."

Mina watched the woman called Aria closely as her father made the statement; she could tell his callous words pained her, but she did a good job of hiding it. What an asshole thing to say in front of everyone, Mina thought. To announce that you weren't afraid of losing your daughter but of her failing and shaming you.

"I won't fail, Father," Aria said boldly.

Director Peterman folded his arms across his chest and slowly nodded, then looked at Mina. "And you will make sure of it. How many can you take in and survive?"

Mina shook her head. "I don't think I could survive alone, no one could. It was a miracle of the God that we got through it once, for feck's sake."

She watched as he leaned his hands on the table and hung his head down, and when he looked up, anger flared in his eyes.

"Your life depends on it. And so does his," he said, looking at Yip. "If you can't take the whole team, how many can you take and survive?"

Mina shook her head again, looking back at him incredulously.

He pursed his lips and stood up straight and snarled, "If the next words out of your mouth are anything but a number, I will kill you right where you sit. So, I beg you to think carefully before you utter a single word. And if you shake your head again, I will have my man knock it off your fecking shoulders. Do you understand me? Now, how many?"

Mina stared at him, wanting very much to rebuke him and fire something back, but her instincts told her this wasn't the time. "One other person," she said evenly.

He shook his head and let out a humorless laugh. "Well, that's not going to happen," he told her. "Do you think I'm stupid enough to send my daughter alone with the likes of you? A dirty criminal?"

"Look, you told me to say how many, and that's pushing it. Yip and I barely made it out. "Going in and out through the marshes is suicide. Maybe... *maybe* coming out would be an option. But if you're telling me I have no choice but to try, I'm telling you the least number of people is our only hope."

"I can go alone with her, Father," Aria interjected, standing, and he glared at her. "It's my Ascension. My responsibility."

"I can't let you go alone," Chello told her, standing as well. "Your safety is *my* responsibility." He looked at the Director and said: "I'll go with her. The two of us and the two of them. The rest of the team can take us as far as the marsh border and await our return. Given what the woman has detailed, I have to agree, the fewer people the better."

The Director began to pace again, and it was clear he didn't like it. But when he turned, his mind seemed made up, and he nodded.

"Alright, Chello. You and Aria go, get Jaxon, and return. The criminals will go with you. Marcus will lead a satellite team to see you in and out." He paused and looked at Mina, who was watching everything intently. "You will keep them safe and deliver them back alive. Or the threats of the marshes will seem like a walk in the park compared to what will await you here."

Mina eyed him and asked, "And if we succeed? Yip and I get our freedom. Agreed?"

The Director smiled, and Mina thought it was more of a sneer. "Oh, most certainly. You have my word."

She didn't like the way it sounded, but had little choice. They'd be made to go on this journey either way.

"The party will leave at first light. The Praector's meet in two hours to go over logistics," the Director barked and then narrowed his eyes as he looked at Mina. "Someone get these two tracked and properly outfitted. And for feck's sake, bathe them. I can smell their stink from across the damn room."

Everyone stood, and Mina and Yip stayed where they were. She saw the woman called Aria staring at them, and then Yip tapped her arm and motioned to the fruit bowl on the table.

"Hey, Director? Can I get that apple?" Mina called out, pointing to the lone apple left in the bowl. "Apples are Yip's favorite."

He looked at her incredulously, as if it would be ludicrous to ask him for anything. He slowly leaned over the table and picked up the apple.

"This apple?" he asked, holding it up in his hand.

Mina nodded, a half-smile on her face.

Everyone stopped and watched, not a sound in the room.

He smiled and shook the apple, then bit into it. Through a mouthful, he said: "No. No, you cannot."

Mina frowned, but before she could retort, hands grabbed her, yanking her and Yip out of the room.

Chapter 3

Mina sat in the corner of the holding cell, watching Yip, who was carefully examining the devices that were strapped to their legs. They looked like small black boxes, no bigger than a fist, attached to a strap that connected just above the ankle. A team in white lab coats attached them and explained that if the device was removed, tampered with, or if they tried to run, it would detonate.

Yip wanted as much information as possible, so Mina followed his gestures and leads, asking the team a series of questions meant to look like they were safety-based. But her questions were geared towards helping Yip understand the device so he could try to remove them later. He loved mechanical puzzles, and Mina knew there was a good chance he could remove them.

"How sensitive is this thing?" Mina had asked as they attached it to her leg. "If I'm trying to get the team through the marshes, and it shifts on my leg, I don't want to blow the Director's daughter to pieces."

"Not that sensitive," a monotoned man told her, and she nodded and continued.

"I don't want to have to worry about this thing killing everyone when I have to focus on getting them through some harsh conditions. There'll be water and grabbing vines."

"Right," the man said, rather disinterested.

"I won't be held responsible if I get to the prison and back alive and then something shifts on my leg, or water gets in it, and I blow everyone up. I mean, how is this going to…"

"Look," he interrupted her. "Nothing is going to happen unless you try to take it off. If the seal disconnects, it will blow. If you try to run away, and they detonate it, it will blow. No pulling or tugging will affect it. It's sensor-based. So just don't worry about it and do your damn job."

Mina saw Yip nod in her peripheral vision and knew he had the info he needed.

She watched him now, analyzing it as they sat in the small holding cell. He had a gift for all things mechanical, he loved to know how things worked and assemble and disassemble them.

"Think you can crack it?" she asked him, and he shrugged and nodded at the same time. "Well, choose your timing wisely. We need to be smart about this."

He gave a thumbs up and then looked at her and frowned. He made a few gestures with his hands and then shook his head solemnly.

"I know. I don't want to go back to Greensk, either. But we don't have a choice."

She thought about how grueling it was and swallowed. Yip made a few more movements with his hands, and she nodded and shrugged.

"Yeah, the odds are slim. But our path is up to the God, and He has done bigger things than this, right?"

Yip nodded and leaned his head back reflectively.

"Remember the tar pits in the south, right at the border of the Spheres?" She watched him slap his palm to his forehead and grimace. "Exactly! So, there's no sense in questioning the why or how of this, Yip-o. If the God wants us on this path, the best thing we can do is put a smile on our faces and play the hand we're dealt. He always has a reason." She thought a moment and then narrowed her eyes. "And you were sent directly from the God! How are *you* the one second-guessing?"

Yip threw a pebble at her and smiled, making a few motions with his hands, and she laughed.

"I know you aren't really second-guessing. And you're right. Going through that again will be terrible, but there must be a reason we're on this path. Let's just be grateful for every breath we get to take, regardless of our sitch, eh?"

He nodded, a faint smile on his thin lips. Before they could discuss anything further, the main gate from the hall opened. After a few moments, the Director's daughter was standing in front of their cell, and Mina and Yip both stood, staring.

"Hello," she greeted in a soft and unsure voice. "My name is Aria. I was at the meeting earlier. I wanted to officially introduce myself since we're going to be traveling together."

Mina stared at her with a furrowed brow, taking her in. Chestnut waves framed a face that was sharper rather than soft, her blue eyes striking even in the dim light. She was fit, built for movement rather than power. There was something familiar about her aura, something Mina couldn't place.

"I understand you must be feeling a certain way about being made to go on this journey, and rightfully so. But it's important to me, so I wanted you to know that I'm appreciative of any assistance you can offer, even if it's forced. I know it seems crazy to attempt, but necessary."

"Necessary to die?" Mina asked, taking a small step forward. "The chances of any of us making it are…slim."

"I know," Aria told her, and Mina sensed something in her face, regret perhaps. "But I have no choice. It's my brother who's being held at Greensk, and I can't bear the thought of no one trying."

"Your father doesn't seem to think it's necessary to try," Mina told her, and she noticed Aria wince at the words.

"Well, I'm not my father," she told her curtly, and seemed to catch herself and smiled. "So, I have to try."

"Trying would be attempting a different way in. Making it out of the marshes is a death sentence, but trying to go in and out, well, that's just suicidal," Mina told her, and approached the bars, putting her hands on them.

Aria looked her up and down with a smile. "You got a haircut."

Mina raised her eyebrows. "Yeah, they took us to the spa. Let us use soap and everything."

Aria let a small smile touch her lips. Mina had her hair pulled back into a ponytail and the sides shaved. Her bangs were still long and flopped into her face.

"I'm glad you're enjoying the amenities," Aria told her.

The comment made Mina smile. She appreciated a sense of humor, even in a situation like this.

"I just wanted to introduce myself. I think you already met Chello, my Praector."

"You're what?" Mina asked, not understanding the term.

"Praector? My team lead?" Aria told her, looking to see if she understood.

Mina nodded. "Ah, ok. Yeah, he was the nicer one. That Greyson is a real nob."

Aria smiled. "That seems to be the consensus, but he's been my father's Praector for a long time."

Mina studied her, noting the flicker of something, discomfort maybe, when her father was mentioned. Definitely more going on here than just pleasantries.

"Huh," Mina said, head tilting slightly. "The Director's daughter. Rich, polished, probably never heard the word 'no.'" Her voice softened, just a touch, curiosity slipping in. "So what's she doing out here, risking her neck for something that's already lost?" A pause. "Especially when her father doesn't seem all that bothered that his son's locked away."

Aria frowned and gave Mina a hard stare. She swallowed and opened her mouth to say something, but then closed it, seeming to change her mind.

"Well, I just came to introduce myself. I'll see you in the morning," Aria told her, and her demeanor changed completely, becoming more guarded.

She turned and started to walk away, and then stopped and came back. She reached into the satchel on her side and pulled out two apples, placing them on the ledge of the bars. Without looking at them or saying another word, she walked away.

Mina stared at the apples, shocked. It was an unprovoked act of kindness, something that she saw very little of in her life.

Yip came up to her and looked at the apples and then raised his eyebrows, wondering if they were ok to eat.

"Yeah, I think so. I think she was actually just being nice."

Yip hit her shoulder and started gesturing, and she walked away from him, knowing what he meant.

"Yeah, ok, ok. Maybe I was a bit of a jerk. But I didn't think she really came to just be nice. Who the feck does that?"

She sat back in the corner, catching the apple as Yip tossed it to her, and replayed the interaction in her head. She smiled and took a bite of the fresh apple. It wasn't often that people surprised her.

***

Aria awoke well before she had to, sleep evasive. She stood out on her balcony, the cool predawn air gently blowing on her flushed face. She was nervous about the journey, the danger of it, but most of all, she was nervous about failing. She knew her father wouldn't tolerate another failure. She wanted to bring Jaxon home, but she knew the prisoner was right; it was an impossible task. And what if, by some miracle, they made it to the prison but couldn't find Jaxon, or worse? Anything less than bringing him home would be a failure, and she would sooner die in the marshes than let that happen.

She exhaled and looked out over the darkness, turning over the weight of her decision. On the surface, rescuing Jax seemed logical for her Vanguard Ascension, strategic, noble, and necessary. But beneath the layers of duty, something else had pushed her to choose this mission. It was a way out of the life forced upon her. A tragic end masked under the cloak of bravery. If she died in the marshes, she would be free. If she didn't and was successful, well, at least she would have her brother back.

She understood that the life her father insisted she live required passing the Ascension; it was the only path forward, the only way to step into the future he had laid out for her. A future she never asked for. And failure? Her father wouldn't tolerate that. He never did.

Aria frowned as she thought of her father's ambition. Love, if it could even be called that, had always been secondary to his relentless pursuit of power. From her earliest memories, she had known the weight of being a Peterman, a name that carried immense expectations. It was more than a name; it was a brand, a symbol of pride and dominance forged by her father's rise. Even her mother had felt that his dominance and pressure were too much, leaving them before Aria took her first steps.

Her father had thrust that weight onto her and her brother long before they could understand what it meant to bear it. He demanded excellence, not for their sake, but for his aspirations. Every lesson, every achievement, every fleeting moment of approval was a cog in the greater machine he was building, a machine designed to elevate the Peterman name to the pinnacle of power.

The city had already revered their family. Peterman was synonymous with strength and protection. Her father had secured his place in history by throwing his weight behind technology and innovation before it had earned the trust of others. It was a bold move that catapulted him to the position of security director, solidifying his influence.

But she knew that wasn't enough for him. He didn't just want to safeguard the city; he wanted to own it, shape it, rule it. His vision of prosperity was one built on domination, where efficiency and progress overshadowed humanity and fairness.

She thought about her life and frowned. She was supposed to fall in line, to carry that legacy forward without question. But with this mission, she saw something else—an escape hatch hidden beneath the guise of duty. This suicide march dressed as valor was more than a mission. It was a way out. If she failed, if the mission swallowed her whole, no one would blame her. They'd call her courageous, a martyr for the cause. But she would know the truth. She hadn't come to be a hero. She had come because part of her didn't want to come back.

It would be tragic, yes, but understandable. Dangerous terrain, impossible odds. They'd write her off as brave. But she knew better. She wasn't just risking her life; part of her was offering it up. Because living under her father's thumb, trapped in a life she hadn't chosen, wasn't living at all.

She closed her eyes and took a deep breath. Thinking of her father and his ambition always unsettled her. At least this way, she'd be going out on her own terms. Dying on this trek would be better than returning to chains, to the future he had carved for her in stone. She loved this city, its bustling streets, and its diverse and complicated people. And she wished there were another way, another life where she could live her own way.

She thought about the prisoner, Mina.

"The Director's daughter. Rich, polished, probably never heard the word 'no'."

It was judgmental and hurtful, and it bothered her, but she couldn't let it. A prisoner couldn't understand the contradiction she carried, how she could both love and hate who her father was.

But none of that mattered now. The only thing she had to focus on was getting to Jaxon and bringing him home. If she could do that, if they both made it back, then maybe surviving wouldn't feel like surrender. Jaxon was the only part of her world that felt like refuge. He understood the weight of their father's legacy because he carried it too. And if they could escape it together, even just for a little while, then living might still be worth something.

She knew the odds were against them, but for some reason, she believed they had a chance. She couldn't explain it, but something about Mina...her presence, her quiet resilience...made the impossible feel just slightly less so. She closed her eyes and let out her breath, torn between the fragile hope of saving her brother and the quiet lure of never having to return. And in the early light of dawn, she wasn't sure which she hoped for more.

Chapter 4

As the light of day began its ascent across the sky, Mina and Yip were brought from their cell and out into the courtyard, where the team had already assembled. They weren't shackled or bound, but their ankles felt the weight of their captivity.

Mina looked around at the group, the same faces from the meeting yesterday. They seemed to be a cohesive unit, all interacting and comfortable with each other. It was a different vibe than she had observed in other cities throughout her travels. This unit, anyway, seemed tight. That was unusual, but Mina liked it. If they cared about one another more than duty dictated, they had to be relatively decent people.

At the thought of decent people, her mind went to Greyson and Director Peterman, and she frowned. She didn't get the same vibe from them; they seemed very different from all these others. As she scanned the crowd, she didn't see either, and for that, she was grateful. She saw Aria and Chello talking to the burly dark-haired guy, Marcus, she thought his name was. They were looking at something, a map perhaps, pointing and discussing.

Three vessels stood at the ready, they looked like the clockwork carriages Mina had heard about when she was little: land vehicles powered by clockwork mechanisms wound by a steam engine or hand-crank. They were covered with brass and metal, their wheels capable of hovering when needed.

"Good morning," a woman said to her and smiled. She nodded toward the vessels and said, "We won't be going the whole way in them, they'll attract too much attention. But they'll be comfortable for the first day of travel, anyway. On the second day, half the group will go ahead by traditional mechanical wagon. I'm Meesh, by the way." She stuck out her hand, and Mina smirked, shaking it.

These were the nicest people she had ever met, she thought, looking at the solid woman in front of her. She was her height but had a thick layer of muscle, and her dusty-colored hair was pulled back into a tight ponytail. Her round, freckled face looked kind, and her eyes, unlike the others in the group, were each the same color: a chocolate brown.

"Mina. And this is Yip," she said, hitting Yip in the shoulder. He nodded but was preoccupied with the mechanical vessels. "I heard about these when I was a kid, but never saw one before."

Yip began an excited motion of gestures, and Mina chuckled.

"Calm down, Yip-o. These may be interesting, but they're essentially bringing us to our death. He loves mechanics. He wants to go explore and check them out. Think he's allowed?"

Meesh smiled and nodded. "I can take him over. Come on, Yip. Let's go take a look."

Mina smiled when Yip's eyes went big, and he hopped up and down like a child. She watched Meesh lead him over to one of the vessels and wondered how it was possible that these people were so successful, so prosperous, and so kind at the same time. That usually wasn't the case, an impossible combination.

She looked over at Aria, who was now standing alone, looking at some items in a satchel. Mina took her in, wondering why someone who seemingly had it all would risk their life for a brother a father didn't seem to care about. Not many spoiled rich girls would take that chance, and Mina frowned at the thought. It was judgmental. She knew nothing about Aria, and perhaps a *spoiled rich girl* was unfair. She let her eyes scan the buildings, the massive one behind them, the Peterman compound. Well, a *rich girl* was at least accurate.

"Ready to roll?" Marcus asked, coming up next to her.

"Do I have a choice? Because if there's an opt-out option, I'll take it," she told him, and he smiled.

"'Fraid not." He scratched his thick black beard and then rubbed his short, wavy black hair. "So, no cuffs, no restraints. I don't want any trouble, ok? This will be hard enough without having to worry about you running off or trying to slit our throats."

Mina couldn't help but laugh at the last part, and he looked at her as if she were laughing at him.

"That funny?" he asked, and his face became a bit more serious.

"No, not funny. I'm just not the slit-throat kind of girl, is all. And I'm pretty sure if I try to run," she said, lifting her pant leg, "this thing would blow me to bits."

"That it would," he confirmed, giving her a skeptical look. "You don't seem bad. I thought you would be more…criminal."

"And I thought you all would be more dickish. But you seem like decent people, truth be told. And my only concern is staying alive and keeping those two alive," she said, motioning to Aria and Chello.

"I'm glad to hear it. I don't want to have to kill you," he told her, staring off at Chello and Aria.

Mina looked at him, furrowing her brow.

He broke out into a smile and then clapped her on the shoulder. "Come on, better get loaded up."

She nodded and followed him, passing by where Chello and Aria were. Mina stopped and looked at Aria, who looked back with a hesitant smile.

"Morning," Mina told her, and then looked at Chello. "Chello, is it?"

"It is. I guess we haven't officially met," he told her, and reached out his hand for her to shake.

She took it with a smirk. *Nicest damn people*, she thought. She let her eyes cut back to Aria, who was staring at her. "Thanks for the apples," she murmured and didn't wait for a response. She walked over to Marcus, who was now with Meesh and Yip, and loaded up into the vessel.

***

Aria sat in the carriage next to Chello and Meesh, across from Marcus, Mina, and Yip. They were in the same vessel by design, Chello wanting them to stay together as much as possible. Aria didn't mind it; she was still trying to get her mind around what she was about to do, and being with those who would be with her was a good thing. Plus, Mina seemed completely unrattled and unnerved, which offered a sort of comfort.

She found herself staring at Mina, assessing her facial expressions and the way she interacted with everyone. She was comfortable, not shying away from conversation. Mina didn't act like a prisoner; she wasn't what Aria was expecting. There was no hostility, no bitterness for being made to do this. She was simply going along with it all as if she knew she had no choice. There was something about her, Aria couldn't quite put her finger on it, an aura of goodness and calmness, a quiet self-assurance and fearlessness. She couldn't deny she was drawn to it, wished for it herself.

"What's with the eyes?" Aria heard Mina ask and pulled herself from her thoughts to pay attention to the conversation the others were having. "Why do some of you have one green eye?"

Aria looked at Marcus, who had a big smile on his face. He and Chello were the only ones in their vessel with the pigmentation. She smiled when he looked at her and nodded, encouraging him to tell the reason.

"It's a symbol of status and honor," Marcus beamed. "When we complete the Vanguard Ascension, we get the pigmentation in our left eye, so everyone in the city knows."

"What is that, the Vanguard thing?" Mina asked, and Aria didn't realize she was staring at her until Mina looked her way, and she quickly dropped her eyes.

"It's something we have to complete to ascend into positions of status and rank," Chello told her. "Prominent families within the city, the highest positions, and such. They must complete the Vanguard Ascension."

"Ok, but what is it, exactly? Because this is one for you, right?" Mina asked, looking at Aria.

Aria swallowed and nodded, crossing her arms over her chest. "Yes, it is. The Vanguard Ascension is an act of bravery, valor, or some task that betters the city, helps it prosper, or provides some sort of benefit for the people. It can be any number of things, really, but it's usually dangerous and requires skill and bravery."

"And your Praector accompanies you. If you're trying to become a Praector, you have to pass your Ascension before becoming one," Chello added.

"And when you complete it, you get the pigmentation as your reward. Shows everyone how badass you are," Marcus said, grinning, and Meesh and Chello laughed.

"But you don't have the eye," Mina told Meesh.

Meesh nodded and smiled as Chello and Marcus ribbed her for it.

"No, I don't. Not yet anyway. As soon as an opportunity arises, I'll apply for the attempt. But I've been on the Peterman team since graduating academy, and there aren't any Praector positions left. I could leave and apply with another team, but I don't really want to. I love working under Marcus for Jaxon."

Aria smiled at her, the woman who had been a part of her brother's unit for as long as she could remember. Her eyes fell back on Mina, who was now staring at her.

"And you have to do this, why?" Mina asked bluntly. "You aren't going to be a Praector, are you?"

"No," Aria told her and inhaled deeply. "But I'll be named Captain of city security under my father, and the position requires it."

"And you picked this, or...? How does that work?" Mina asked.

"Usually, there's a list of tasks for you to choose from," Chello told her. "None are ideal, all are dangerous, but you can petition for something and try to get it approved if you want to do something specific."

Aria watched Mina nod, noting the contemplative way she looked at her. It made her feel as if she had to justify herself, her choice of Ascension.

"I wanted this," Aria told her, and it came out more defensive than she intended. "I mean, I chose this because of my brother."

She felt Mina's eyes on her and looked away, trying to seem confident in her decision. Her father had scoffed at it and didn't want to approve it, but she begged him. He may view Jaxon as a failed liability now, but he was her brother, and she couldn't sit idly while he rotted in the Greensk prison, a result of his own failed Ascension.

"It's a noble cause," Chello announced, showing support.

Meesh and Marcus nodded in agreement. "And it helps the city because Jaxon is brilliant with tech-no. He's a gifted engineer," Marcus added.

"What landed him in Greensk?" Mina asked.

Aria looked at her and swallowed uncomfortably. She thought of how he didn't want to go, how he said he wasn't ready for the Ascension attempt, but their father insisted.

She could still see the plea in Jaxon's blue eyes, silently begging her to stand beside him, to help him convince their father not to send him on the Ascension. But she had said nothing. Fear of disappointing her father had sealed her lips, and in that moment, she had failed Jaxon when he needed her most. That failure clung to her, a shadow that never faded, a guilt that gnawed at her every step.

"It was…" Marcus started, about to answer Mina, but stopped and looked at his hands, which were folded in his lap.

"It wasn't your fault, Marcus," Meesh told him.

Aria watched as Marcus slumped, the weight of Jaxon's failure heavy on him, his Praector. She sat up straight, not wanting him to feel this way, to look at Jaxon's failure as a foreshadowing of their own.

"There was nothing anyone could do," Aria told Mina, the change in her tone evident. "Jaxon was sent to obtain a piece of tech, and it backfired. The intel we had wasn't conclusive or complete. He shouldn't have been made to go. He was sent on a fool's errand."

"I should've seen it coming, and I didn't," Marcus muttered.

Meesh reached across the small space and put her hand on his knee. "No one could have."

Aria leaned her head back and closed her eyes, refusing to think about it. The entire situation felt off as if Greensk knew Jaxon was coming. Her father's scoff at the news of Jaxon's capture seemed surprising, yet not surprising at all. None of it felt right.

"This is why we can't enter the city," Aria said, eyes still closed and head still back. "When Jaxon went, they took the city route. Someone must have suspected them and tipped off the guards. They were waiting for him. That's not a chance I'm willing to take."

She opened her eyes, and Mina nodded, and she could tell she was trying to make sense of it. Her eyes were sympathetic, something that surprised her. Why would a criminal who was being forced on a dangerous mission feel any sympathy for the person making them do so? She couldn't figure Mina out at all.

"I get it," Mina told her, then she turned to Marcus, who was still hanging his head in somber reflection. "We'll get him back."

Aria looked on in awe as Mina placed her hand on the back of his neck and lightly shook him in a gesture of kindness. Marcus looked up and nodded, forcing a smile.

Aria squinted, studying Mina. She wasn't behaving like the criminal her father had portrayed her to be, and it was driving her crazy. It made no sense at all.

"What did you two do to end up in prison?" she couldn't help but ask.

Mina didn't seem offended; she smiled and held up her hand to Yip, who was hitting her rapidly, trying to gesture. She scratched the back of her head and then shrugged.

"Nothing, actually."

"The common criminal answer!" Meesh jested, and they all laughed.

Mina looked at her with a smile, and Aria caught herself noticing how it lit up her face.

"No, I'm actually serious," Mina told them. "I have no problem admitting my sins, trust me. But this time we were...surprised."

"What happened?" Marcus asked, coaxing her on. "If you didn't do anything?"

Aria watched as Yip hit her arm and gestured rapidly to her, and Mina nodded.

"Ok, ok. Yip is insisting I tell you the truth," she told them, her eyes briefly stopping on Aria.

Aria held her stare, curious to know the story. Mina didn't seem like a common criminal. Her easy-going nature, the way she comforted Marcus, none of it added up.

"There was no record of what you did or even of who you are," Chello told her. "I was surprised Director Peterman knew you existed."

Mina nodded and looked across at Aria again, who this time dropped her eyes. Her father was so rude to Mina and Yip, it was embarrassing.

"We were only in your city for a few days. We were looking for someone, have been for years."

"Who?" Marcus asked curiously.

Aria noticed emotion flash across Mina's face, but she seemed to stifle it quickly.

"The person who killed my family," she said evenly, and the group went quiet.

Aria looked at her, a sadness in her eyes.

"Who killed your family?" Meesh asked in nothing more than a whisper.

"I don't know. But I'm looking for him, and when I find him, I will have my vengeance."

"I'm really sorry, there, Mina. I didn't mean to pry," Marcus told her.

Mina shrugged and said, "It was a long time ago. I've been looking for him for fifteen years, I guess. He betrayed my father and killed my entire people, the whole city. I was only twelve years old, but I remember bits and pieces. Yip and I watched it happen. He stole my father's pocket watch, so that's who I'm looking for. The man with the watch. It's a mechanical invention my grandfather made. It has gold blades that spring out when you push the top. Made from the green rock of Velho. It's different, has a raw sense of beauty."

"You're from Velho?" Chello asked, incredulous. "The people blessed by the God?"

Mina nodded, staring at the ground.

"I thought everyone from Velho was destroyed," Chello told her. Mina shrugged. "All but one," she said with a forced smile.

Aria watched her closely and felt a tug in her heart. To be orphaned at such a young age was heartbreaking to hear.

"So," Mina continued, "we were asking questions about the watch when we got here, as we do in every city we come to. Maybe it had been spotted or pawned or something. No one had seen it, of course, but then that night we were at the inn, eating, and some city guards were watching us. I thought maybe I was imagining it. But the next night they were back, and one of your friends was with them, that Greyson guy."

"That doesn't track. We don't go to the local pubs. We have our own," Marcus said, looking around at the others.

"Well, he was there. I recognized his face when he came to my cell the other day." Mina looked at Chello, and Aria saw him nod in agreement.

"He did seem surprised that you recognized him," Chello admitted, "But I agree with Marcus, it would be unlikely that he was there."

"Well, he was. And he was talking with the guards. Yip and I were eating, minding our own business, and a guard walked by and bumped into me. I mean, he really gave me a shove, so much so that I spilled my broth. I stood up to get out of the way of the spill, and before I knew what was happening, they had me in their grip, cuffing me, yelling that I was causing trouble."

Aria watched Mina speak and saw no sign of deceit, she believed what she was saying. Yip started flailing next to her, and Mina put her arm around his shoulder and shook him.

"Yip is trying to tell you it's true. They threw us in your prison and that was that," Mina told them, and the group looked at each other, no one sure what to believe. "Believe me or not. You asked, so I'm telling you. That's what got us in your shitty prison. We had only been out of Greensk for the handful of days it took to get to your city, and then just like that, back in the cells. What fecking luck."

Aria thought about her story and didn't think she had a reason to lie. It made her wonder how her father knew she was in prison if there was no record. And surely, he knew about the arrest if Greyson was there.

"Well, that's shitty luck if what you say is true," Marcus told her and looked over at Chello and then Aria. "But I guess your shitty luck is our good luck. I really hope you can get Jaxon back."

"We will," Aria told him with conviction. She needed to show strength and confidence, even if she wasn't sure herself. "We have no choice but to succeed."

She felt Mina's stare and looked up at her, and they held each other's eyes for what felt like a long time, each trying to figure out the other.

Yip started gesturing again, and Mina looked over at him. "How long has he been there?" Mina asked, nodding at Yip.

"Just over a month," Aria said somberly.

"Forty-six days," Marcus told them. "I've been counting."

They were silent, and after a few moments, Mina said, "I think you need to be prepared that your brother might not be the person you remember." She looked at Aria, who looked back with a furrowed brow. "The things they do to prisoners in Greensk…it changes a person."

They went quiet, the only sound was the movement of the wheels outside as the group let Mina's words sink in. Aria swallowed, knowing she was right.

Yip tapped her on the leg and made a few gestures, and Mina shook her head. "They don't need to know that," Mina told him in a low voice.

"What did he say?" Marcus asked somberly.

"He said the dreams are the worst part because, after a while, you stop knowing where the nightmare ends. Whether your eyes are open or closed, it all feels the same. The things they do to you... your mind plays it over and over, twisting it, stretching it. You wake up gasping, but you're never sure if you actually woke up at all," she said quietly as she stared off, trying not to recall the memories of her time there. "They're obsessed with their experiments, it's really fecked up what they do."

"Feck's sake," Meesh whispered.

Yip banged his hand on the bench, causing them to look at him. He pointed to his mouth and then looked at Mina, who put her arm around him again, half hugging him.

"They get the point," she told him, and then looked at them all, seeing that they wanted to know what Yip said. Mina let out a sigh and said, "They cut out his tongue."

Aria felt tears in her eyes and blinked them back, not wanting to show any emotion. She looked at Yip, who was nodding, and felt such sorrow. Not just for Yip and Mina, but for what her brother might be going through.

"I'm sorry that happened to you," Chello told him sincerely, and the others nodded.

They sat in silence for the rest of the way, each one contemplating their thoughts and each other until they stopped where they would be camping for the night.

Aria was the last to step out of the vessel. Mina stood at the exit, hands on her hips, watching the team set up a makeshift camp in the shallow woods.

"Why did you bring us the apples?" she asked when Aria stepped out.

Aria blinked at the unexpected question. When she didn't answer, Mina finally looked at her.

"Why? Really?" Mina's hazel eyes locked onto hers, sharp and searching, as if the answer mattered more than it should.

Aria swallowed, caught in the weight of that gaze. "I felt bad for how my father acted," she admitted, barely above a whisper. "And I wanted you to know I'm not like him."

A slow smile spread across Mina's face. "You're not bad, Richy. You might be the Director's daughter, but you're not that bad, Richy."

"Don't call me that," Aria muttered, turning away, but not before stealing one last glance at Mina, who was grinning. Aria caught herself smiling, then quickly looked away

Chapter 5

Mina sat next to Yip in front of the fire and listened to the group banter back and forth. She couldn't get over how nice they were, no one was treating them like prisoners. It was difficult to understand. She glanced around, taking in their easy camaraderie. They joked and teased each other with a familiarity that seemed far deeper than just members of the same unit. Her curiosity got the better of her, and she looked at Chello, who was sitting on the other side of Yip.

"Tell me something," she asked him, and he looked up at her with a smile. "I don't understand. You're all so... kind. Even to me and Yip. How is it that you're all so close?"

The chatter from the group died down, and all eyes turned toward them.

"Well, we're more than just guards," Chello told her, his voice tinged with a note of pride. "From the moment we graduate from the academy, we're assigned together as a team. And that team becomes our world. We train together, eat together, and fight together. We live our lives as one."

"Yeah," Marcus agreed. "Each team, for each family or leader, is formed with purpose, picking the right people to balance out skills and temperaments. We're raised together, bound by the same oaths and goals. It's not just about duty… it's about trust. About family."

Mina nodded, and her eyes flickered to Aria, who was staring at the fire with a slight smile on her face. She looked rather pretty with the glow of the flames bouncing across her face. Mina pulled herself away from the thought and then asked:

"Doesn't that get… I don't know, old? Always being with the same people all the time?"

A ripple of laughter passed through the group, but it wasn't mocking. It was warm and understanding.

"Sometimes," admitted Meesh from across the circle. "We fight. We argue. But that's what families do, isn't it? The difference is, we can't afford to hold grudges. When your life depends on the person beside you, you learn to resolve things quickly. To forgive."

"And to celebrate!" added Marcus, smiling. "Every victory, no matter how small. Every milestone. We bond over celebration as often as we can. But all in all, the most important thing to each of us is the people we protect, the ones we're assigned to."

Mina glanced around again, seeing the truth of their words reflected in their faces. The way they laughed together, the ease with which they talked. She had spent so much of her life alone, Yip aside. This kind of bond felt foreign to her, but she felt a small tug in her heart towards it.

"That's so different from what I've seen in other cities. It's kind of nice," she told them.

"It is," Chello agreed. "But it's not always easy. It takes work, trust, and time. Years of it. Which is why most of us are put together after graduation. The ones that come and go adjust quickly, too, though."

Mina nodded and again looked at Aria, who was looking back at her. Mina smiled a small smile and wondered what it might feel like to belong to such a place with such people.

***

Aria stared into the fire, listening as Chello spoke about the bond they all shared, and it stirred something deep in her chest. What he said was true. She'd felt that bond with him for years, her Praector, her steady shield. More like an older brother than a bodyguard. It made her think of Jaxon and everything still ahead of them. The road was uncertain, probably deadly. Mina had been honest about that, and Aria didn't need convincing to know the odds were slim.

She frowned as her thoughts turned to her father, to the life waiting for her if they made it home. But this time, she wasn't thinking about escape. She was thinking about survival, just not her own. If Jaxon could make it back, if Chello could walk away from this alive, then maybe that was enough. She had made her peace with what might happen to her. But Jaxon and Chello deserved to live, and she hoped that Mina could get them through.

There was laughter across the loose circle they all sat in, and she looked at the two prisoners, sitting side by side as if they were a part of the Fusian people. Mina kept letting her eyes flicker over to her, but they never seemed to settle, always darting away once Aria met her stare.

Aria had a feeling about her but couldn't describe it. There was something about her, a survival instinct that seemed ingrained in her. Mina didn't deny the danger or stupidity of this trek, but she didn't shy away from it, either. She didn't seem scared at all, but rather cocky and confident. For some reason, that made Aria feel a bit better, a tiny bit safer. She found herself grateful to the God that these prisoners were on the trek with them and hoped they survived and got the freedom they deserved.

***

As the first light of morning crept over the horizon, Chello, Aria, Yip, and Mina stood behind the wagon carriage, checking their gear. They had been given new clothes: practical, matching outfits of spandex and breathable cotton. Mina was relieved by the snug fit; anything too loose could be a hazard in the vine fields of the marshes. She shrugged on the lightweight button-up overshirt they'd provided, drawing Aria's gaze.

Aria hadn't meant to look, she hadn't meant to *notice*. But the moment Mina moved, shrugging into the thin overshirt, her eyes betrayed her. The ripped sleeves revealed arms that were impossibly defined. Cords of muscle that spoke of strength, of survival, of someone who didn't just fight but *lived* in the fight. Aria's breath caught.

She scrambled to cover her reaction with a half-joking question. "Did you rip the sleeves off for a reason?" But the words felt flimsy in her mouth.

"I don't like sleeves," Mina replied with a shrug and a grin.

Aria gave a small nod and turned away, embarrassed. She'd never had the luxury of noticing anyone. Not like this. Not with wonder curling in her stomach and heat rising to her cheeks. Attraction, noticing others...those were things other people got to explore. Her path had been mapped before she was old enough to understand what it meant. Her father had already chosen who she would marry. Someone strategic, someone useful, someone who fit into the vision he had for her life. There was no room in that vision for someone like Mina. And yet… here she was, unable to look away. Something about Mina—her presence, her strength—unsettled everything Aria thought she knew about herself. And for the first time, she felt the weight of everything she'd been told she could never have.

Mina didn't miss the flicker of something in Aria's expression as she looked away. Letting it pass, she shifted her focus to the bags Chello and Aria had packed. They had kept things compact, one bag filled with food and nutrient packs from the tech-no team, another with essentials like a med kit. Their only weapons were Chello's daggers and Aria's staff, which pulsed with some technology Mina had never seen before. The staff retracted, and when it opened fully, there was a crackle of laser light at the end, bright and sizzling blue.

"That will attract more attention than we want," Mina told her.

Aria smiled and spun it in her hands, showing off her adeptness with it.

"We're better off using glow balls for light when needed," Mina said.

"This is more than a light," Aria told her, and Yip jumped back when she slammed it on a log nearby, and it exploded the piece of wood.

"Don't worry, I won't use it on you unless I have to," she teased.

Mina smirked. "I'll try to behave then." She turned her gaze to Chello. "What's the plan? They aren't coming with us?" she asked, motioning to the rest of the camp.

"Marcus and Meesh and a few others will see us as far as they can with the wagon. The rest will stay here."

Mina nodded and took in a deep breath. She hoped they were ready for this. They had to be. They had no choice. She looked at the sky and took in another steadying breath. It was time to go back to what she had escaped. She had clawed her way out once. But now she was going back with others, and the weight of their lives pressed heavier than the dangers of the marshes ever did.

Chapter 6

The four of them stood at the threshold of the marshes, where the world seemed to shift into something unnatural. A dense, purple haze coiled above the bog like a living thing, pulsing in slow, deliberate waves. The air was thick, laced with a faint hum that wasn't quite sound but something deeper, something that settled in their bones. It was an uneasy vibration, as if the land itself was aware of them, waiting. The marsh exhaled a damp, rotting scent, the kind that clung to the skin, seeping into every breath. Shadows twisted in the mist, indistinct and shifting, never quite forming shapes but hinting at something watching. Something hungry.

Mina swallowed and took a slow, deep breath. This was it. There was no sense in dreading it; they were here, and this was their path. She nodded to herself and looked over at Yip, who was staring stoically out into the marshes, his face unreadable.

"You wanna do this?" she asked him, pointing to the sky, and he nodded. They took a few steps away from Aria and Chello, who were both looking at them. "Give us a minute, will you? We need to pray to the God for protection and guidance."

Aria and Chello exchanged glances before walking over to them.

"Mind if we join you?" Aria asked, and Mina raised her eyebrows in surprise, nodding.

They stood in a loose circle, Yip and Mina holding hands, Chello resting a hand on Yip's shoulder before taking Aria's. Mina inhaled sharply when she felt Aria's warm fingers wrap around hers. No one spoke for a moment until Chello said:

"You're the Velhoian, go for it."

Mina nodded, letting her eyes cut to Aria, and then closed them before saying:

"To the God who watches over us. Guard our steps as we walk into the unknown. Let no danger find us without your shield, no fear rise without your voice to still it. Strengthen our hearts and set fire to our resolve. You have called us to this, marked this road with your purpose. Remind us, even in the darkness, that it's not without meaning. Help us see with your eyes when ours begin to falter. You have put us on this path for a reason, and we ask that you help us remember that. Protect us, guide us, and let our steps bring honor to your name."

"Well said, Mina. Thank you," Chello told her. "May the God bless us all."

Mina watched as Yip patted Chello on the chest, and they started to move back to where the bags were. She looked down, realizing that Aria was still holding her hand, and looked at her, seeing a silent fear in her eyes. Mina swallowed and nodded at her, giving her hand a gentle squeeze.

"I'll get you to your brother. I promise," she whispered and meant it.

Aria let out a breath and nodded, squeezing Mina's hand before letting it go. She wiped her eyes and turned and walked away.

Mina watched her walk over to Chello and hug him, wishing him luck. She looked at Yip, who seemed perfectly calm, and she knew the God would be with them. She flexed the hand that Aria had just held, feeling a tingling sensation. May the God be with them all, she thought.

***

"It's important to remember that everything here wants to kill you," Mina told them. "Your instinct will be to fight, to strike, and to protect yourself. In the vine field, that will be to your detriment."

"What do you mean?" Chello asked.

"If you strike a vine, they'll swarm you. They're more like animals than plants and react to light and sensation. If one wraps around you, don't panic, don't fight or strike it. Try your best to stay calm. If they swarm, none of us will survive."

Yip motioned to the water and made a few gestures, and Mina nodded.

"Right. There are things in the water, creatures you have never seen before. Again, the key to survival is not to panic. Keep yourself steady and even. The creatures you can fight, but don't touch the vines."

"How big is the vine field?" Aria asked.

"I don't know. It feels never-ending. This, we are standing on, is a salt bank. It keeps the vines away. But once the water dilutes enough, the vine field starts. It'll lead to the gas flats, and while they seem clear of danger, their very essence will try to choke you. The purple haze comes from its vapors. We can't breathe it in. But first things first. Let's get past the marsh entrance and the vines."

"We'll take your lead, Mina," Chello told her.

She nodded and seemed to think, then said, "It'll be hard, but you need to trust me, ok? Do exactly what I say when I say it," Mina told them, and Aria and Chello looked at her. "I'm good at escaping and evading, it's what the God blessed me with. But that's because I trust my instincts and don't hesitate. When the God shows me something, I trust it and I survive. What I'm asking is a lot, to let your guard down and do exactly what I say when I say it, but it's going to be the difference between life and death in this place."

They looked back at her, trying to understand, and then Chello said:

"We'll try our best, Mina. And we appreciate you leading us into this."

"Don't thank me yet," she muttered and looked at Yip. "Ready to do this again, Yip-o?"

He gave the thumbs up and nodded, and then pointed at Mina, then Aria, then Chello, then himself. Mina nodded and looked at Chello.

"He wants it to be me first, then Aria, then you, then him. And remember, don't touch anything. And mind where you step, there are holes all over."

They moved off the salt ledge and into the marshes, Mina keeping her eyes focused on each step ahead. As they moved, they saw ripples in the water, evidence of life, and kept up a slow and deliberate pace. Mina led the way, every step a calculated shift to avoid the sinkholes that dotted the ground. She could see them in the thin water and knew they were deadly to step in and disturb what lived in them.

Behind her, Aria moved silently, her eyes scanning the mist that sat on the water's surface for movement. Chello walked closely behind her, his hand on the hilt of the blade at his waist, trying to remember *not* to draw it. Yip swept his eyes from side to side behind them, his sharp senses alert to the unnatural hum that seemed to rise from the marsh itself.

They all could feel it, the marsh was alive. Strange hisses and guttural croaks echoed from unseen corners, and now and then, something splashed faintly in the murky water. They moved slowly, their senses heightened, but they still weren't ready for the first attack.

The water at Mina's feet erupted, a spray of sludge and weeds giving way to a dark, glistening form. A creature, no larger than a dog but hunched and bristling with needle-like spines, arched in the water. Mina jumped back, knocking into Aria, who was close behind her.

Aria lost her footing and fell to her knees just as the creature resurfaced and lunged for her. Its translucent skin revealed writhing organs, and its wide, lidless eyes reflected the dim purple light. It was hideous and terrifying.

Mina's senses flared just in time. She saw its path to Aria a heartbeat before it lunged. "Roll!" she shouted, leaping back and kicking at the creature mid-charge.

Through the sheer terror of seeing such a thing, Aria managed to roll to her side, plunging into the murky water and muffling a scream.

Chello was already moving, drawing his dagger in one fluid motion. He waited, watched Mina's kick connect, then drove his blade down into the creature's skull. It let out a screech, limbs flailing.

Yip ran forward, grabbing Aria and pulling her from the water just as more shapes rose from the muck, their low croaks swelling into a sharp, deafening chorus.

"Eyes up! More are coming!" Mina called out.

Chello drew his other dagger, but this time handed it to Mina. She took it without hesitation and looked at the forms surfacing, their numbers too many to fight against.

"We need to move!" she yelled, trying to press against the panic in her chest.

They followed her step for step, Chello now behind her and Yip and Aria hand in hand behind them. Creatures lunged, and they swatted and kicked, occasionally driving a blade into one. As they moved, Mina lost her focus and stepped into a hole, a small howl escaping her mouth. Chello was there, pulling her up, and when she pulled her leg out, it was covered in a black tar-like substance, oily and thick. She saw a vision flash in her mind of Yip, and she turned to warn him.

"Yip!" she called out, but it was seconds too late. The creature launched out of the water and landed on his chest, pushing him backward into the murky marsh. The other creatures moved in that direction, sensing an opportunity for fresh flesh.

Mina grabbed Aria by the hand and pulled her away from the rippling water, all while keeping her eye on Yip, who was on his back, grabbing and pushing at the swarming creatures. She knew they had to move; she saw it in her mind and grabbed Chello's arm, but he shook off her grip and dove for where Yip was.

Chello pulled him from the water, creatures clinging to him, their teeth already sunk into his flesh. Yip's mouth was open in a silent scream, the pain evident in his expression. Mina rushed forward, stabbing the ones she could, but it was overwhelming. There were too many of them, and the taste of Yip's blood had driven them into a frenzy.

Mina looked around frantically, with no image or vision of escape in her mind. More creatures came as if in a wave, and they slashed their blades from left to right, black, oily blood spilling from the creatures. It was too many, and Mina wondered if this was really the end. But then a flash of light sparked from behind them, and Mina turned to see Aria with her staff extended, blue light crackling at the end. The creatures recoiled, the light seeming to hurt their eyes, and she swung the staff around in an impressive circle.

It was the lapse they needed, and they pulled the remaining creatures off Yip and tugged him forward, Aria urging them ahead. She kept the staff low to the water, lunging it at everything that moved at their feet. They rushed ahead, the creatures thrashing in frustration at the strange light, but slowing their chase. They moved nimbly to a slightly elevated ledge of dry land and stopped, all of them breathing heavily.

"Lower the staff, the light will agitate the vines," Mina told her in a huff, and Aria did so, the light dimming and then disappearing altogether.

Mina looked at Yip, his shirt torn to shreds, blood oozing from the bites all over his midsection. "Yip?" she asked, concerned.

He looked at her with frustration on his face and punched her in the shoulder. He made a series of gestures, tears streaming down his face.

"I know, and I tried to escape. But he wouldn't leave you," Mina told him, motioning to Chello.

"You ok, kid?" Chello asked, not fully understanding the exchange between them. He reached into his bag for the med kit to see what he could do about some of the deeper lacerations.

Aria was crouched down, her eyes scanning behind them, waiting for the next attack.

They caught their breaths for a moment, Chello patching up Yip's bites as best he could, and Mina squatted next to Aria.

"Are you ok?" Mina asked quietly, her eyes scanning the surrounding marshes. It had gone eerily quiet.

"Not in the least," Aria told her, but kept her voice from cracking.

Mina put her hand on her shoulder and offered a small squeeze, and then stood and turned to Yip. "You gonna live?" she asked him, and he gestured at her and then pointed at Chello. Mina nodded and shrugged. "I guess he did."

Chello looked at Mina expectantly, and she looked out over the vines that were ahead of them and said, "Thanks for saving him. He appreciates it."

Chello put his arm around Yip and half hugged him, and then looked at where Mina was staring off to, the thick forest of vines that seemed endless.

"Are there creatures in the vines?" he asked, and Aria moved next to them to hear.

"Probably something different from what we just saw. I wouldn't worry about creatures, though. The vines are dangerous enough."

There was a hitch in her voice that she couldn't help, and she swallowed it back. She didn't know how she would get them all through the vines, plants with animal-like instincts. Yip stood, and again they all looked out over the black vines, the eerie quietness seeming to exude its own danger.

"There is no path I can see." Chello told her.

Mina nodded. "We have to make our own. Remember, touch as little as possible. If something grabs you, don't panic. And Aria, keep the staff in the bag. The light will wake them."

Aria nodded and wiped the sweat from her brow with the back of her hand. It was already too much. She hadn't expected to be this scared, to feel it so sharply. She wasn't okay, still badly shaken from what they'd just faced. But there was no time to dwell on it. They had to keep moving.

"Alright, same rules apply," Mina told them, and stepped off the ledge, slowly walking towards the darkness of the vines. She took a deep breath, summoning her strength.

Move like a shadow. Breathe like the dead, Mina told herself, and stepped forward, letting the darkness close around her. Panic was a noose in this place; tighten it, and the vines would do the rest. She kept her breaths shallow, her pulse steady. *The only way through is to become untouchable.* She put her fear aside and focused on the God and the path that began to come to life in her mind.

Aria watched Mina go and then followed, her heart beating rapidly in her chest. As she took in a steadying breath, she could feel her fear, and hated it. Ahead of her, Mina crouched low, her every movement deliberate as she tested the ground before committing to each step. They came to the first patch of vines, and Aria took a deep breath and asked the God for courage.

They moved slowly, Mina stepping a slow path before them. The vines spread across the ground like a dark web, their spindly tendrils intertwining and pulsing faintly with a life of their own. Some stretched upward, coiling around each other, while others lay dormant, or seemed to. Aria couldn't shake the sensation that they were watching, waiting.

"Careful," Mina whispered, her voice barely audible over the distant croaks and rustling that filled the air. "Touch as little as you can. No sudden movements."

Aria swallowed hard, her mouth dry. Courage. That's what she needed right now. She could almost hear her father's voice in her mind, his insistence that fear was a choice and not one that a Peterman could afford. *"Fear is a choice, Aria. Choosing it is a weakness you must not allow yourself."*

She frowned, not wanting to think of him or her fear. Instead, she focused on Mina, weaving through the labyrinth of vines, planting her feet where Mina had just been. Out of the corner of her eye, something shifted.

Her heart skipped a beat, and she turned her head slightly, careful not to make any sudden moves. There it was again, a vine, slithering along the ground like a serpent. She froze, her breath caught in her throat, watching as it coiled slowly around another vine before lying still.

It's just a vine, she told herself, though the pit in her stomach begged to differ.

She glanced at the others. Mina was too focused on leading to notice. Chello's face was stoic, his steps measured. Even Yip, jittery as he was, seemed oblivious.

Another vine moved, this time closer. She clenched her jaw and forced herself to move forward, carefully placing one foot in front of the other, side-stepping the vines in her path.

"Mina," she whispered, her voice trembling despite her efforts to steady it. Mina glanced back. "The vines. They're moving."

Mina's gaze flicked to the ground, then back to Aria. She nodded, her expression grim. "I know. Just keep going."

Aria nodded, forcing her legs to obey. She couldn't let herself falter. *Courage*, she thought, and forced herself to move. Her breath came in shallow huffs as she pressed on, her senses heightened to every sound, every shadow. The vines were everywhere, and she swore they were closing in. She paused briefly, just to wipe at the sweat dripping down her face, then froze as the faintest pressure curled around her ankle. Her breath hitched, her heart hammering. Slowly, she looked down.

A vine, sleek and deep black, had coiled around her boot like a snake. Fear surged through her, hot and immediate. Her instincts screamed at her to pull away, to kick, to scream, but she knew better. Mina had told her that it would be a death sentence for them all if she panicked… the vines didn't simply tighten; they swarmed.

She fought against the panic in her chest. *Breathe,* she told herself. *Don't move. Don't fight.* But the words felt fragile against the rising terror inside of her.

"M-Mina…" she whispered, her voice barely audible.

Mina turned, her gaze locking onto Aria's boot. Her eyes widened for a fraction of a second before her expression hardened.

"Don't move," Mina commanded.

"Feck," Chello huffed out.

"You and Yip stay completely still. Do not move," she told him.

Mina crouched slowly, her movements deliberate, and placed a steadying hand on Aria's knee. "You're okay. Just stay calm."

Aria watched as Mina's eyes darted from left to right, surveying the patches of vines closest to them. They were thrumming, almost vibrating with anticipation. One wrong move would end them all in a swarm.

Aria's breathing turned ragged, every inhale catching in her throat like it might be the last. Panic scraped at the inside of her chest, sharp and unrelenting, and she bit down hard to keep from gasping. She felt the vine tighten slightly and had to purse her lips to keep a scream from escaping from her throat. Out of the corner of her eye, she could see other vines shifting, as if waiting for the slightest provocation to strike.

"I…" Aria started, tears beginning to leak from her eyes, but Mina cut her off with a sharp shake of her head.

"Stay quiet," Mina murmured. "No sudden movements."

Aria watched as Mina seemed to be looking at something only she could see, her eyes squinting off to the side, focused on nothing. And then with what felt like agonizing slowness, Mina reached down, her fingers brushing against the vine. It reacted instantly, shifting its grip, its tendrils twitching like the tongue of a snake. Aria flinched, and Mina's grip on her knee tightened.

"Aria. Look at me," Mina told her, her voice low but firm.

She tore her gaze from the vine and met Mina's eyes. There was no fear there, only steady determination.

"Breathe with me," Mina told her, inhaling deeply and exhaling slowly. "In. Out. Focus."

Aria nodded, following Mina's lead, her eyes locked on the hazel pools before her. Something in Mina's steadiness reached her— subtle, like the shift of wind before a storm breaks. Aria didn't know what it was, only that it helped. Her heartbeat began to slow, the fog of panic lifting just enough for her to think clearly.

Mina moved her hand closer to the vine, her fist in a ball, and her arm extended. She let her thumb brush against its surface just slightly. It shifted again, loosening its grip on Aria's boot and slithering up toward Mina's wrist. Mina didn't flinch as it coiled around her, instead, she let it wrap around her arm.

Aria stifled a gasp, more tears leaking from her eyes.

"Good," Mina murmured, her voice soothing. "You're doing great, Aria," She told her quietly, "Almost there."

Aria watched in awe and terror as Mina gently lifted her arm with the vine away from her boot. She slowly removed her hand from Aria's knee and took the blade from her waist, and put the tip of it on her arm, very close to the vine. The vine began to slither around the blade, coiling up and off Mina's arm.

She slowly placed the blade into the ground, and the vine slid its way off and into the tangled mass on the ground. It disappeared without a sound, merging seamlessly with the others.

Mina picked up the blade and slowly stood, turning to Aria. "You're okay," she said, her tone soft now.

Chello put his hand on Aria's shoulder, and she gripped it immediately, needing comfort.

"I'm here," Chello whispered.

Aria nodded, her legs trembling beneath her. She opened her mouth to speak, but the words caught in her throat, and nothing came out. She could only feel fear in her chest, raw and rattling. And beneath it, threaded through like something she didn't quite recognize, was complete gratitude. Mina had stepped in without hesitation, steady and sure in the face of chaos. Aria didn't know what to say to that. She only knew she was thankful, more than words could carry.

Mina smiled faintly, almost as if she could hear Aria's thoughts. Aria wanted to throw her arms around her and beg her to take her out of this mess immediately, but she only swallowed and nodded at her.

"Let's keep moving. Slowly," Mina said quietly.

The group resumed their trek through the vines, the tension tangible in the air. Aria's heart was still racing, but she kept pace with Mina, stepping where she stepped. Chello, sensing when she needed comfort, would occasionally put a gentle hand on her shoulder and squeeze.

It was a slow and anxious walk, often stopping for vines to slither past or to watch as they seemed to circle them. Mina never stopped leading them, and after some time, the vines began to thin, and there was nothing but murky water on either side of them.

They walked through ankle-deep water, wading cautiously, eyes darting side to side. Aria could feel the pressure of anxiety in her chest; it was heavy and made it difficult to breathe. Finally, when she wasn't sure how much more she could take, they came to an embankment, and Mina pulled them up one by one. There was more water on the other side, but they took a moment to catch their breaths and release the tension they'd been holding.

"Aria, are you ok?" Chello asked her, concern in his eyes.

She nodded, trying her best to put on a brave front. There was a tug at her side, and she nearly jumped out of her skin. But it was only Yip.

"He wants to make sure you're ok," Mina told her, and there was a small smile on her lips. "He was scared for you."

Aria glanced at the mute man, who looked entirely too young to be grown, and put her hand on his shoulder. "I'm fine, Yip. Thank you," she whispered, but she felt like she was falling apart. She wasn't prepared for this, and none of this was ok. In the back of her mind, she was trying to come to terms with the fact that they would have to cross back this way again, and she wanted to burst into tears.

"Flats are next. But if we can get across them, we only have to climb the ridge, and there is a good chance at safety for the night," Mina told them.

"I have these," Chello said, and went into the satchel on his side and pulled out mouth masks.

"Whoa, where did you get those?" Mina asked, and there was a bit of excitement in her tone.

"Tech-no, of course. When you mentioned vapors in the meeting, we asked them for something to wear that was lightweight. They're filtered, but not knowing what's in the vapors, they couldn't promise that they'll keep everything out," Chello told her, handing one over.

Mina smiled and passed it to Yip, whose face lit up as he took it and put it on.

"This is going to make a huge difference, Chello," Mina told him. "The worst part of the vapors is the burning sensation in your lungs, so if these help with that even a little, it'll be great."

"What else do we have to be aware of?" Aria asked, and she hated how weak her voice sounded. She wasn't okay and could feel herself coming unraveled.

"Holes in the ground with liquid that splashes up. It's like acid, so don't touch it," Mina told her and put on her mask. "Step where I step."

Mina led the way, and Aria walked close behind her, watching where she stepped. It was difficult to keep her eyes on Mina, her gaze moving between the fissures and the sluggish ripples of green liquid seeping through the cracks. The thought of what it might do if splashed made her skin crawl.

Aria's thoughts were rolling with anxiety as they moved, considering that a single misstep could send someone plunging into a fissure or splashing into the acidic liquid. Even the vapors themselves felt like a threat, making her head feel light, as though her thoughts were being tugged in different directions.

A sudden hiss erupted from a nearby fissure, the gas igniting into a brief flare of pale purple flame. Aria flinched, but Mina didn't break stride.

"Keep moving," Mina urged. "It's unstable here."

The group pressed on, weaving between the cracks and jagged protrusions of stone. Aria wasn't sure how long it had been, but she heard a skidding sound and turned to see that Yip had stumbled, his foot sliding dangerously close to a bubbling pool of green liquid. He waved his arms for balance, trying to push himself forward so he didn't fall into the acidic pool.

Chello moved quickly, grabbing him by the arm and yanking him upright.

"Easy, Yip. You ok?" he asked, his voice low.

Yip's eyes were wide with fear, but he threw his arms around Chello's neck and squeezed him in thanks.

"Keep moving," Mina whispered, and Aria watched as Chello put Yip in front of him, so he was in the rear.

The tension was palpable, every step a careful calculation, every breath shallow to avoid inhaling too much of the tainted air, even with the masks. This flatland was a predator, patient, and indifferent, waiting for one of them to falter again. Aria felt as if it were all alive, just waiting for its opportunity.

They finally reached solid, unbroken ground, and Mina exhaled, pulling off her mask. The air felt different here, less like poison, more like breath. They were far from safe, but the first part was over, and they were alive. And for that, she thanked the God.

She glanced back at the others, their silhouettes emerging one by one through the haze. Bruised, shaken, but still standing. She hadn't expected it, not all of them. Not like this. A tight knot loosened in her chest, something she hadn't realized she'd been carrying. Her lips moved in a silent prayer, a whispered thank you to the God who had seen them through. There would be more danger ahead, more to lose. But for now, they had made it through. And that was enough.

Chapter 7

Mina looked at the others, a mix of exhaustion and fear on their faces. "We're through," she said. "We just need to climb the ridge."

"And what awaits us there?" Aria asked, removing her mask, her face a sweaty mess from the environment and from her anxiety.

Mina looked up the ridge and sighed, seeming to remember something from the past. She looked at Yip, who frowned, and then she rubbed her face with her hands.

"The plants embedded in the cracks are spitting plants. They spit thorn-like darts with some sort of secretion. Yip got it bad when we crossed. It's painful and irritating, and, honestly, hard to avoid."

"So what do we do?" Chello asked, eyeing the ridge.

"Just move as fast as you can. If you get hit, just keep moving. We can deal with it once we get to the top."

They followed Mina up the rocky ridge as fast as possible, and when they reached the top, they all had at least a handful of thorns stuck in them, but not as bad as Aria thought it would be.

The top of the ridge was flat with a rock wall to the back, but plenty of room for the four of them to get some much-needed rest. They took turns removing thorns and applying a balm from the med kit, and Chello asked about a fire.

"I honestly have no idea, but I wouldn't chance it," Mina told him.

They sat with their backs up against the rock wall in a row, each trying to recover from the events as best they could. Chello passed out food, which was a sealed package of meat, bread, and blue liquid.

"What is it?" Mina asked, wary of the fluid.

"Dried beef and bread, and an electrolyte boost. You should drink it, it's going to help with endurance and muscle fatigue."

She nodded but didn't open hers right away.

Yip was struggling to open his package, his fingers slipping off the corners before he could grip the tabs. Chello got up and walked over to where he was sitting and squatted next to him.

"Here, let me help you. These things are sealed so tightly, they can be tricky."

Mina watched as Yip handed over his package, and Chello showed him the best way to grip it and peel it back, opening it.

"There you go, kid. Try to eat it all, you'll need the strength." He stayed next to Yip, opened his package, and started eating.

Mina squinted, thinking of how Chello backtracked for Yip in the marshes. He could have easily left him. What would a Fusian soldier care if Yip died?

"You aren't so bad, you know," Mina told him.

He looked up at her with a grin. "Is that supposed to be a compliment?"

She shrugged nonchalantly. "I'm just saying that you aren't so bad."

"So, a compliment," Chello confirmed, and Yip silently chuckled beside him. Chello nudged him and said, "I knew she liked me."

Yip made a motion with his hands and then nodded and pointed at Chello while looking at Mina.

"Of course, I like him, Yip. He has weird eyes, but seems ok," Mina told him, and Yip nodded, looking at Chello's different-colored eyes.

"How do you know what he's saying?" Aria asked from where she sat.

Mina shrugged. "We sort of made up our own communication when we were locked in Greensk. Yip was in the cell across from me, and when they cut his tongue, we started using signals and stuff. We're well-connected, so it's not hard to know what he's thinking. Plus, the God lets us know when we need to."

They were silent for a while, and then Chello asked quietly, "Do you mind if I ask why they did that to you, Yip?"

"Because they're unhinged psychopaths," Mina said bluntly. "They love experimenting on human subjects, and poor Yip had one word too much to say about it one time when they came to my cell." Mina went quiet, remembering the moment. She thought for sure they would kill her. "They liked to see how much the prisoners could tolerate. They came in and rubbed some sort of salve on my back, claiming it should lessen the pain. They wanted me to let them know if it did and how it felt. But it burned just the same, each time they dropped acid onto my flesh, I screamed. It hurt so fecking bad." Her eyes stared out at nothing, remembering the pain. "Yip was across the hall, screaming in his cell, trying to get out, begging them to stop. They did stop, but only to beat the shit out of him and clip his tongue. I didn't see most of it, I was in and out of consciousness from the pain. Probably the worst day we had in there, eh, Yip?"

Yip nodded, covering his face with his hands and then making a gesture as if he were wiping tears away.

"Yeah, I know you felt bad, but what could you have done?" Mina asked him. "Makes your shitty prison seem like a dream," she said, looking at them. Both Chello and Aria looked sick, as if they couldn't believe such things occurred.

"Feck's sake, I'm so sorry, you guys," Chello said somberly, and he placed his hand on Yip's shoulder, squeezing it.

They sat in silence for a while, eating and contemplating. After a while, Aria asked, "How did you know what to do with the vines?"

Mina stared at the blue packet of liquid in her hands and shrugged. Yip kicked at her and then made a motion with his hands, causing Mina to roll her eyes.

"They already know the stories, Yip," Mina told him.

Chello raised his eyebrows. "What stories?"

"Of Velho," Mina told him, taking a drink from her blue packet of liquid. It tasted sweet.

Chello nodded, having heard the stories. "People blessed by the God."

"Yeah," Mina said evenly and thought about her knack for escape. "I can't really explain it. I just sort of see things in my head sometimes."

"So, like a vision?" Aria asked, intrigued.

Mina shrugged. "I guess so. I saw the vines wrap around my wrist, and then the dagger just before I tried to help you. And as we walked, I saw where to move to avoid them. But 4 of us were too much, which is why Yip here almost lost his head in the marsh," she said, kicking at Yip, who tried to kick her back but missed.

"You get that from the God?" Aria asked.

"My mother used to tell me I did, yeah. She said the Velhoian people have something special from the God."

"What happened to Velho?" Chello asked, his voice somber. "I heard that they were wiped out, the underground city imploded, or something of the sort."

Mina nodded, swallowing at the memory. "Traitors. They came claiming to want to swap knowledge. I don't remember a lot of it, I was just a kid. But they were curious how we lived below the ground, how to get air and water below the surface. They had uninhabitable lands they wanted to expand into. But then another group came and claimed they were a part of the original group, and once we showed them the internal structure, they used it against us and blew the whole place up. I still remember the man talking to my parents and grandparents right before he killed them. I don't remember much, but I will find that man and take my vengeance. The man with my father's watch is the man responsible."

"Feck's sake," Chello murmured. "I'm so sorry, Mina."

"It was a long time ago. But I'll have my vengeance. I promise you that."

They sat in silence until they were done eating and then lay down to sleep. Yip moved over to sleep on the far side of Mina, and he made a few gestures and slyly pointed at his ankle, and Mina nodded.

"Be careful, though," she told him, and he gave the thumbs up. She casually flopped her leg over his torso, so it looked like she was using him as a footstool. But neither Chello nor Aria looked twice, both too tired to notice.

Mina drifted off into sleep as Yip worked on her ankle device, and eventually, all of them fell into slumber.

***

Mina lifted her head and wiped her eyes, sleep falling away from her. Yip was asleep, the ankle device still on her leg. Her pant leg was rolled up, so she pulled it back down and froze, movement catching her eye. She squinted and saw Aria standing on the ledge. She slowly stood and walked out to where she was, the dim purple haze reflecting off her.

Aria was gazing out over the horizon in the direction they had come, and as she approached, Mina couldn't help but notice how beautiful she looked in the dim glow.

"If you jump, I'll never get this thing off my leg," Mina told her, motioning to her ankle.

Aria smiled but didn't look at her. "Asking me to stay alive for you, then?"

"I don't ask anyone for anything," Mina told her and looked out over the purple, hazy valley they had just come through. "It's actually sort of pretty when you look at it from up here."

Aria huffed out a chuckle. "I suppose if you can forget everything down there wants to kill you."

Mina smiled and looked at her. "You ok?"

"No, but it's my job to be ok," Aria told her and furrowed her brow.

"Such a tough guy," Mina chided and folded her arms across her chest. She swallowed and then looked away from her, saying: "You did good today."

Aria looked over at her to see if she was serious or making fun of her.

"I mean it," Mina continued. That wasn't something everyone could survive, mentally or physically. You're stronger than I thought."

Aria swallowed and let out her breath. It was an unexpected compliment. "I was scared to death, truth be told."

Mina finally looked over at her. She once again found herself taking in Aria's features in the dim light. "You'd be crazy not to be."

"Does that make you crazy, then?" Aria asked her, nudging her with her elbow.

Mina smiled and let out a low chuckle. "I think we both know I am."

They laughed quietly, and Aria let out a deep breath. "Thank you for what you did for me. I..." She stopped and swallowed, her face pulling into a tight expression as if what she was saying was difficult. "I don't think I've ever felt a fear like that, with the vines." She looked at Mina, who was staring back at her with sharp eyes. "I don't like needing people, Mina. But thank you. You kept me from panicking, and that would have killed us all."

"No big deal, Richy," Mina told her with a shrug, but there was a soft understanding in her eyes.

"I don't understand how you can stay so calm, so nonchalant about it all. I'm a ball of fear and nerves," Aria admitted, and frowned a little, looking at her.

Mina shrugged again. "It's not that I'm not scared. But I trust the God. We're taught as kids that even the bad things have a purpose. So, I never see the sense in letting fear control me. If I die, it's the way it's supposed to be. Why drive myself mad, fearing everything? He knows what He's doing."

"What a completely simple way of looking at things. It seems to serve you well," Aria told her.

Mina smiled. "Well, it's taken a lifetime of practice, and when you're forced on your own at a young age, you learn it pretty quick."

They were silent for a while, and Aria let out a long sigh. "It'll get worse, won't it? That was just the start."

Mina nodded. "Yes. The flats continue on the other side and will have poisonous gas fissures. That will give way to quicksand and swamps with venomous reptiles that we don't even have names for."

Aria exhaled and closed her eyes, shaking her head. "I never thought such things truly existed as what we saw in the marshes, but this, this seems worse," she told her honestly and was grateful to speak freely.

Mina nodded. "It'll be worse going back because we know what's waiting for us."

"How does one recover from these things, even if they survive?" She looked at Mina, who had dropped her eyes and was staring at the ground. It occurred to her that Mina had survived this once before and was being forced to do it again. "Mina."

Mina looked up at her, and Aria reached out her hand and put it on her shoulder. Aria felt her tense, but didn't stop. "I'm sorry that you're being made to do this again."

Mina looked at her, she saw that she was sincere and swallowed. "I suppose I could run away, but then you'd blow me up, so I guess I'm stuck."

"I wouldn't," Aria told her quietly, and Mina stared at her. "I didn't even take the detonator. I left it with Marcus," she admitted and shrugged.

Mina looked at her with a furrowed brow. It made no sense; it was the only protection she and Chello had from them. Not that they needed it, they weren't going to hurt them, but they didn't know that.

"I don't understand," Mina said, looking at her with confusion. "You don't know anything about me or Yip. Why wouldn't you want to take the detonator to keep yourself safe?"

Aria let a soft smile touch her lips and shrugged, crossing her arms over her chest. "I don't think you're going to hurt us. And if you want to flee, you should. I won't stop you."

Mina shook her head in frustration. Aria was too nice, too trusting. However, her world was sheltered; she didn't understand the true horrors of the real world, always kept safe in her fancy house with her guards and Praector at the ready.

"You shouldn't be so trusting," Mina said, the words coming out more bitter and jagged than she'd intended.

"Maybe," Aria replied, her gaze drifting out over the purple haze. "But I don't think you're bad. And this is a chance at freedom for you and Yip. I know that must mean something." She hesitated, then added quietly, "No one should live under the thumb of another."

Mina looked at her, catching the edge in her voice, the way the words seemed to echo something personal. She thought of Aria's father... rigid, commanding, all control and no warmth. It didn't take much to see it. Aria knew what it was to be owned, imprisoned, in a different sort of way.

"Freedom's relative," Mina said, her voice quieter now. "Not all prisons have bars."

Aria turned to her, throat tightening. Part of her wanted to say it, to tell her that she hated the life waiting for her back home, that this mission, this Ascension, was her rebellion, her chance to end things on her terms. And for the first time, she felt like someone might actually understand that.

Mina didn't press. She just stood there, steady and quiet, leaving space for the truth if Aria wanted to offer it.

But Aria held it in. How could such things be admitted, and to a perfect stranger? But something about Mina seemed to pull at her, to make her *want* to tell her secrets. But she knew she couldn't. Some things were best left buried.

"Well," Aria finally said, "bring Jaxon back alive, and you'll have your freedom."

Mina chuckled. "I'm not stupid enough to believe you'll let me have my freedom if we survive this."

"Of course we will, my father promised," Aria told her with a frown.

Mina looked up at her and saw that she believed what she said, even if not true.

"It wouldn't be the first time a man in power lied to get what he wanted."

"I give you my word, Mina. If we make it out, you'll be free. I promise."

Mina looked into her blue eyes, and they were hard, solid. She meant every word.

"I almost believe you, Richy. Let's work on getting through this alive before we argue over false promises."

Aria crossed her arms and looked out over the valley, considering that Mina may have never had someone keep their word to her in her entire life. It made her sad. Mina wasn't what she expected, she felt herself wanting to like her, to befriend her. Or at least ensure her father kept his promise to her. After everything she was doing, she deserved that much.

"You should get some more sleep," Mina told her. "This is the only place we'll have a chance to rest without danger."

Aria nodded and asked, "What about you? Why aren't you sleeping?"

"Habit," Mina said simply. She shifted her weight, leaning forward to look down over the edge of the ridge. "People like me don't sleep easily."

"And what kind of person is that?" Aria asked, her eyes flickering over to Mina's.

Mina looked up, her eyes meeting Aria's. For a moment, the air between them felt charged, their gaze holding on to each other for a bit too long.

"The kind you're probably not supposed to be around. You know, the criminal kind," Mina told her, her tone light and a smile playing at the corner of her lips.

"You don't seem so bad. Certainly not the criminal I had you pegged for. You're almost... *civil*," she jested, and she couldn't hold her smile back.

Mina's smirk returned. "Careful, Richy. You're starting to sound like you actually like me."

Aria felt a flush rise to her cheeks but forced herself to stay calm. "Don't get ahead of yourself." But her voice betrayed her, a hint of a smile slipping through.

Mina chuckled, a quiet, genuine sound that made Aria's chest tighten. "Fair enough."

They stood in silence for a while, and then Aria told her, "Thanks, Mina, for what it's worth. We'd be dead already if you weren't here."

Mina stood still as Aria lifted her hand and cupped her cheek, albeit briefly, and then turned and went and lay herself down next to Chello, who was sprawled out and lightly snoring.

Her cheek felt hot where Aria's hand had been. Staring out over the land they had crossed, she thought of the moment the Fusia guards arrested her and Yip, how there had been no vision of escape. Maybe the God had put her here for this reason, to be Aria's guide, to help her get her brother back.

Mina exhaled slowly and nodded her head as she let her eyes flicker up to the faded purple sky. Closing her eyes, she said a quick word of thanks to the God for their survival and guidance, and for what felt like two of the kindest people she had ever met. She put her hand on her face where Aria's had been, a small smile touching her lips. She turned and went back to lie next to Yip to get some more sleep.

***

Mina awoke to the sound of Chello's voice, and when she sat up, she saw him and Yip sitting across from each other, drawing something on the gravel ground. She looked over at Aria, who was sitting against the rock wall with her eyes closed.

She stretched and noticed the feeling on her ankle. She reached down, and the device was gone. Yip had removed it without blowing them to pieces.

Aria opened her eyes and smiled as Mina stood, and she smiled back and nodded at her. Mina felt a flicker of something in her chest and pushed at it, not wanting to feel anything. It would make things too difficult if she let herself like these people more than she already did. She walked over to Chello and Yip, and Yip handed her another meal pack.

"Perfect timing. I was about to wake you," Chello told her. "Yip is trying to show me the lay of the land near the prison tower."

Mina sat next to them and opened her meal, looking at the loose lines and symbols drawn in the dirt, recognizing what Yip had done.

"Yip knows it. He's the one who planned our escape, so this will be accurate," she told him, chewing on whatever dried meat was in the pack.

"How do you know all this, Yip?" Aria asked as she came and sat down next to Mina. Their arms brushed together as she did, and Mina swallowed tightly, again feeling an energy in her chest.

"Yip wasn't arrested with me in Greensk," Mina told them, and Yip nodded and gestured to the drawing and then to Mina. "I was caught in their security hub, trying to find any indication that they had something to do with the destruction of Velho. I heard it was them who came to ask for help, wanting to develop the marshlands."

"That actually sounds familiar," Chello said, his face contorting as if trying to remember.

"I was arrested and thrown in their prison, and Yip did what he does best: he saved me." She put her hand on his head and pushed a little.

Like a kitten at play, Yip batted at her hand with both of his and shoved her away.

"He did recon, surveyed the area, and planned the escape. Then he got himself arrested so he could get to me," Mina explained.

Aria and Chello stared at them, not believing what they were hearing.

"You purposely put yourself in prison to get Mina out?" Chello asked, staring at Yip.

Yip nodded and shrugged as if to say, *Of course, what else would I do?*

"Maybe you're more of a Fusian than I thought!" Chello told him and clapped his shoulder.

"So, take me through it. What's the plan?" Aria asked, and she leaned in to point to the prison tower in the sand. As she did, she passed very close to Mina, who felt the heat of her closeness. "This is the prison. How do we do this, find Jaxon, and get out?"

The four of them sat huddled together and went over the plan, a hybrid of what Mina and Yip had done and something new. Mina had no idea if it was going to work, but she never trusted herself, only what the God showed her. She was confident that this was going to be the right path. She exhaled, and they all looked at her, ready to listen.

Chapter 8

They focused on Mina, listening to her every word as she pointed and gestured to the makeshift map in the dirt.

"First, we descend the other side of the ridge. There will be more fissures and vapors, but it will quickly give way to marshy lands, holes filled with quicksand. If you get caught in the quicksand, stay calm and as still as possible. If you try to get out, it will suck you in deeper."

Chello moved quickly over each hole, but his last step was into a mushy patch that he immediately began sinking into. At first, he thought it was just loose ground, but it quickly began to suck him in. When the others got to him, he was already waist-deep, the suction a painful force on his midsection. "Stop fighting it, let your body go slack," Mina told him, and it was difficult to go against his instincts. "Put your arms around my neck, like you're hugging me. Don't pull or use your legs at all, just hang on," she told him, and he did so, panic starting to well up inside of him. He put his arms around Mina, who tried to use her weight to pull him up. "Aria, wrap your arms around my waist. Yip, you do the same to Aria. On three, we all gently tug our weight backward. Don't pull, just let yourself go backward with your weight." Chello watched the three of them line up, almost like a giant group hug. They pulled, and he felt himself coming loose, and eventually, they pulled him out. He had tears in his eyes, throwing himself on top of Mina, who was catching her breath on the ground. "Thank you, thank you!" he huffed, his breath ragged and his eyes frightened. "No offense, but you're not my type," she joked, pushing him off her, but hugged him briefly before doing so.

"Once we make it through the rest of the flats, the ground will give way to wetlands, marsh, and half-dead trees filled with creatures. Everything is dangerous. Take nothing for granted. We know for sure there are fat, poisonous frogs in the waters; they have some sort of secretion that burns."

They waded through the wetlands, ripples of water moving around them as if what lay underneath was waiting for its chance. Yip stopped and began gesturing, and Mina nodded. "He wants to catch some frogs for later. Yip, don't touch them, use your scarf," she told him, and he took a bag from Chello and began trying to catch the frogs. It was easy enough, the hungry creatures almost rushing to him when he put his hands in the water. But he fell in the process, and Aria pulled him up just as a large two-headed serpent slithered over and sprang from the water, ripping a frog out of Yip's hand. She used her staff to fight it back, and the creature retreated into the depths of the marshes. "Maybe you have enough frogs?" Aria asked him, and he nodded with wide eyes.

"Next will be the prison moat. Once we cross onto the shelf ledge, the back of the prison tower will be in front of us, surrounded by a moat. Inside that water are the dwellers, half human, half creature. The waters are fed from the sewage drain, filled with human waste and who knows what else. But that's our entry point, the only way in."

"How do we get up into the drain without going in the water?" Aria asked, and Mina frowned.

"Unfortunately, we have to get in the water to reach the grate. But Yip and Chello will go around this way, to where they have the moat gated off. There's a large swath of water and land here that they try to keep clean because it leads to the main city road. Yip and Chello will cause a distraction and draw the dwellers in that direction. That will hopefully attract the attention of the guards inside as well. Aria, you and I will have to move quickly and get into the sewer, through the tunnel, and into the prison. We'll have to find your brother and get back out before the commotion stops."

"No, no, I need to stay with Aria," Chello protested.

"I know you want that, but I can't let you two go into the prison alone. Either Yip or I has to go with you. You'll never find your way."

Chello shook his head. "I can't leave her. If something were to happen…she's my responsibility. I'm her Praector."

"If you two go in alone, you won't come back out," Mina told him in a steady voice. "I appreciate what you're saying. I don't want you to think I don't understand. Yip's not crazy about leaving me, either. But it would be suicide." She looked at Chello, who had a deep pleading in his eyes. "Chello, I'll keep her safe. I promise."

Chello looked at her and then at Aria, who Mina saw nod slightly. He rubbed his face with his hands and seemed to really struggle with the idea of leaving her. Mina respected that; he clearly cared about her and took his job as her protector seriously. She knew this would be a struggle.

Mina lifted her hand, trying to explain the importance, and was shocked when Aria reached over and put her hand on her forearm.

"Chell," Aria said, and she gave Mina's arm a gentle squeeze before releasing it. "You have to trust Mina. It's the only way this will work. I trust her."

Mina stared at Aria, her insides thrumming. And when Aria met her gaze, she felt lightheaded, as if she were swimming in new and unknown emotions.

"Go with Yip and keep him safe. Make sure you both do your part, or none of it will matter, anyway," Aria told him, and he begrudgingly nodded, understanding it was the only way.

Chello and Yip moved swiftly, keeping low to the ground as they made their way around the tower. Their eyes locked on the rusty metal gate submerged in the water, a barrier meant to keep the dwellers away from the city. Its surface was slick with algae, the dark water beneath stirring with unseen threats. Yip pointed at the gate and made a quick gesture. Chello squinted, trying to grasp the plan. "I get it, but how are we supposed to..." he stopped mid-sentence as Yip reached into his satchel and pulled out a familiar-looking device. Chello's eyes widened. "No way," he huffed, grabbing Yip's pant leg and yanking it up to confirm what he suspected. "How the feck did you get that off without blowing us to pieces?" Yip's grin was equal parts smug and sheepish. He shrugged and pointed to the device and then to the gate. Chello nodded and took the satchel of frogs from Yip. He motioned for Chello to toss them into the water, a distraction to draw the dwellers away from the gate while he set the explosive

device. Chello hesitated only a moment, then nodded. They exchanged
a quick fist bump and moved.

"Where do we meet afterward?" Chello asked, "Assuming all goes to plan?"

Yip pointed to where the flats met the marsh, tapping his finger in the dust.

"It is going to have to be quick and careful," Mina told them.

Chello nodded and put his fist out in front of him. Aria covered it with her hand, and Yip quickly did the same. Mina swallowed and put her hand on the pile, looking each of them in the eyes, her gaze lingering on Aria for a bit longer. She prayed that the God would keep them safe. She realized that she *liked* Chello and Aria and wanted them to survive this suicide mission. *If the God wills it,* she thought, and then told them:

"May the God watch over each one of us. Let's go."

***

Aria sat at the entrance of the sewer tunnel above the water, her breath heaving in her chest. The stench of putrid wastewater filled the air, but it wasn't the smell that made her stomach churn. Across the narrow space, Mina was on her back, chest rising and falling as she caught her breath.

"Did it bite you? Are you okay?" she asked Mina, her voice tight, the words trembling as they escaped her lips.

Mina propped herself up on an elbow and shook her head. "I'm good." Her voice was steady and calm as if what had just happened was nothing. She reached out across the grimy floor, her hand settling lightly on Aria's knee. "What about you? Are you okay?"

"I'm fine," she lied, though her voice cracked on the words.

Physically, she was unscathed, but mentally … she was far from okay. She closed her eyes and took a breath. The image of the dweller lunging at her from the murky water, its grotesqueness beyond anything she had ever imagined, flashed in her mind. The moment replayed: how she froze, how she couldn't even scream, let alone fight back as it lurched for her. It was a bloated and pale monstrosity, its eyes a vacant black, and its teeth jagged and hungry.

"You're lying," Mina said gently, not moving her hand. "But that's okay."

The memory burned in Aria's brain. Mina was quick to act while she stayed paralyzed in fear. Mina was almost into the tunnel but had flung herself down onto the humanesque creature, wrestling it back into the water long enough for Aria to scramble up to safety. Even when other dwellers came, gnashing and writhing, Mina fought them off before climbing to the safety of the tunnel.

"Just got the boot, not me," Mina told her, brushing off the encounter like it was nothing. But it *was* something. It was terrifying, and Aria wanted to burst into tears.

Mina shifted to sit beside her. "We need to keep moving."

Aria's insides screamed in protest, but she nodded, forcing herself to her knees. They began crawling, and the tunnel grew narrower the farther up they went, the stench thick and oppressive.

"This is going to get tight," Mina told her. "Let me go first. You follow."

Aria nodded, keeping her eyes down, but Mina stopped, lingering.

"Hey, Richy, look at me."

The nickname was ridiculous, and out of annoyance more than anything, she looked up at Mina. "Don't call me that," she muttered, the faintest quiver in her voice.

Mina smirked, but her eyes softened. She reached out, cupping Aria's chin with a hand surprisingly gentle for someone so tough. "You're doing great. This is a lot, more than anyone should have to deal with. But you've got this, okay? Your brother is just up ahead, through the grate. We're almost there."

Aria's throat tightened, her eyes stinging. She blinked rapidly, embarrassed by the tears threatening to fall. She wasn't supposed to cry, to be scared.

"Hey," Mina said again, her thumb brushing lightly against Aria's cheek. "Look at me, Richy."

She looked at Mina and there it was, that maddeningly calm, cocky grin. It was absurd how she could be so composed at a time like this. But it reached something deep inside, and Aria gave a small nod.

"You're stronger than you know," Mina told her. "You've already exceeded my expectations, truth be told."

Aria let out a shaky chuckle, wiping at her tears. Something shifted inside her, a tiny ember of resolve catching fire. She wasn't just surviving for her brother. She wanted to do it for this maddening, annoying woman who somehow made her feel like they could do this, they could get to Jaxon and bring him home. Somehow, Mina made her feel like it was possible that she could be strong enough to get through this.

"Atta girl." Mina gave her a nod of approval. "Now let's go get your brother and get the feck out of here."

Aria took a deep breath, squaring her shoulders. "Let's go."

Chapter 9

Are you alright?" Aria asked, her breath labored. She had Jaxon in her arms, but her eyes were on Mina, who was clutching her side, leaning her head against the wall of the tunnel.

"I'm fine. We need to move. They're going to realize what's going on and come after us. Go on, you go first with him, and I'll be behind you."

Aria looked at the blood oozing out over Mina's fingers where she held the gash on her abdomen and frowned. They had moved with urgency once they were in the prison, happy to see that the distraction Chello and Yip caused had drawn most of the guards out. But not all of them.

The first attackers came quickly, men in uniform with daggers and taser-like weapons. Aria stepped into the fray, her staff whirling as she deflected strikes and landed blows with precision, her training in action.

Even in the chaos, she found herself marveling at Mina's skill. Mina flowed like water, anticipating every move before it happened, her body a blur of grace and ferocity. And she never killed any of them, somehow managing to knock them out or incapacitate them instead.

They were on a speed search then, looking in cell after cell for Jaxon. Mina led Aria through the corridors like a ghost retracing its death. Each cell they passed clawed at her memories, whispers of past screams, the scrape of iron chains, the suffocating weight of captivity. Her breath was tight in her chest, her hands curled into fists to keep them from shaking. Memories were thick, flashes of her time locked in this nightmare.

Then Aria found him.

Jaxon was huddled in the corner of his cell, little more than skin and bone. His dark hair hung in filthy strands over a face mottled with bruises. The stench of sickness and rot hit them like a wave, but it was the emptiness in his eyes that made Aria stagger. He knew her, Mina could see it in the flicker of recognition, but something inside him had unraveled, lost to the darkness of this place.

Mina squatted at the cell door, her mind screamed at her to run, to get out before the past locked her back in. Instead, she forced herself to focus as Aria fumbled with the stolen keys, her hands shaking as she unlocked the door. Prisoners howled from their cells, the air thick with desperation, but Mina kept her gaze on Aria, who was now kneeling beside the brother she had fought so hard to find.

Aria got him on his feet. Mina noticed that Jaxon was tall and lanky, and his facial features were like his sisters. Despite his height, his shoulders were hunched in, a clear sign of the toll this place had taken on him. She saw the tears rolling down Aria's face, and she placed a gentle hand on her shoulder as she passed on their way out of the cell.

They made their way back to the sewer, and they thought it was done; they were out. But two guards were hiding in the shadows and attacked them as if anticipating their point of escape. One lunged forward, a dagger aimed directly at Jaxon.

"No!" Aria screamed, but Mina was faster.

She threw herself between Jaxon and the guard, throwing a punch that landed, but so did the guard's blade. The dagger sank into her midsection with a sickening sound, and Mina crumpled with a gasp of pain.

Rage and fear surged through Aria. She swung her staff with deadly precision, unleashing crackling currents of energy that sent the attackers convulsing to the ground. When she turned to Mina, despite her injury, she found her already urging them forward and out of the prison.

And so that is where they sat, back in the sewer tunnel, Jaxon dazed, and Mina badly hurt.

"Mina, I think you should…"

"Don't be scared, Richy," Mina told her and tried to force a smile through her pained breathing. "Slide down and when you get to the end, stop. I'll be right behind you."

Aria looked at her and hesitated, but noises from above made her nod, and she took Jaxon and moved down the tunnel.

Mina grimaced when they were gone, lifting her hand and looking at the area where the blade had sliced her. It missed her organs, but it was a deep cut that would need to be stitched. She took off her shirt and tore it, but not in half, just enough to make it long enough to wrap around her midsection. The pain was intense as she pulled it tight, doing her best to create a makeshift tourniquet to stop the bleeding. There was a clamoring from above, and she knew she had to move.

She grabbed the grate and struggled to pull it back shut. The guards would know this was their exit, but that was the point. She sat for a minute, wedged against the wall, her eyes closed, trying to compartmentalize the pain. More noise from above made her move, and she reached down to the bag on her hip and fished out the altered contraption Yip had made from her ankle device. She looped it around the latch and then turned and slid down the sewage tunnel, her hand on her stomach, and her eyes wincing in pain.

***

Aria sat with Jaxon at the end of the tunnel, wondering what was taking Mina so long. She should have slid down right after them, and she felt worried. "Jaxon, are you ok?" she asked, and he nodded, his breath still labored. "I need you to sit here while I go check on Mina. Stay exactly where you are, and whatever you do, don't jump down into the water, do you hear me?"

He nodded at her, lifting his hand to touch her face again, as if still in disbelief that she was real.

"Stay right here."

Aria turned and scrambled up the tunnel, heading back towards the top, hoping that Mina was ok. She stopped at the first turn, hearing clatter ahead. She tried to listen, and moments later, Mina came crashing into her.

"Feck!" Mina yelled out.

Aria used her legs to stop them from sliding.

Mina saw it was Aria and relaxed a bit. "Missed me, huh?"

"I was worried. What took you so long?" Aria huffed out; they were face to face in the small space. She felt Mina's labored breath on her face.

"Had to set the device."

"What device?" Aria asked, confused.

Mina grimaced again as she shifted her position. "We need to get the feck out of here before it blows, Richy."

Mina leaned in, and Aria's eyes widened. She sucked in a breath as Mina wrapped her arms around her, then hooked her legs around her waist.

"Hold on," Mina whispered in her ear.

With a sudden pull, they tipped forward and began sliding down the tunnel. They plunged downward, tangled together, until they crashed into the tunnel's opening. Mina thrust her legs out, stopping them, letting out a painful grunt.

"Aria?" Jaxon called out in a hoarse voice.

Aria pulled herself away from Mina and went to him. "Here, Jax. Let's get you up, we have to get out of here."

"You still have the bag?" Mina asked her.

Aria nodded, unclipping it from her waist and handing it to her. "I hope they're still alive."

Mina wasted no time untying the bag. "They'll have to do, dead or alive. Get ready to jump, we don't have much time to pull this off. The device will detonate as soon as they open the grate."

"What device?" Aria asked again.

Mina smirked and winked at her, lifting her pant leg to show the missing ankle device.

"How…" Aria asked incredulously, but Mina grabbed her side and grimaced, and Aria sucked in her breath. "Mina, that's bad," she said, staring at the blood-stained shirt.

Mina ignored her, moving to the opening and looking below. She could see ripples in the water where the dwellers were bobbing, waiting, and hoping for them to fall and be devoured. She felt her insides swirl, her instincts triggering, and stared off, seeing the vision that crashed into her mind.

Aria looked at her, watching her eyes glaze over. She had seen Mina look this way before, seeing something no one else could, one of her visions, as she called them.

"Mina?" Aria asked, concerned.

Mina's eyes flickered to her, and then she gave a small nod. She took two frogs out of the bag, their secretion stinging her hands. She tucked them into the waistband of her pants, one on each hip.

"I don't know how well this is going to work anymore, there are more dwellers that came back," Mina told her. "I'm not sure how many are down there. But listen to me, once you hit the water, you don't stop. For anything. Do you understand?"

"Mina, I think we should all…"

"Aria," Mina said, cutting her off, her voice low and firm. "You got what you came for. Now finish it." She thought of her vision and added, "No matter what you hear, what you see, you take him and get to the edge. You do not turn back. No matter what happens to me."

Aria flinched at the words, her head slowly shaking before she could stop herself. No. That wouldn't work. Mina had to live. She was the one who could lead, the one who could get the others through. Aria had already made peace with what this mission might cost her. She told herself the marshes were a fitting end. Better to die out here than return to the cage her father called home.

But as Mina stepped closer, the space between them vanishing, her hand landing steady on Aria's shoulder, something in Aria cracked.

"Promise me," Mina said quietly.

Aria met her gaze, and the world narrowed to those fierce, unwavering hazel eyes. Something stirred in her chest, a sudden ache, unfamiliar and sharp. Regret? Longing? She wasn't sure. All she knew was that for the first time in her life, someone looked at her like she wasn't just a pawn, a daughter, a duty. Mina saw *her*. And Aria didn't want to disappear anymore. Not like this. She began wondering what a *different* life could look like.

Her hand reached up almost on its own. She took Mina's from her shoulder and held it between them, grounding herself in its warmth.

She nodded once, her voice barely above a whisper. "I promise."

They stood looking at each other for a moment, a swirl of some unexpected energy moving between them.

Jaxon coughed, bringing them back to the present. Mina blinked and quickly moved away to the far side of the opening. She glanced down and again saw ripples in the sewage water. She looked back at Aria, who had Jaxon under her arm, and nodded.

"On my signal."

"Jax, we are going to jump and swim as fast as we can. Our lives depend on it," Aria told him, and he nodded, moving to the edge and looking over.

Mina opened the bag, reaching for a fat frog. She pulled it out, again feeling the sting from the secretion, but ignored it. She winced as she threw it into the water, watching as the dwellers moved towards it. She grabbed two more and threw them. After a moment, she turned to look at Aria.

"Now!" she yelled.

Aria wasted no time pulling Jaxon and jumping off the ledge into the raw sewage below. They submerged, and she kicked until her head broke the surface, never letting go of her brother. She swam as fast and as hard as she could while towing him along, her insides fighting between making it to the edge and turning back to look at Mina.

Mina watched them jump, and when they hit the water, she ripped the bag and threw it as far as she could, frogs flying everywhere as the bag sailed through the air. She jumped in the opposite direction, the pain in her stomach not allowing for much push.

When she hit the water, she swam as fast as she was able to, pain ripping through her midsection. The edge of the embankment came into view, and she thought she had made it and would survive this a second time. But then she felt hands gripping her legs, and they pulled her under, all sight of the shore gone.

***

Aria hauled herself onto the slick shelf of land, breath ragged, limbs trembling from the swim and the fight. For a moment, she felt the dizzying rush of survival. Of *hope*.

And then she turned and saw that Mina was gone.

The surface of the water churned violently for a beat, then stilled, the last trace of her, an outstretched hand, dragged beneath.

Aria stared, her blood turning to ice. "No," she breathed. "Mina!" She scrambled to the water's edge, mud caking her hands as she searched the dark surface, willing Mina to rise. "Mina!"

But nothing broke through.

Her heart thudded against her ribs, desperate and wild. She looked back, and Jaxon lay gasping behind her, barely conscious. Alive. Mina had done that. Mina had saved him.

And she had saved *her*, too.

Aria had stepped into these marshes ready to die. She had made peace with that. But somewhere along the way—somewhere between Mina's sharp words and steady hands—she had felt it. The pull. The ache. The terrifying spark of *wanting* to live. Not for her father. Not for duty. For *herself.*

And now the one who had lit that spark was gone.

She pressed her hand to her chest, as if to hold the breaking pieces in place. "Please," she whispered to the water. "Please."

Her eyes searched, waiting for Mina to break the surface of the sewage like she did before, but she didn't. Aria had promised, but she couldn't let Mina drown. She couldn't not try to help her. Before she could act, Jaxon let out a groan, and when she looked back, she saw a twisted and deformed reptile emerging from the hollow trunk of an old tree, saliva oozing from its barred teeth.

"Jax!"

She ran over to him and kicked at the creature, who hissed. In a fluid motion, she reached for her staff, extended it, and swung it in the direction of the creature. It scurried away, recoiling. Aria looked back at the water, but there was still no sign of Mina.

She ran to the water's edge and scanned desperately for a sign of anything. To the far side, the surface rippled. The dwellers were still thrashing, distracted by the frogs Mina had thrown. But there was no movement near her, no sign of Mina. She had been under for too long.

A strangled sound escaped Aria's throat, a broken cry, half of Mina's name. And then, without warning, the water directly in front of her burst apart.

Mina exploded upward, gasping, coughing, fighting for air. Aria didn't hesitate. She lunged forward, gripping her under the arms, dragging her toward solid ground. Mina collapsed onto the embankment with a wet thud, panting, her chest heaving. Blood soaked her midsection, her forearms shredded with teeth marks. She looked like something torn from the deep.

"Mina! By the God, speak! Say something!" Aria dropped to her knees beside her, hands cradling her cheeks, slick with blood and water. Her voice cracked. "Mina?"

Another ragged gasp. Mina's eyes fluttered open as she choked up murky water, coughing hard. When her gaze finally landed on Aria's, she tried to smile through the pain.

Relief crashed into Aria like a wave. Without thinking, she fell forward and wrapped her arms around her, holding her close, needing to feel the warmth, the solidness, the *life* still inside her.

"Easy now, Richy," Mina rasped, her voice torn but teasing. "Your brother's gonna think you have a crush on me."

Aria let out an unexpected, breathless sound as she pulled back, sitting on her heels. "I was worried, but I can tell by your mouth that you're just fine."

Mina tried to sit up, the smirk still on her lips until it twisted into a grimace. She clutched her side, breath shallow. "Frogs in the waistband. Works every time."

She reached out, and Aria took her hand, helping her sit fully upright.

"We need to get out of here," Mina said.

Aria nodded, then gestured to the blood still soaking her side. "We should clean that. You've been swimming in sewage. It's going to get infected."

"We don't have time." Mina's eyes flicked to Jaxon. "Can he walk?"

Aria turned, moving quickly to her brother. "Yes," she said, helping him to his feet. "Come on, Jax."

Mina stood slowly, unsteady at first, but she straightened, inhaled deeply, and locked her focus ahead.

"Stay close. Stay quiet. And don't touch anything," she ordered.

And just like that, they moved out, three survivors with no time to waste, and no promises of what waited ahead.

***

The relief Chello felt when he saw all three of them coming across the marsh and onto the flats was so immense that he actually cried out.

"Thank the God!" he yelled, and Yip jumped up from where he was sitting and they both ran to the ledge, helping them up as they approached.

"Chell!" Aria cried out, and they embraced tightly, tears in both of their eyes. "I wasn't sure I would see you again!"

"Are you ok, are you hurt?" he asked, pulling away to look at her, his hands on her shoulders. He assessed her, and she looked ok. There was blood on her face, but it was dried smears and not her own.

"I am, you? Is Yip?" she asked, looking at him and then over at Yip, who was hugging Mina.

"We're ok. A few close calls, but we made it." Chello let his eyes slide to Jaxon, who was sitting on the ground, hunched over. "By the God, you found him."

He went over and kneeled next to Jaxon and hugged him.

"He's a bit disoriented, but I think ok," Aria told him, squatting down next to them. Jaxon looked at them with a bit more clarity and tried to smile.

"Glad to have you back, Jax," Chello told him and put his hand on his head. He stood and looked over at Mina, closing the space between them. He threw his arms around her, pulling her close.

"Thank you. Thank you for keeping her safe," he told her, and Mina grunted in pain.

"My pleasure."

Chello furrowed his brow. "You're hurt."

"I'll be alright," she told him as he bent down for a closer look.

"She was cut with a dagger, saving our lives," Aria told him, walking over.

Yip put his hands on his head, jumping up and down in frustration.

"You wouldn't have been able to help, Yip. He came out of nowhere, and I barely saw it. I reacted too late," Mina told him, and grimaced when Chello peeled back the swath of shirt she had tied around her.

"Oh gosh," he said, looking at it, and knelt on one knee. "Yip, grab my bag, will you? Let me clean this the best I can before we get going."

"We don't have time," Mina protested.

Aria put her hand on her shoulder. "Please. Let him clean it."

Chello made a mental note of the way Aria and Mina were looking at one another and filed it away, taking the med kit from Yip.

"This will sting, but just bear with me, Mina," he told her and uncapped a small vial. "Can you lie back?"

Mina sat and lay back while Chello hovered over her, and Aria kneeled next to her, taking her hand. Yip was pacing in a circle, making all sorts of animated gestures, angry that he wasn't there to protect her, the very thing he existed for.

Chello poured the vial out into the cut, and Mina gritted her teeth and closed her eyes as she felt the burn of the liquid.

"You need stitches, but this is the best we have. Hopefully, it slows the bleeding," Chello told her, and put a piece of sterile gauze over the wound, and then wrapped a bandage cloth around her waist.

"That fecking hurts," Mina huffed out.

Chello nodded. "I know. Let's get out of here, and I can take a better look up on the ridge."

Mina nodded, and Aria helped her up, their hands staying connected for longer than necessary. They both felt the pull of the unseen energy that was humming between them.

"Can Jax walk?" Chello asked.

Aria let go of Mina and nodded, walking over to him. "Yes. He's a little slow, but he can."

Mina looked at them and then out across the flats, grimacing. "Ok, let's go."

Before they could start, Yip walked up to Mina and made some adamant gestures, which Mina shook off.

"No way. You take up the rear and keep your eyes on them."

But Yip shook his head, his gestures insistent. Mina let out a resigned sigh, knowing that sometimes Yip knew better, and this was one of those situations, given her current state.

"Ok, Ok. Yip will lead, I will follow him, and Chello, you bring up the back." Mina told them, and they all nodded and fell in line, slowly starting their way back.

***

They made it to the ridge with a handful of close calls, Chello slicing through a creature that grabbed Yip near a hollow tree, and Aria using her staff to push back salamander-like creatures that seemed insistent on attacking Jaxon. They moved slowly through the flats, and once the quicksand started to disappear and give way to the fissures, they all breathed a bit easier.

It was a slow climb up the ridge, Mina not being able to move fast enough to avoid the bulk of the shooting thorns. She got it worse than the rest, but Yip was quick to pull them out of her once they reached the top and apply a balm.

Mina sat against the rock wall, her breath labored. She felt unwell, her vision was foggy, and her body felt like it was hot, burning. Her wound throbbed, and she felt weak.

Chello passed out meal pouches, and he handed Mina and Jaxon an additional blue bag of fluid. "You both need these more than we do."

Mina sat with hers on her lap, not trying to open anything.

"Let me help you," Chello told her, and he eyed her cautiously. "I don't think you're ok, Mina."

"I can't argue with you," she told him.

Yip kneeled next to her, concerned.

"I don't feel good, something isn't right," she admitted, shifting her weight with a grimace.

"I'm sure it's infected from the sewage," Aria told her, lifting the fluid to Jaxon's lips as he drank. "We need to get you back to the city."

"Well," Mina announced and put her hand on Yip's shoulder. "I'm not sure if I can commit to that."

Yip began a flurry of gestures and had tears in his eyes, clearly upset.

Mina smiled a weak smile. "You might need to get them home, Yip-o."

"Don't talk like that. We're all leaving here together," Chello told her.

Mina looked at him with knowing eyes. "If I have to choose between dying in your prison and here, I choose here."

"You aren't going back to prison! I already told you that!" Aria told her, and there was irritation in her tone.

"I doubt that's what your father has in mind," Mina said weakly and looked at Chello. "Am I wrong?"

Chello didn't answer; he simply tore open the food pouch and placed it in Mina's hands.

"Eat all of this," he ordered.

"Chell?" Aria asked, sensing that he knew something she didn't. "That isn't true, right?"

Chello stood and rubbed his hand over his head, looking at Aria. He couldn't lie to her, nor did he want to. He looked at Mina and Yip, two people he thought were decent when they started this journey, but now considered his friends, the trauma of their shared experience bonding them together.

"He …" Chello started and then exhaled. "Your father made it clear that if Mina and Yip didn't make it back, no one would be too concerned about that. It would actually be...*preferred*."

Aria stood and looked at him incredulously. He looked back with sorrowful eyes, and shrugged a little, knowing that Aria wouldn't just be upset about the news, but about the fact that her father was the one who said such.

"He didn't," she muttered in a low voice, but she knew the truth. She had known it the moment Chello spoke. The promise had been a lie.

Something shifted inside her, like a tide turning. Anger rippled through her, quiet but consuming. Her eyes found Mina, still battered, still breathing. Aria felt it settle in her chest like a vow. If her father wouldn't honor the promise, *she* would. That alone was worth living for.

"See, Richy? Told you so," Mina huffed out and grunted as she shifted her side.

"Well, that's not going to happen. We're all making it out together!" Aria told her and looked at Chello.

"Of course we are!" Chello agreed and nodded at her. "They've saved our lives! We owe them to keep the promise made to them."

Mina closed her eyes, her breathing heavy, and wondered if it was destined that they all survived this. She felt the pain in her side and thought that maybe the God had other plans. She didn't see any visions, no sign of anything, and wasn't sure if that was good or bad.

"Rest, Mina. You'll need your strength," Chello told her, patting her shoulder, and Mina nodded, closing her eyes.

Sleep came in waves, and Mina awoke with a chill. She opened her eyes, and Aria was lying against her, her head propped on her shoulder. She sat up, and Aria awoke as well.

"Are you ok?" Aria asked her in a sleepy voice.

Mina croaked out, "Thirsty."

Aria reached for the water and handed it to her, but Mina didn't attempt to reach for it. She was shivering, her lips trembling. Aria opened the canteen and lifted it to her lips so she could sip it.

"Ttthank yyou," Mina stammered out.

Aria put her hand on Mina's forehead. "By the God, you're fevered," she said and stood, going to where Chello was sleeping on the other side of Jaxon to get the med kit. She fished around in it and pulled out a small packet of pills. "Here, take one of these. They don't work as well as the tonic, but I think it'll help."

Mina took the pill with a shaky sip of water and pressed her hand to her stomach, the pain cutting through her. Her thoughts swam in a fog, her vision blurring as she fought to stay awake.

"Can you promise me something?" Mina asked in barely a whisper.

Aria shrugged off her shirt, leaving her in just a tank top. She draped it gently over Mina, the thin fabric functioning as a makeshift blanket, before sitting beside her and pressing a cool hand to Mina's burning forehead.

"I can try," Aria replied softly.

Mina clutched the shirt close to her chin, her body trembling.

"I need you to make sure Yip is okay. I don't know how it works, if he can live on without me. But if he does, take care of him. Don't let him go back to prison."

Tears pricked Aria's eyes, and she shook her head, swallowing the lump rising in her throat. She didn't want to hear this, didn't want Mina to start giving up.

"Mina, you're going to be fine. We just need to get you out of here, back to the city."

"Hey, Richy. Promise me," Mina insisted, her weak hand reaching for Aria's. "He's too sensitive to be on his own. Please. Just promise?"

Aria squeezed her hand, her thumb tracing slow circles over the back of it. "Okay. I promise. But you've got to promise me something, too. Don't give up, alright?"

Mina's attempt at a smile barely reached her lips, her eyes fluttering open and shut, glazed with fever. "I'll try. But I think I'll hurt you more than help you. Especially with those vines. But you can do this. I know you can. You're more than halfway there. And then you can get your weird green eye." A faint grin broke through her exhaustion, and Aria tried to return it, though tears threatened to spill. "And Richy?" Mina's voice pulled her back.

"What is it?" Aria asked, her gaze locking on Mina's face, wet with feverish sweat.

"You're more than your father's expectations, okay? Try to remember that."

The words hit Aria like a stone, breaking through years of self-doubt. Mina had touched a wound she rarely let herself acknowledge, one she was prepared to die for.

"Believe that," Mina continued, her voice a fragile thread. "The God has a path for you. Don't be afraid to seek it out, to embrace it. No matter what your father thinks. You're so much more than his plans and expectations."

Tears rolled down Aria's face. How could this near stranger see her so clearly, speak to the hidden parts of her soul? She looked at Mina, who lay there with her hair plastered to her forehead, trembling, yet somehow stronger than anyone she had ever known. She was a gift from the God, sent here to see them through. To see *her* through. She was sure of it. Any lingering thoughts of letting herself go, of disappearing, were shattered.

"You have your path, Mina. And it doesn't end here in the marshes. Do you hear me? We're getting out of here. All of us together," she whispered. "Now rest. You'll feel better in the morning."

It felt like a lie, but Mina nodded and held Aria's hand, drifting off to sleep.

***

It was slow and miserable, but they made their way across the flats and stood at the beginning of the vine field. Jaxon and Mina slowed them considerably; the first getting better, but the latter getting worse. Yip was worried, staying by Mina and helping her walk, stopping when she needed to.

Aria and Chello stared at the vines, a cold knot forming in their stomachs. A deep unease settled between them; without Mina leading, the path ahead felt impossible.

"How are we going to do this?" Aria asked Chello, and he shook his head.

"I don't know. Very slowly and with help from the God, I guess."

"Don't touch them or strike them," Mina wheezed out, and she tried to stand and move forward. "I can lead."

"We remember the rules. You're going between me and Aria with Jaxon." Chello told her.

She shook her head. "No, I'll go last with Yip. But keep your eyes up, Chello. Remember how they move."

The apprehension was thick enough to choke on, but Chello nodded anyway and swallowed hard, praying he didn't make a fatal mistake. He glanced at Aria. Keeping her safe had always been his duty. But now? Now the weight of all their lives pressed down on him, and he had to find courage. He took a deep breath and steadied himself.

"Ok, let's go. Slow and steady," he told them. He let his eyes flicker upwards to the God, very much hoping He was with them.

They moved gingerly through the vines, and Mina could barely keep her focus. To her, it looked like the vines were moving all around them, swarming immediately.

Yip was at her side, tugging her along, and occasionally, he would stop and maneuver around a set of vines, leading Mina carefully. Once, when they were about halfway through, a vine coiled and rose like a snake in front of Chello, who drew his dagger out of reaction but held it very still.

"Chell, don't," Aria whispered, and they all froze, their hearts hammering.

Chello held his breath as it inched towards him, and before he could react, Yip was by his side and slowly slid in front of him.

"What are you doing?" Chello yelled in a whisper.

Yip carefully reached behind him into the satchel and pulled out the remaining dead frog.

He took two steps to the side, so he was almost in a mass of vines, and motioned for them to slowly move past. The vines moved with Yip, coiling and swaying at the scent of the frog. The others moved slowly, Mina hanging on Aria's shoulder for support. Once they were passed, Yip very slowly dropped the frog and carefully moved away from it. A vine coiled around it, and others seemed to take notice and joined. Yip scurried to the rest of the group, who didn't stop. They move purposefully through the maze.

They were almost out, each of them moving slowly as they prayed to the God in their own way. The salt ledges weren't far ahead, and they knew the vines had to be coming to an end.

Mina was behind them, walking slowly with a dazed wobble, and fell to her knees, unable to keep her focus. Yip was ahead of her and stopped, looking back. He frowned, sensing a shift in the air, but it was too late.

It came out of the marshes in a giant plume, and all Mina could do was stare at it in shock. Her eyes went big, taking in the size of the slick-skinned black creature. It looked like a vine had come alive, almost like an eel with a large bulbous head. It had no distinguishable facial features, no eyes or nostrils, just slick black skin and a large open mouth with rows and rows of razor-sharp teeth. She watched it stretch up out of the marshes and tower over her. She tried to stand but was too weak.

"Oh, feck! Mina!" Chello yelled, but they were too far ahead.

The creature already had her in its sights, the smell of her blood drawing it out of its slumber. The other vines recoiled at the emergence of the enormous creature as if it dominated all of them.

Mina tried once more to stand, her limbs shaking, useless. She collapsed back into the muck, bracing for the inevitable. Nothing was triggering inside of her, no visions or paths of escape. This, she thought, was it. The God was calling her home. She watched as the creature lunged, its massive jaws parting... but then Yip was there.

He moved without hesitation, moving silently into the creature's path, his small frame a wall of loyalty in front of Mina. For a moment, just a breath, the air around him seemed to be still. No sound. No fear.

The creature's jaw closed around him. It flung him into the air like he weighed nothing, caught him again mid-fall, and slammed him to the ground with bone-crushing force. Mina let out a pained groan, something close to a weak scream.

Yip lay broken and still, and something about him shimmered, barely visible like heat rising off a stone. Then it was gone.

Mina was left staring at him, her eyes wide, her heart pounding. She felt the sting of tears in her eyes and swallowed a dry lump. It always hurt when she lost Yip, and she really liked this version of him. But she knew this was part of the deal as she tried to crawl away.

Aria and Chello watched in horror as the creature's tentacle pierced through Yip, front to back, the slick black coil going completely through him as it picked his body up off the wet ground.

"NO!" Chello yelled, and he took off running towards them.

The creature slowly pulled Yip backward into the marshes, Mina locking eyes with him for a few precious seconds. There was a silent exchange, a thankfulness, and a promise to see each other again in that look.

Mina fell back, unable to crawl any longer. Chello ran past her to the edge of the marshes, but Yip was gone, dragged under the murky water, with nothing but bubbles left. He stared in disbelief, his thoughts unable to comprehend that Yip was gone. His eyes stayed frozen on the ripples, almost as if he stared hard enough, Yip would resurface. But there was nothing but the quiet truth as the water stilled.

Mina moaned, and Chello turned to her, rushing over. "Mina, I'm so sorry," he whispered, but she shook her head.

"We have to move," she wheezed out, and he hoisted her up and helped her walk over to where Aria and Jaxon were both staring in disbelief. Aria had tears rolling down her cheeks, a shocked expression on her face.

Chello dragged Mina and yelled to Aria, "Come on, the vines will be back, we have to keep moving!"

The four of them moved on through the vines, which were distracted enough that none were near them. They went as fast as they could, Chello dragging Mina, and Aria helping Jaxon. They saw the open marsh and then the salt ledges ahead and knew they were close.

"We're so close, the vines are nearly done. Just keep moving," Chello huffed.

Before they could get into the openness of the marshes and the safety of the salty water, a vine slithered out and began to wrap around Mina's leg. When he couldn't pull her, Chello looked back.

"No, no, no!" he yelled, letting her fall to the ground.

Mina held up her hand. In a fragile voice, she huffed: "Go. Get to the ledge, you're almost out."

"We can't leave you, come on," Chello told her, pulling at her leg.

Mina let out a scream, and Chello jumped back as the vines reacted and one reached for him.

"Go, you fecking idiot! You made it! You're almost out!" Mina scolded him, and she saw black spots in her vision, consciousness threatening to leave her.

Aria urged Jaxon to reach the ledge and then hurried back to Chello, who had stepped a short distance away from Mina.

"Aria, please go. You have what you came for. I won't make it," Mina told her weakly, trying to keep her leg still to avoid the other vines.

Aria pushed past Chello, kneeling in front of Mina. "I'm not leaving you, Mina. Tell me how to get you out."

"Listen to me, Richy," Mina told her and tried to smile. "Get them out of here. I'll cut the vine, and they'll swarm me. That's your escape. You did what you came to do. Now finish it."

"No," Aria told her firmly, and tears leaked from her eyes. "Tell me how to help you."

"Come on, Richy. You're far too beautiful to die in this place," Mina said, attempting to lift her hand to Aria's face but lacking the strength. She fell back, her breath coming in labored gasps, as other vines began to shift and coil around each other.

Aria stood and jumped back as another vine slithered to her feet. She looked at Chello and then back at Jaxon, who had moved ahead a bit, something in the water moving beside him.

"Go!" Mina gasped from her back, her breath ragged as the creeping vines drew closer, their tendrils inching toward her like some deadly embrace.

"It's our only way out." Chello's voice was thick with regret, the words almost tasting bitter as they left his lips. He met Aria's eyes— sad, resigned, yet strangely understanding. The weight of the decision pressed down on him like an iron chain.

Aria didn't move. Her heart pounded against her ribs as she looked back at him, her eyes wide with panic, silently pleading.

"Go! Before it's too late!" Mina's voice broke, raw with desperation.

For a moment, time stretched thin. Chello's gaze flicked to Aria, her face twisted with the same struggle he felt, torn between doing what was necessary and trying to help the person who had seen them through this, who had saved their lives. His mind screamed at him to run, to take Aria and escape. This was their chance to survive. The vines were closing in, but leaving Mina felt wrong. Like betrayal.

His chest tightened, and his pulse quickened. He *couldn't* leave her. Not like this. Not after everything. He looked at Aria again, and she was shaking, her jaw clenched as if holding herself together by sheer will. And then he saw it, the truth in her eyes: she couldn't leave Mina, either. Not after all they'd been through.

"Feck it." Chello's voice cracked with the weight of the decision. "Let's do the right thing."

Aria let out a shaky breath, her shoulders slumping in relief and fear all at once. She nodded, her eyes glistening. Thankful. So thankful for Chello, for this decision, but also terrified. She couldn't leave Mina. Not now. Not like this.

"Use the staff. I'll grab hold of her," Chello ordered, his tone shifting to the fierce command that came naturally when lives were on the line. "The staff will attract them, but not before stunning them. We have to be quick."

Aria nodded, the weight of the moment settling in her chest. The vines were almost upon them, and more had coiled around Mina's legs. They didn't have time to second-guess. It was either this or watching Mina die.

"Ready," Chello huffed, and Aria extended the staff, blue light crackling.

As soon as he saw the light, he tugged Mina up with all his strength, Aria slamming the staff down on the vines that had her legs. They retracted and squealed, and Chello hoisted Mina up and over his shoulder, moving as fast as he could.

Aria swung the staff down in a low circle. The vines retracted for a moment, but only a moment. Then the water rippled. A deep, unnatural tremor ran through the marsh. There was a brief moment of stillness, and then an explosion from the water. The vines were coming. *All* of them.

Aria turned and ran. Behind her, a tidal wave of black vines coiled and rose like a living nightmare, writhing and twisting toward her. The air crackled, thick with the scent of damp earth and decay. She didn't dare look back.

She caught up to Chello in the marsh, his grip tightening around Mina's limp form. Aria ducked under Mina's other arm, bracing against the dead weight as they staggered forward. The ground sucked at their boots, each step a fight.

Ahead, Jaxon had reached the salt ledge. He was hunched over, gasping for breath, his face pale with exertion. His eyes went big as he saw the scene before him.

"Move!" he wheezed. "Faster!"

Behind them, the vines shrieked, an unnatural, high-pitched sound like metal grinding against stone. The air shifted, growing thick, pressing against their backs as if the marsh itself was breathing down their necks.

A tendril lashed out, swiping against Aria's back. She gasped, nearly pitching forward, but she kept moving, a small cry escaping her throat. More came, snapping and writhing, hungry.

They hauled Mina forward, their muscles burning, their lungs searing. They were so close, the salt ledge within reach.

With one final, desperate lunge, they threw themselves onto the ledge. The moment their bodies hit the salt-crusted surface, they turned and saw that the vines had recoiled, shriveling back like burned paper.

Chello put his hand on Aria's shoulder as they tried to catch their breath, their chests heaving rapidly. Aria put her hand on his briefly and then turned her attention to Mina, who was motionless beside them.

Mina was slipping into unconsciousness, and Aria was the last thing she saw, a blurry vision looking down at her, saying something she couldn't hear. Mina's eyes rolled back in her head, and everything turned dark.

Part II.
Love.

Chapter 10

Aria slowly opened the door to the med lab recovery room, and her eyes fell on Chello, who was sitting on a backward chair at the end of the bed.

"Chell, what are you doing here?"

"Just checking on her, I guess," he told her, and shrugged a bit, as if he was caught doing something he shouldn't be.

Aria nodded and entered, quietly shutting the door. She walked over and stood next to him, and looked at Mina. She was in the same position as this morning, on her back, face flushed and motionless.

"Any news?" she asked.

"They think they have the infection under control, but she's still fevered and not conscious much."

Aria nodded and sat in the chair next to him. She leaned back and looked at Mina, the fever evident in her flushed cheeks.

It was a grueling journey back, even after they exited the marshes. Aria wasn't sure Mina would survive. When they arrived back in the city, she barely had a pulse. The medics and tech-no teams had been working on her nonstop for three days, trying to remove the infection and get enough medicine into her without killing her.

"You know what I can't understand?" Chello asked her. "Why did they stay with us?"

Aria looked at him, her brow furrowed. "What do you mean?"

Chello folded his hands on top of the chair back and rested his chin upon them. "She had the device off. They both did. They could've left at any time and made their escape. But they stayed with us and went through the whole terrifying ordeal, voluntarily. Why?"

Aria stared at Mina and nodded. She had given much thought to the same question.

"Doesn't make sense," Chello told her, shaking his head. "She thought she would end up back in prison, so why stay for that fate when you could leave at any time?"

They stared at Mina and considered it, only one answer coming to the surface.

"She's a gift from the God. She knew we needed her help. Yip, too. She saved our lives. Both of them did."

"True enough," Chello agreed, and after a bit of silence asked: "Did you speak with your father?"

Aria leaned back in her chair and exhaled. "I did."

"And?" Chello asked, wondering if the Director had warmed to the fact that Mina was back in the city.

When they returned, he barely spared a glance for his daughter or son. He was preoccupied with the news that Mina was with them, badly injured, and his face darkened with something colder than disapproval. His mouth thinned, arms crossed tightly over his chest as if restraining the words he wanted to say aloud. He hadn't expected her to survive. In truth, he'd made it clear she shouldn't.

The questions that came weren't ones of concern, but condemnation cloaked in diplomacy: *Why bring a criminal back? Why risk everything for someone like her?* There was no joy, no relief that his children were alive. Only a quiet, seething disappointment that they hadn't followed his unspoken directive. It wasn't the warm reception they were expecting. Chello saw the way Aria's posture stiffened, the way her eyes searched her father's face for something...anything...but found only judgment. Instead of celebrating their return, she was forced to defend it, to explain why they chose compassion over obedience. And that, Chello thought, had cut deeper than any wound they'd brought back from the wasteland.

"Mostly the same as when we arrived," Aria told him. "He isn't thrilled that Mina's here. Even though he knows she saved my life. He doesn't seem to care." She thought for a few moments and added, "And he still hasn't said much about Jaxon. It's almost like he's embarrassed that he's back."

"How is Jaxon?"

Aria shook her head and rubbed her eyes with her hand, exhaling. "Physically, he's fine. They said he's malnourished and dehydrated, but they're treating him for that. He has some strange scarring on his back and arms, but hasn't said what it's from. He hasn't said much about what happened, and honestly, after what Mina told us about the Greensk prison, I'd rather not force him to talk about it."

"Perhaps he will in time. How is he otherwise?" Chello asked. "Does he seem to be coming back to himself?"

Aria shrugged and nodded. "A bit. He's happy to be home. And every time I see him, he gets emotional. He said he thought he would die in that prison." She paused and thought about her father and added: "My father hasn't seen him apart from our initial return. I don't understand how he can be so cold. I understand that Jaxon failed his Ascension attempt, but his son is home and alive; shouldn't that be enough?"

Chello watched the frustration and disappointment wash over Aria's face and put his hand on her shoulder. Director Peterman wasn't a sentimental man, all business all the time. Chello knew that the family name was the most important thing to the Director.

"I'm sure he's relieved both you and Jaxon are home, Aria. He just…he concerns himself with city matters first, unfortunately."

Aria grunted and stood, slowly walking over to the head of Mina's bed. She looked at her flushed cheeks, her brow dotted with sweat. She reached for the cloth on the side table and carefully dabbed her forehead. There was a gash on the side of her head which had been stitched, and bruising under one of her eyes. How did she survive it all? How did she save them all?

"Kind of amazing that she's alive," Chello said as if he read her mind. "I wonder if she'll understand what happened to poor Yip?"

Aria felt tears in her eyes at the mention of Yip. "Poor Yip."

"Saved my life. And the way he threw himself in front of Mina, he didn't fight or hesitate. Just gave himself up for her." Chello recalled, emotion on his face.

"What a special man he was," Aria whispered and looked back at Mina. "What a special woman, she is."

Chello nodded and swallowed. He suspected that there was something yet to be acknowledged within Aria when it came to Mina, so he politely excused himself so she could be alone with her.

"I have the Praector meeting to get ready for. Will you be okay?" he asked, standing.

Aria looked back at him and nodded, and for some reason, she stepped forward and hugged him. He hugged her back without hesitation, the silence between them heavy with all they'd endured. Theirs had always been a strong bond, but something had shifted, solidified. Surviving what they did had fused them in a way that words couldn't touch, like two edges tempered in the same fire.

"I'll see you at the meeting, Chell," she told him, and he smiled softly and nodded.

"She'll be ok, Aria. The worst is over," he reassured her, and she nodded as he left.

The room became quiet, the only sound remaining the faint rhythm of Mina's breathing. Aria pulled the chair close to the bed and sat, staring at her. Mina's face was calm and peaceful, a stark contrast to the fierce energy she had grown used to seeing in her.

Her thoughts were a mix of gratitude, worry, and something she wasn't ready to name. She leaned forward slightly, resting her elbows on her knees, and let out a quiet sigh.

"What am I going to do with you?" she murmured under her breath, her voice barely audible.

The memory of Mina pulling the vine from her boot flashed in her mind, and she closed her eyes. The way Mina sprang into action, calm and determined. She hated needing help. Hated feeling vulnerable. But she couldn't be more grateful for her, the way she took such care in keeping her safe, even when she didn't have to. She could've left, run off, and saved herself at any time, but didn't. It was a debt Aria wasn't sure how to repay, and the thought made her chest tighten.

Mina had shifted something in her. In the marsh, she hadn't just protected her. She *saw* her. Saw the person beneath the title, the one buried under a lifetime of expectations and silent obedience. Somewhere in the tangle of fear and vines, that quiet act of seeing her, truly seeing her, had made Aria want to live.

Aria swallowed a lump in her throat and thought of her father, his harsh words.

"She doesn't belong here, Aria. She's a criminal. People like her are trouble."

"He's wrong about you," she whispered. "You're not trouble. You're...something else."

She wasn't sure when it had started, this pull she felt towards her. Perhaps it had been in the marshes, or maybe it was in the quiet moments on the ridge when they had time to talk.

Admitting it, even to herself, felt dangerous. But sitting here, watching Mina breathe, the thought of her leaving, or worse, not recovering, was unbearable.

"You're staying," Aria said softly, the words a quiet vow. "If you want to, you're staying. I'll make sure of it. He'll just have to understand."

Her eyes drifted to Mina's hand, resting limply on the blanket. She slowly reached out and took it in her own hand, her thumb rubbing over the back of it.

"You're going to be fine," she said, more to herself than to Mina. "You have to be."

She didn't know what the future held, but she knew one thing for certain: she wasn't ready to let Mina go.

***

Jack Peterman sat stone-faced, barely listening as the med team lead droned through her report. He wished she would stop talking. The list of injuries, the condition of the Vanguard Ascension team, it was all irrelevant noise. He didn't care who was bruised, broken, or bleeding. Aria had succeeded. That was all that mattered. Her name would be etched into the Book of City Heroes, and he would use that success like a blade, precise, effective, to place her exactly where he needed, solidifying the power and authority of the Peterman family name.

"And I'm pleased to report that all of Jaxon's tests came back clear. He's physically fine, sir. Nothing to worry about."

The med team lead paused as if she thought he would want to comment on the news, but he kept still. The others at the table were looking at him expectantly, and he stifled an agitated sigh and forced a smile.

"Glad to hear it," he told her.

She shuffled the parchment she was holding uncomfortably and then hesitantly added,

"Our only area of concern with Jaxon is that he's still suffering from dreams and night terrors. We've given him something to help with that."

"But bad dreams are to be expected, after such an experience, right?" Aria asked.

Jack narrowed his eyes. He didn't want Aria to be softened by her brother's return. She had a bigger role to play in this city, one Jaxon wasn't cut out for.

"Dr. Shale, I appreciate the report. If there's nothing else, I think we can adjourn," Jack told her.

Aria looked back at him, and he again forced a smile.

"The only other report I have is on the prisoner who came back with the team."

"She isn't a prisoner," Aria corrected, causing Jack to glare at her.

He was furious that the criminal had been brought back. He had made it clear to Chello that it would have been preferable if neither prisoner returned. His eyes shifted sharply to Chello, seated beside Aria. He liked the man. Chello was loyal to her, and she would need that loyalty as she stepped into her new role. But his blatant disregard for his subliminal orders was infuriating, and it would not go unpunished.

"Right, I apologize," Dr. Shale told her, and then looked at Jack. "She's passed all of her tests as well. She's just about recovered, and there's no need to keep her in the recovery ward."

Jack stared at the doctor, wondering if there was a way he could get her removed. Why she thought he would give a feck about the fate of that *criminal*, he didn't know.

"Meeting adjourned." It was his only response, and Dr. Shale furrowed her brow and nodded, gathering her things.

Jack watched as Aria lingered, almost as if she wanted to say something, but then just smiled and nodded at him and took her leave.

He spun in his chair from side to side, the irritation of the criminal flowing under his skin. If Chello weren't so weak, she wouldn't have returned. Now it was something he had to deal with.

"We should've killed her when we had the chance," he told Greyson, who nodded. "Either back then or the moment we knew she was here."

He stood up and went to the window, which overlooked the city, his hands behind his back.

"I don't think she will stay very long, sir," Greyson told him. "She's an interloper, moves from place to place."

"Yes, I know. Looking for her vengeance," Jack said stoically. "I don't like her here. Keep an eye on the situation. I don't want her lingering."

"Yes, sir," Greyson told him, and Jack waved his hand dismissively, letting him know he wanted to be alone.

No, he didn't like her. Didn't like her look, her mouth, or her attitude. And he certainly didn't like her bullshit heritage. He didn't want her here, and if she didn't leave on her own, he would be happy to help with that. As he thought about the possibility, Jack Peterman did something he rarely did. He smiled.

Chapter 11

Mina couldn't stop eating the ice cream—the cold, creamy concoction they had brought her when she woke two days ago. She had requested it every meal since. It was sweet and creamy, and if she were on her deathbed and offered one final bite of food, this would be it.

"You really never had ice cream before?" Chello asked incredulously. He leaned against the wall, arms crossed, a smile on his face as Mina scraped the bowl clean with her spoon.

"No, never," Mina told him with a smile, her gaze flicking to Aria, who stood on the other side of the room, smiling softly. "I saw it once, though. At some festival, when Yip and I passed through a city."

The mention of Yip made her pause, and a faint, bittersweet smile touched her lips.

"I'm so sorry about him, Mina," Chello said, his voice gentle.

Aria stepped closer, stopping at the end of the bed. "Me too."

Mina looked between them, nodding slowly. "It's always hard. I'll miss that Yip."

Chello frowned slightly, exchanging a glance with Aria, who seemed equally as puzzled at the way Mina said *that* Yip. Before either could respond, the med tech interrupted, setting down her tray.

"Alright, Mina. I just need you to hold still while I remove these IVs."

Mina straightened her arm, watching the woman deftly remove the lines and press small bandages over the puncture marks.

"There you go. You're officially released."

Mina raised her hand in a mock salute, grinning. "Didn't think I'd come back from this one, truth be told."

Chello chuckled, shaking his head. "You and me both."

"This is a healing agent," the med tech told her, handing over a small vial of white cream. "The internal damage has been addressed with an enhancer, but apply this twice a day over the scar to prevent irritation."

Mina turned the vial over in her hands before slipping it into her pocket. She hesitated, glancing at Chello and Aria from under her lashes. She had no idea where this was heading. Every time the door opened, she braced herself, expecting Greyson, or worse, Director Peterman himself, to come and drag her off to prison. But they never did.

Chello and Aria were the only ones who came. And they came regularly, always happy to see her healing. She hadn't felt any warnings or triggers, and she trusted that after all they'd been through, at least one of them would have given her a heads-up if she were going back to prison. Aria would, she thought.

Her gaze flickered to Aria. She thought about how often Aria came to check on her, how their conversations felt effortless, mundane, even, like old friends killing time. It was...nice. A small smile tugged at Mina's lips as she realized how much she enjoyed that. But the smile faded when she realized that she would have to leave before Peterman changed his mind and sent her back to a cell.

Mina stood up out of bed, her hand moving to her midsection where the scar was. It didn't hurt; whatever combination of med and tech they used was brilliant. She looked at Chello and then Aria.

"So, I guess I'll go," she told them, looking at her feet. She swallowed and then asked: "Think you could find me a room at the inn? Just for tonight."

Chello laughed. "You think we're letting you stay at the inn? Come on!"

Aria smiled and crossed her arms over her chest. "I had one of the guest rooms in my quarters prepared for you. It's perfectly comfortable, and I'm sure we can find a way to get some ice cream brought up, too."

Mina looked up with a smile, thrilled that this wasn't goodbye. "Here I thought I was going back to prison, and I get a room at the finest house in the city?"

Chello chuckled while Aria frowned.

"It's not the finest house in the city!" Aria protested, her prestigious family position slightly embarrassing to her.

"Close to," Chello jested, and Aria looked at him with a curt smile.

"Alright, Richy," Mina said, her smirk returning as she nodded at Aria. "Show me what you've got."

Chello clapped his hands together excitedly and headed out of the room, but Aria lingered, her gaze locked on Mina's. Something flickered in those bright blue eyes, gratitude, fondness, and something else Mina couldn't quite name. She smiled and they followed Chello out the door.

***

Mina looked around the guest room with wide eyes. It wasn't just a room, it was its own apartment, complete with a sitting area and fireplace off the entrance and a separate back bedroom. It was decorated with fine linens and ornate touches and was easily the nicest room she had ever stepped foot in.

But it made sense, given that Aria truly did have her own quarters. They took an underground corridor that led to the Peterman compound, and it spilled out into the grand entrance. There was a dual staircase, a huge crystal chandelier, and artwork everywhere.

"The stairs lead to my father's quarters and offices," Aria told her nervously, and Mina nodded as she followed her under the big chandelier to a set of glass doors that looked like they led to a garden. "To the left are Jaxon's quarters, and to the right are mine."

Mina was shocked at the grandness of it all, and Aria's quarters were practically a separate home altogether. There were several rooms, like the guest room she was staying in, plus a library and other communal spaces.

"There's no balcony in this room, I'm afraid," Aria told her as Mina approached the floor-to-ceiling windows in the bedroom. "But it does afford a nice view of the gardens."

Mina stared out in awe, shaking her head. "Amazing." She turned to face Aria. "Thank you, really, for letting me crash here tonight."

Aria smiled and crossed her arms. "It's no trouble at all. And you don't have to just crash here, Mina. You can stay as long as you'd like." She paused and then added, "I'm glad you're staying here."

Mina watched a blush creep into Aria's cheeks and felt her insides stir. Aria had dropped her eyes but had a slight smile on her lips.

Mina swallowed a lump that popped up in her throat, and then said in a quiet voice:

"For the first time, I don't know where to go. So, I appreciate this."

Aria looked up at her, and Mina felt her chest tighten at the beauty in those bright blue eyes. There was something there, something she couldn't find a word for. It pulled her in, and she couldn't drop her gaze.

"Like I said, stay as long as you'd like. You don't need to have it all figured out right now."

For a moment, the air between them felt charged, as if the words they hadn't spoken hung there, waiting. Mina thought about how strange it was to feel so unmoored yet so grounded in Aria's presence.

"Yeah, right. One step at a time," Mina said in a low voice.

Aria smiled. "I'm two doors down if you need anything. Make yourself at home, Mina. Please. I mean it."

"Careful, you've already set the bar pretty high here, Richy," Mina told her with the cocky grin Aria liked best.

"That mouth of yours," Aria told her with a smile and a shake of the head. She headed out the door, a blush flooding her cheeks.

"It'll be here all night," Mina called after her, and couldn't help the genuine smile that spread across her face.

***

Time passed quickly when they were together, it was hard for Mina to remember that she was an outsider. It had only been a few days, but the more time she spent with Aria, the more comfortable she felt and the more she was drawn to her. It was easy to forget the path she was on before her time in Fusia.

They spent almost every moment together when Aria wasn't tied up in meetings or sessions. Aria seemed genuinely happy to show Mina the corners of her life: her favorite hidden nooks in the city, the lush gardens where the air always seemed sweeter, and even the sprawling training grounds where she honed her skills.

As they wandered through the city, Mina learned that Aria's love for Fusia was a part of everything she did. The pride in her voice as she spoke of its prosperity, and the genuine affection she held for its people. She cared so much about them, it made Mina want to be a part of it.

They stood on the top of the old watch tower, the city sprawled out before them.

"They don't use it as a watch tower anymore, but I used to come here all the time when I was younger. I would pretend I was running away and sit up here for hours, staring out at the city." Aria told her with a small smile.

Mina nodded, staring out over the city. It was a beautiful view, and out ahead of them, the Peterman compound rose above it all, the most well-situated structure that Mina could see.

"I can see why. It's amazing up here, really something," Mina told her. "It makes me think twice about leaving this place." She leaned back against the short wall and crossed her arms over her chest.

Aria felt her face frown, and as she looked away, she asked, "Do you really want to leave?" The thought made her chest tighten. She loved having her here, someone to spend time with who wasn't obligated to.

But the truth was, everyone loved having Mina here, well, everyone but her father. He exploded when she told him Mina was staying in her guest room, and barely had spoken to her since. But she wasn't concerned about that. She had found something in Mina she didn't realize she was looking for, and she didn't want to give that up, even if it meant disappointing her father.

Mina looked at Aria and shrugged, letting out an incredulous breath, as if staying in such a place was an actual option.

"Even if it were some crazy possibility to stay, I'm looking for someone. I can't give that up," she told her and then smiled. "But I will say, it would be easy to fall into a false sense of belonging here."

"False?" Aria asked, and for some reason, the word bothered her.

"Not false in a bad way," Mina quickly corrected. "You're probably the nicest people I've met in my life. You haven't made me feel like an outsider, even when I was fresh out of the cell."

"And that's a bad thing?" Aria asked, walking around in front of her, leaning on the opposite wall so they were facing one another.

"It's a confusing thing," Mina told her, staring at her with a small smile. The early evening light was reflecting off Aria's face, and she couldn't help feeling the familiar stir inside. The more Mina got to know who Aria was, the more beautiful she became to her. "I don't belong here."

"Where do you belong?" Aria asked, and she slowly raised her eyes to gaze into Mina's. There was a thrum in her chest, an energy that she seemed to feel more and more around her.

Mina wasn't sure she could speak, Aria's eyes holding her captive. Her breath was heavy in her chest, and she felt a pull she had never experienced before. Her head was light, her heart hammering, and she thought to herself that she could easily belong with Aria. She would be perfectly fine with her, the rest of the world be damned. She cleared her throat and dropped her eyes before she could give herself away.

"Nowhere and everywhere, I guess," Mina shrugged, smiling. "I haven't belonged anywhere in a long time. My home has been the road, the search for the man who killed my family. It's the only home I've known for the last fifteen years."

Aria looked at her with sad eyes, trying to imagine such an existence. The thought of Mina and Yip, two children, alone in a cruel world, was difficult to think about. She looked up at her, her voice soft.

"I don't understand how you made it, Mina. You were so young, what, barely twelve?"

"Yeah, just twelve. But I wasn't alone. Never am. The God had His hand on me and still does. There's no way two kids from a closed-off world survive without Him. We got captured a lot and forced into labor camps. In the south, they used kids for coal mines and rock quarries. It was awful." She paused, looking out over the horizon thoughtfully. "But looking back, every bad place we ended up in had a purpose. Maybe it was to help someone else, or maybe for a reason I still don't know."

She glanced at Aria, half-expecting her to be rolling her eyes, but instead, she saw she was looking back intently. It gave her the push to make the rare move of letting her guard down and sharing her true self.

"I believe the God puts us where we're meant to be, even if we don't always understand why. Like us." She motioned between them, her voice soft but certain.

Aria's breath caught at the word *us*, the possibility seeping into her.

Mina continued, "Greensk was the worst, probably the most hopeless situation I've ever been in. But if I hadn't gone through that, I wouldn't have escaped through the marshes and ended up here. And if I weren't here, I couldn't have helped you get your brother back. Everything happens for a reason."

Aria stared at her, her heart beating fast in her chest. To think that the God led Mina to her, *for* her, it made her insides swirl.

"Do you ever get, I don't know, lonely moving around so much?"

Mina's face dropped a bit, thinking of all the times she had prayed for a place to call her own, for her vengeance quest to be over so she could settle somewhere to call home.

"Of course. Especially when Yip is gone. We used to talk about stopping somewhere and finding a place where we could belong. I always thought that would be amazing, you know, finding people to call our own." She smiled and looked up at the sky, thinking of Yip, making her miss him. "And we will someday. Once my search for vengeance is over."

Aria felt emotion in her eyes, thinking about Mina settling somewhere, perhaps with someone else. She wanted to ask her to stay, to settle here, but she knew Mina wouldn't. She would want to continue her search for the man who did her wrong, and Aria couldn't blame her.

"Wow," Mina said, breaking Aria from her thoughts. "Look at those clouds, I've never seen anything move like that. Is that a storm coming?"

Aria looked out over the horizon at the swirling clouds, trying to steady herself, and nodded. "We don't get many storms, but yeah, that looks like one forming off the mountains." She hesitated before adding, "When I was little, the storms scared me to death. The wind would howl, and I'd cry in my bed, clutching my blanket. The garden wind chimes would clank and rattle so loudly, I thought it was something coming to gobble me up."

"That sounds terrifying," Mina told her. "Especially for a kid. Could you go to sleep with your family, or…?"

"I told my father once," Aria said with a small, humorless smile. "He had more wind chimes added to the garden below my balcony."

"What?" Mina turned and looked at her incredulously. "Even though he knew they scared you?"

"He said I needed more of them to overcome my fear. I thought he'd comfort me, maybe stay with me until the storm passed. Instead, the next storm was worse. The chimes drowned out the wind, and I hid under my bed and cried. I never told him my fears again."

Mina swallowed, her face reflective. She wasn't sure how someone could be so cruel to their child.

"He believed fear could be overcome through exposure to it," Aria continued. "But when you're a kid, all you want is someone to hold you and say it'll be okay." She paused. "I think the only time he hugged me was at my academy graduation, and even then, it was just a one-armed hug." She gave a hollow laugh. "I learned love had to be earned, and even then, it could disappear."

Mina looked at her with sad eyes, and Aria laughed a humorless chuckle. She motioned to her house off in the distance, the large Peterman compound.

"You think I have it all," Aria told her in a sad tone. "And materially, I do. But all I've ever wanted was to feel loved, really loved, without having to earn it first. Unconditionally. As if such a thing exists."

For a moment, the evening air seemed to hold its breath, the distant storm clouds rolling, cheering them on. Mina looked at Aria, wondering about the same sort of love, one where you could be who you were and that was ok.

Aria looked back, Mina's gaze piercing through the guarded layers she had spent years building. It felt dangerous, almost intoxicating, to be seen so completely.

"Imagine that," Mina said, almost involuntarily, in a low voice. "A love where someone saw you, the real you. Knew every shadow of your past and loved you anyway." She let out a breath as if something so pure could exist.

She seemed surprised by her words, a lump forming in her throat. Aria looked at her, eyes glimmering with an intensity that made the space between them feel electric.

Mina's pulse quickened as she pushed off the wall, her movements deliberate yet hesitant. Her chest tightened with the possibility of rejection; thoughts of the situation being read wrong slamming into her. But she felt the pull of Aria's gaze, her nearness, the unspoken gravity between them. She moved slowly, Aria's eyes wide, her face flushing. The world seemed to stop as Mina leaned closer.

"There you are!" Marcus called out.

Both Aria and Mina were startled, jumping back, seeming shocked at the revelation that other people existed in the world.

"Chello said he thought you were up here."

Aria put her hand to her forehead, feeling dizzy, and tried to steady herself.

"Marcus. Is Jaxon alright?" she asked, concern washing over her face.

"Yeah, yeah, he's fine. He's getting his treatment in the tech-no lab," he told her, walking across the narrow bridge to where they stood. His eyes cut to Mina, and he smiled. "Looking a lot better, Mina. Almost normal."

"Almost," Mina said, smiling, her face flushed from her interaction with Aria. She had to slow her breathing and calm herself.

"So, we're all set for tonight. Chello has it set up, and he's going to come get you at eight, good?" Marcus looked at Mina and added, "And you have to come."

"What's tonight?" Mina asked curiously, rubbing her hand over her bandaged midsection. The scar was almost healed; whatever miracle medicine they gave her worked wonders.

"Aria's Vanguard Ascension celebration!" he told her, putting his arm around Aria's shoulders and shaking her a bit. "We're all so fecking excited to celebrate with you!"

Mina smiled at his energy but said, "I thought that was tomorrow night?"

"The formal ceremony is tomorrow. Tonight is just for the team," Aria told her, and she suddenly found it difficult to look Mina in the eyes.

"You better be there! You have just as much to celebrate as the rest of us!" Marcus told her, punching her shoulder.

Mina smiled and looked at Aria. "I suppose if the guest of honor wants me there…and lets me borrow some more clothes…I'll be there."

"Of course, I want you there, you idiot. Marcus is right, you have just as much to celebrate as the rest of us," Aria told her, and then cocked her head and squinted. "And I think I have just the outfit for you, something with ruffles and floral prints?"

Marcus laughed, imagining the tough Mina in such a feminine outfit.

"Well, sounds like it's settled, then," Marcus told them, and they all left the tower laughing and talking about the night ahead. Aria and Mina both felt like their insides were on fire and wondered if the other felt the same.

***

The party was in a private underground tavern that the security teams had access to, so they didn't have to go out into the city pubs. Mina marveled at the liveliness of it, the stone walls and wall sconces giving it a medieval vibe. There were community tables scattered about, lively music, and an area for dancing, and barkeeps were keeping drinks full at a rapid pace.

When Chello led Aria in, the crowd erupted into cheers, and they swarmed her with congratulations and genuine happiness. Mina trailed in behind them, a smile on her face. Everyone was dressed rather casually, and she was glad she convinced Aria to let her wear an old pair of khaki linen pants and a white long-sleeved shirt, which she promptly tore the sleeves off of. She felt comfortable and happy for Aria.

"Glad to see you here!" Meesh told her, throwing her arm around her shoulders. "They said you were recovered, but you look much better than I imagined. Nice shirt, by the way."

"Thanks. This is quite a party."

"We're good at what we do, in all things," Meesh told her with a wink and started pulling her towards the bar. "What're you drinking?"

"I guess whatever the Fusia specialty is," Mina told her, and she cut her eyes to Aria as Meesh pulled her away.

Aria smiled at her, and Mina smiled back, letting Meesh drag her across the tavern.

There wasn't a dull moment, and everyone acted like Mina was a part of the group. There was no awkwardness or uneasiness, and she talked and drank with them, laughing at jokes and stories they told. She couldn't remember a happier bunch than these people, and it was contagious, the natural joy seeping into her.

She sat at a long table with Chello, Marcus, Meesh, and some others, her eyes always falling on Aria, who was sitting at the next table with her brother and some of his friends.

"And I have to be honest, Mina," Marcus told her, his face flushed from the drink, his eyes glossy. "If you don't end up joining Chello and his team, you should consider joining my squad."

"Yes! We'd love to have you!" Meesh called out, and Mina smiled, her face a bit surprised.

"Join your team?" she asked, and Chello put his arm around her and clinked her glass.

"If you'd like, of course. You're practically a part of us already. But we'd love for you to stay and officially join us," he told her, and the entire table erupted in a cheer, raising their glasses.

Mina smiled, her heart warming at the fact that they wanted her here. "I'll definitely think about it."

Everyone fell back into conversation, and Mina sat and watched them all banter and laugh, and she couldn't help the smile on her face. She kept an eye on Aria, the shining star of the night. There was a genuine glow about her, and Mina could feel herself being pulled in by it.

She took a drink of her ale and thought about how she had misjudged her. She had grit, determination, and, above all else, heart. She cared. About everything and everyone, it was so opposite of how Mina lived; she couldn't help but be drawn to it. Plus, she was beautiful, Mina couldn't deny that. Aria looked over just then and caught Mina staring, and Mina didn't look away. She smiled and lifted her chin, and Aria smiled back.

"Enjoying yourself?" Chello asked, smiling at her.

"I am. Everyone seems genuinely happy for Aria."

"The Vanguard Ascension doesn't always end happily, so when it does, we celebrate well."

Mina looked at him and nodded, her eyes drifting back to Aria, who was smiling at her. Mina winked, and Aria quickly looked away.

"I'm glad you came to this, Mina. And believe me when I tell you, I'm not the only one," Chello told her sincerely.

Mina looked at him, and he smiled, his face flushed from the drink. She shifted in her seat and looked at her cup, not sure what to say to that.

"And what Marcus says is true. We're all ready to fight for you to join our teams, should you want to stay. You have more than proven your loyalty, something you didn't have to do. I'll never forget it, Mina."

He held up his cup, and she picked hers up and nodded, taking a drink.

"Same to you, Chell. You could've left me for dead, and I don't think anyone would have cared if you did. I hope you know that means something to me."

He smiled, putting his arm around her. "You have a good heart, Mina. I would never kill anything with a good heart. You're more than meets the eye, and I hope you stick around. You fit here."

Mina looked at him and saw the truth in his eyes. No posturing, no hidden agenda, just genuine kindness. She shook her head, not out of disagreement, but in quiet disbelief. *How could such good people exist in such a broken world?*

They had welcomed her without hesitation and offered her a place in their existence. She wasn't used to that. Not anymore. The longer she stayed, the more it chipped away at the walls she'd built around herself, walls she'd thought were permanent.

She thought about what it might look like to stay, to belong. The idea felt delicate, almost dangerous, like something she could ruin just by holding on too tightly. Still, the thought warmed her. But then the weight returned, the reminder of what waited beyond this place. The faces she still saw in dreams, the vengeance that hummed beneath her skin like a second heartbeat. That mission, that shadow, had followed her too long to simply let it go.

Her smile lingered, bittersweet. She wanted to stay. She truly did. But she wasn't sure the past would ever stop chasing her long enough to let her. She took a drink from her cup and her eyes cut to Aria, who was being pulled up by someone for a dance. She looked past her and saw Jaxon sitting alone on top of a table across the room, his head against the wall.

Mina excused herself and walked over to him, sitting beside him. "Hey, Jaxon. Having fun?"

139

He looked as if he was struggling; the reality of being home was difficult to embrace.

"I'm doing ok, Mina. How about you? Enjoying a taste of the Fusia elite?"

She laughed and watched as the dance floor came to life, enough drink being had that everyone was letting go of their inhibitions.

"A bunch of drunkards, more like it," Mina told him.

He laughed and nodded. "I've missed this so much, though. These people."

She looked over at him and saw tears in his eyes, and she patted his leg. "It's hard to put yourself back into the right headspace. Greensk can feck you up in more ways than one."

He looked at her and seemed to be contemplating something, and then looked back out at the others dancing. "It's like I know how I'm supposed to act and feel, but part of me doesn't know how to do that."

Mina took a slow drink, her gaze drifting over the crowd. She winced at the memories before speaking, her voice low.

"For days after we broke out, I'd wake up screaming. Even though I knew we were out of Greensk, I could never shake the feeling that I was still trapped. I'd dream about it, then wake up drenched in sweat, unable to tell if it was real. Poor Yip... he didn't know what to do with me."

Jaxon nodded his head, a rogue tear leaking down his face. "Me too." He pressed his palms to his eyes. "I should probably leave. I don't want to ruin the party."

"It'll get easier, Jax. It won't ever leave your mind, but you'll start replacing the thoughts with happier ones. I promise," Mina told him, placing her hand on his leg. "It's ok to feel fecked up."

"I do feel fecked up," he told her and laughed a humorless chuckle. "It feels good to admit it out loud."

"You come find me any time you want to admit it," Mina told him with a smile. "I get it. I've been there."

Jaxon wiped his eyes and nodded, and Mina looked over at Aria, who was staring at them with concern, a frown on her face.

"What do you say we go make fools of ourselves on the dance floor? Surely, that'll replace the thoughts in our heads," Mina told him.

He laughed. "I can't remember the last time I danced."

"I promise you I can't either. So, what do you say? You and me?" Mina asked him, opening her palm to him, and he smiled and took her hand.

"Thank you, Mina," he said, and she smiled and went to stand, but he pulled her back. "For all of it. For me, for her," he said, motioning to Aria, "For everything. I don't care what my father has to say about you or me, for that matter. He won't ever understand. So, thank you."

Mina's smile threatened to turn into a frown at his words, wondering what the Director had been saying. She knew he didn't like her here, but decided it didn't matter, not tonight. Tonight was about Aria, not her asshole father. She smiled and pulled him out to the dance floor, and they did their best to forget where they had been.

***

They were an intoxicated mass of bodies, swaying in the flashing lights to the music. The room pulsed with energy, a hypnotic rhythm carrying everyone along like a tide. Bodies swayed and collided; laughter bubbled up in every corner.

Aria had barely moved from her spot, her eyes fixed on Mina. She'd seen the transformation on her brother's face, how Mina had turned him from sad to happy, and was now making him laugh with her ridiculous, mismatched dance moves. The sight touched something deep inside her, warming her chest with something more potent than gratitude. She couldn't look away. She felt so much for Mina, her interaction with Jaxon increasing whatever that was.

Her feet seemed to move on their own, weaving through the crowd until she reached the edge of the floor, where Mina's attempts at rhythm were hopelessly out of sync with the beat, and Jaxon was laughing. It was messy, uncoordinated, and utterly beautiful.

As if sensing her, Mina looked up, her movements slowing. Their eyes met, and the air seemed to thrum with a different kind of electricity. The crowd blurred and faded; it was just the two of them now, tethered by an invisible thread. Jaxon noticed, too. He leaned in, his voice soft but audible over the music.

"Thank you, Mina," he said, placing a quick kiss on her cheek.

Then he turned to Aria, pressing a kiss to her cheek as well before throwing his hands in the air and plunging into the crowd. He disappeared in the direction of Marcus, his laughter trailing behind him.

Mina stopped completely, staring at Aria.

"Don't stop," Aria told her. "I think you're just a few moves away from inventing a new dance trend."

Mina laughed, the sound low and rough. She stepped closer, leaning into Aria. "I don't think Fusia is ready for my...*innovation*s."

"Oh, I think it's overdue," Aria replied, her lips twitching into a smirk. Then she became slightly serious and said, "Thank you for what you did for Jax. He's struggling, and to see him smiling and laughing, it really is a win, Mina."

Mina's eyes held hers, a flicker of something undefined crossing her face. "He's a good guy. He's a lot like you."

The words hit Aria with unexpected force, and she looked up into Mina's eyes as she continued to sway with the music.

"I mean it as a compliment," Mina told her. "You're both so genuine, and you feel so much, so deeply."

Aria swallowed, feeling like Mina was looking inside of her, seeing something no one else had bothered to uncover. The distance between them felt impossibly small now, and her pulse quickened, her skin prickling with awareness. Mina looked like she wanted to say something more, but the words never came. Instead, she stepped back, her hand brushing against Aria's for the briefest of moments, a touch so quick it could've been accidental, but Aria felt it jolt through her.

For a second, Aria wanted to ask, to push past the unspoken tension and demand to know what Mina was thinking, what she was feeling. But the fear of hearing the wrong answer rooted her in place. They were so different, Mina was strong, courageous, and adventurous; she couldn't possibly be feeling what Aria was.

"Aria! Here! Come here!" Chello yelled over the noise, and both Mina and Aria looked in his direction, where he was holding up tubes of bright blue liquid.

"I think you're wanted by your man," Mina told her in a low voice, and Aria looked at her with eyes that wanted to ask so much more.

"Yeah," Aria said, her voice soft, almost reluctant. "I should go." She hesitated, her eyes flicking back to Mina one last time before she turned and disappeared into the crowd.

Mina stayed where she was, her heart hammering in her chest. She told herself it was the music, the noise, the press of the crowd, all of it swirling together to make her feel unsettled. But deep down, she knew better. It was Aria. It had always been Aria. Since the moment she came to her cell and handed over the apples, an act of pure and unexpected kindness. It was Aria who was burning into her heart.

Mina looked over to where Chello was toasting her with the shots of blue liquid and shook her head. She had to stay focused. Aria didn't feel the same, there was no way she could. Aria was everything she wasn't, and glaringly so. She was rich, accomplished, and educated. Still, she was grateful for her, for the opportunity to be a part of this group for whatever amount of time the God allowed her.

She thought about what Chello had said, about staying and joining them. There was a flicker of desire in her chest, and Mina closed her eyes and took a deep breath. Maybe, she thought, if the God wanted it, she could return here once her mission for vengeance was over.

She opened her eyes and looked around the room, seeing the smiles and genuine care for one another. Maybe, she thought. Perhaps it could happen that way. She saw Marcus jumping up and down to the music and smiled, making her way over to him, refusing to think about this coming to an end. There would be a time for that, but this wasn't it.

Mina swayed with the music, letting herself enjoy it. When Marcus moved behind her in his own awkward dance, she laughed, his burly frame moving to the beat of the sounds. Meesh came up in front of her, and the three of them swayed and laughed, a trio of mismatched rhythm. Mina saw the way Meesh was looking at Marcus and smirked, recognizing the eyes of desire. She wrapped her hands around Meesh's waist, and after a few off-beat moves, she casually turned her in a circle that ended with Meesh face to face with Marcus. They wasted no time in moving into one another, lost in the drink and the intoxicating sound of the music.

Blue tubes of liquid were passed around continuously, and Mina lost count of the number of shots she took, but she was having the best time of her life. She wasn't guarded, wasn't afraid. She was just herself, blending and moving with people who seemed not to mind who she was or where she came from. She saw Aria dancing close by and fell into a blurry sort of dream state, everything slowing and Aria the only one she could see.

When Aria locked eyes with her, they gravitated closer, and soon Aria was in front of her, smiling and moving with rhythm and grace. Mina moved closer, their bodies touching, and Aria raised her arms above her head and twirled her wrists, moving to the music. Mina couldn't help it, she was drawn into the moment, into Aria being so close to her. She raised her hands to Aria's and slowly ran her fingers down her arms, to her shoulders, and finally to her waist, where they stayed, holding her in place. They moved and swayed, their eyes staying locked in the flashing lights. It was mesmerizing, it was intoxicating.

Mina let herself be herself for the night, and she wasn't sure she had a better time. She felt like she was a part of something, and she couldn't help but enjoy every moment of it. She only wished that Yip was there to have fun with them, but she knew he would turn back up in due time.

She kept her eyes on Aria, her heart trying to wedge something open that had always been closed. Marcus came over and picked them both up in a hug, lifting them off the ground, and Mina smiled and laughed and felt like a normal person for the first time in fifteen years.

Chapter 12

The early afternoon sun seemed to taunt their headaches, but Mina and Aria walked the back gardens after a late brunch, hoping the fresh air would clear their heads. The night ended in a blur, too much drink being had by everyone, Chello dragging them to their rooms at some early morning hour.

Mina awoke fully clothed in her bed, barely remembering how she got there. When Aria knocked on her door just after midday, Mina was still a disheveled mess, which Aria laughed at.

"You look horrible," she had told her, and Mina couldn't disagree.

"I feel horrible. How is it that you look so *good?*" Mina asked her.

Aria blushed at the compliment. "Tech-no has a serum for nights like that, I'm sorry I didn't think to give you anything."

They ate a light meal and then Aria suggested they stroll the back garden to get some air. Mina did take a vial of something Aria gave her, something that was supposed to help her recover, but she still felt groggy, as if in a fog. The outdoors and fresh air did help, and as they walked, Mina was awed by the amount of garden space.

"I can't believe this is all yours," Mina told her.

They were standing at the water feature, a large gray stone fountain with three fish on the top spitting water that cascaded down three tiers into a small pool that was filled with small fish.

"This is my favorite place to come and think, I love the sound of the trickling water," Aria told her. There was still an electricity humming between them, something tangible that both felt.

"I see why. It's beautiful," Mina agreed.

She saw that Aria was staring at her, and it made her insides swirl. Every time she looked at Aria, she felt a current hum through her, and it made her insides sway, and her head feel light. "We didn't see much water back home."

"Your city was in the barren lands, right? In the uninhabitable Sphere?" Aria asked, sitting on the bench in front of the fountain.

Mina nodded, and Aria watched her dip her fingers into the rippling water at its base.

"Water was manufactured; we didn't have a natural source."

She watched as Mina looked at her wet hand, snapping the droplets off.

"Your people must have been incredibly resourceful and smart. To create an entire city where others deemed the land uninhabitable."

Mina nodded and looked off into the distance, seeming to remember a different place at a different time. "A lot different from here, that's for sure. You really have it all, Richy." Mina smiled and sat beside Aria on the bench, crossing her arms over her chest.

Aria caught a glimpse of Mina's muscles flexing in her short-sleeved t-shirt, and her heart gave a small, unexpected lurch. She couldn't help but wonder what it would feel like to be wrapped up in those strong arms, held tight. The thought sent a wave of heat through her. She quickly shook her head, embarrassed by the sudden rush of feelings, and forced herself to focus on the conversation instead.

"That statement is relative, I guess. But yes, we're very fortunate, and that isn't lost on me."

"I know it isn't, and I hope you know how rare that is. Most people who have it all don't care that they have what others would kill for. You're different, Richy."

"I hate it when you call me that," Aria told her and narrowed her eyes. She broke out into a smile when Mina said:

"Yeah, I know."

They laughed and watched the water trickle in silence for a while.

"Is it really required for you to do that thing to your eye?" Mina asked, breaking the silence.

Aria nodded. "Yes, it symbolizes the success of the Vanguard Ascension. It's a great honor to have one pigmented eye."

"Too bad. I really love your eyes," Mina told her nonchalantly.

Aria stared at her, her mouth suddenly very dry. She swallowed and said, "Thank you. It's just the left eye, though. The right stays its normal color."

"Still," Mina told her, leaning back on the bench and placing her hands behind her head in a cocky and confident manner. "Your eyes are beautiful. It's a shame to alter them."

Mina's compliment made Aria's heart beat faster, and she felt a nervous flutter in her stomach. She bit her bottom lip and focused on the fountain, trying not to think about the fact that Mina thought she had beautiful eyes.

"I should probably go get ready for that, it's later than I realized," Aria told her, and she didn't want their time to end. Every time she left Mina, she wondered if she would ever see her again, as if she would disappear. "You're coming tonight, right?"

"If it's anything like last night, I wouldn't miss it," Mina told her, and they stood, looking at one another.

Memories of their dancing flashed in Aria's head, and she blushed.

"Well, it's not. It's more formal and ceremonial, and not everyone from last night will be there. But I'm glad you had a good time last night."

Mina smiled, closing one eye and looking at the blue sky. "It was the best time I've ever had in my life. It's going to be hard to leave."

"I wish you would stop saying that. You don't have to leave, Mina. There's definitely a place for you here," Aria told her, almost desperately.

Mina chuckled and put her hands in her pockets. "Oh yeah, Richy? What would my place be? In the cells in the basement again?"

"No!" Aria exclaimed. "You're so smart and skilled, Mina, strong and resilient. You'd have a place here, with me." She paused and then added awkwardly: "On my team, I mean."

A slow smile spread across Mina's face.

"And what would I be doing for you, exactly?" she asked and began walking in a slow circle around her.

Aria watched Mina smirk, and she blushed, a curl of heat rising in her stomach.

"Be at your beck and call like Chello?" Mina asked.

"Of course not. Chell's my Praector. It's his job to be with me nearly everywhere I go."

"So, then, what would my job be, Richy? What would you have me do?"

Mina had moved behind her, and Aria felt her pulse increase as she slowly turned to look at her. When their eyes met, it was as if a jolt had shocked her. What would she have Mina do? Her imagination started to get the best of her, and when Mina took a step closer, Aria held her breath.

Mina smiled and said in a low voice, "If I can't be with you nearly everywhere you go, what would be the point?"

They stood staring at each other, with very little space between them, and Aria felt her world tilt a bit. She let her eyes drop to Mina's lips, and her insides flared with heat.

"Madame?"

Aria startled and jumped back, looking over at Gretchen, who was standing in the pathway behind them.

"I'm so sorry, I didn't mean to frighten you," Gretchen told her. "They're almost ready for you."

"Yes. Yes, of course. Thank you, Gretchen," Aria said quickly, trying to pull herself together. She looked at Mina, who was still looking at her intensely. "You're staying, right? You'll be there tonight?" Aria asked her, and it came out with too much intensity, almost as if it were a plea rather than a question.

"I'll be there, Richy," Mina told her with a smile. "Wouldn't want to miss the new eye."

Aria smiled and rolled her eyes, feeling more herself. She was grateful for Mina's easy-going disposition, which always put her at ease.

"Gretchen, will you help Mina with something to wear tonight while I'm gone, please?"

"Of course, Madame."

Aria looked at Mina, paused, and said: "Think about it, at least. My team or Jaxon's, both of us would love to have you."

Mina nodded and watched her go, wondering what a lifetime in this place would be like. She looked at Gretchen, Aria's maidservant, and chuckled as if it were all an impossible dream.

***

Mina walked through the doors of the banquet hall to the sounds of string instruments playing, and her eyes took in the scene before her. It was something out of a fairytale; crystal chandeliers hung from the ceiling, and ornate flowers and decorations were scattered throughout. Well-dressed people in fine fabrics roamed about with drinks in their hands, and those in uniform weren't wearing everyday fits but dress uniforms with sashes and medals. Mina swallowed and laughed silently, finding it ludicrous that she was in such a situation.

"Yip would get a kick out of this," she muttered under her breath, and she nodded when a servant presented a tray of drinks for her to choose from. She took a glass of what tasted like wine and scanned the room, looking for anyone she recognized.

She inched her way through the crowd, people smiling at her as if she belonged. She was glad that Gretchen insisted on her upping her outfit game, wearing a fine velvet short blazer with a silk shirt and dark blue pants that had a gentle flare to them. She wanted to rip the sleeves off the shirt, but it wasn't hers, and she didn't want to ruin it.

"So glad to see you here!" Chello called out, and Mina smiled as he came up to her and put his arm around her, smiling with genuine joy.

"Hey Chell," Mina greeted him, and her eyes moved to the woman with him. She was younger than Chello, maybe Mina's age, with reddish blonde hair, a fair complexion, and bright blue eyes.

"Mina, this is my girlfriend, Sara," he introduced.

Sara stuck out her hand and shook Mina's. "A pleasure, Mina. Chell hasn't stopped talking about you since his return."

"That's hardly true," Chello said in a low tone, embarrassed.

"He's a bit obsessed with me," Mina joked, and the three shared a laugh.

"So, are you fully recovered? I understand you were quite ill with a bad infection and wound," Sara asked her.

Mina nodded. "Yes, thanks. Your medical staff here are miracle workers, that's for sure."

"And I should probably thank you for saving this one's life, Mina. He's rather annoying, but I'm not sure what I'd do without him. From what I heard, we owe you several thanks."

Mina shrugged indifferently and took a sip of her drink. "Likewise. I'm sure he should've left me for dead and chose not to, so I think we're even."

They held some conversation, and soon others joined them. Mina did her best to stay focused, but she found herself constantly scanning the room, looking for Aria. She couldn't find her, no matter how often she looked.

"Looking for someone specific?" Chello asked, leaning in with a sly smile.

"Maybe," Mina told him with a smirk.

He motioned with a nod of his head to a group not far from them. Mina saw her then, speaking with people she didn't recognize.

"You really do make her your business, don't you?"

"That's my job," Chello laughed. "Even off the clock, it's a habit."

Mina watched as a tall, broad-shouldered man with clean-cut brown hair and two different-colored eyes stood close to Aria, occasionally placing his arm around her shoulders or touching her arm. *Who the feck is that?* she thought.

As if he read her mind, Chello said, "That's Burrow Renfold. He's a good friend of the Peterman family."

"He seems… comfortable," Mina muttered, and she felt a prick of jealousy that caught her by surprise.

She had never been jealous of anyone before. Living only for yourself meant that jealousy wasn't anything to worry about. But she was thinking of someone else now, and that let in other feelings.

"He is. His family is very powerful and well-known."

"What do they do?"

"They run the tech-no lab and own just about everything that comes out of it. Their funding gives us the advanced technology we need to live as we do and protect ourselves as we are able. All our gadgets and weapons, even the eye pigmentation, come from them. They're very powerful and have a ton of influence in the city. Jack knows that and has been trying to get forged with them for years."

Mina nodded and took another sip of her drink, her eyes watching the way Burrow was interacting with Aria. She didn't like it. She wanted to be the one next to her. And as if Aria heard her thoughts, she looked over, and Mina's breath caught in her throat. She saw the eyes and smiled, she couldn't help herself. She was still so damn beautiful, even with one green eye.

Aria smiled back, and it brightened her whole face.

"I'm pretty sure that smile isn't for *me*," Chello chided, and Mina threw a soft elbow into his ribs.

"Excuse me," she said barely above a whisper, and took a few steps away from the crowd she was with.

She let her breath out when she saw Aria do the same. They moved toward one another until they were face to face. Mina smiled when she saw Aria's hesitant expression as if Mina wasn't going to like her new look.

"Weird," Mina told her, looking closely at her eye, and couldn't keep the laugh suppressed.

"You're such a jerk," Aria told her, hitting her shoulder, and then looked her up and down. "But even with my new eye, I can see that you look amazing. You clean up well, Mina."

Mina nodded and looked at her shirt, a deep red made of fine silk and ruffled sleeves. Probably the most feminine article of clothing she had ever worn.

"Thanks. You look pretty good yourself, Richy." Mina thought for a moment and then leaned in closer and whispered: "Still the most beautiful eyes I've ever seen." She winked when Aria looked at her with a blush.

A quiet, helpless sound almost escaped Aria, but she bit it back, clinging to her composure as best she could. Yet, hearing the words sent a flutter of excitement through her. Mina had no idea what she was doing to her.

"Thank you." Aria stammered. "It's a little to get used to. And thank you for coming tonight. I'm glad to have you here."

"Well, you're lucky. I don't really have anywhere else to be at the moment," Mina told her, and they once again locked eyes as if they were the only two in the room.

Mina felt something stir within her, a warmth she hadn't realized she'd been missing. It felt like it would be so easy to be who she really was with Aria. The thought was unsettling, yet strangely comforting. Almost as if the layers would crumble, and all of a sudden, she wouldn't be a wanderer looking for vengeance, but a real person rooted in a real life.

"Mina!" a voice called out, and both Mina and Aria were startled as they came back to the present, both smiling a bit at the reality of them being lost.

Mina turned and saw Jaxon approaching and smiled. "Hey Jaxon, how are you?"

He wrapped her in an embrace and shook her from side to side. "Still hung over but happy to be here. I'm so proud of her!" he told Mina and put his arm around his sister.

"Thank you, Jax."

"Mina, I know this isn't the forum for the conversation, but I was talking to Marcus, and I hope you'll consider staying on. There's certainly a place here for you on my team if you wish."

Mina laughed and shook her head. "By the God, you all do make a woman feel wanted."

She cut her eyes over to Aria, who was staring at her. If only Aria were the one wanting her, not as someone to join her team, but in a more personal way.

"Hey, hey now! Look who's back!" Burrow called out with his signature booming voice, striding over to Jaxon with open arms. He pulled him into a bear hug, patting his back with enthusiasm. "I'm so glad to see you!"

"Thanks, friend. Mina, this is Burrow," Jaxon introduced as they pulled apart. "He's a very close friend of our family and my mentor in the tech-no lab."

Mina nodded politely, though her expression remained guarded, colder than she intended. "Nice to meet you," she offered curtly.

"Mina, I've heard so much about you," Burrow said warmly, his tone curious and genuinely friendly. "How are you feeling?"

"Just fine, thanks," Mina replied, keeping her words clipped. Her eyes flicked to Aria, who shifted uncomfortably.

"I developed the enhancer they used when treating you!" he announced proudly. "It's incredible that you're up and about so soon. Honestly, you were near death when they brought you in. Infection that bad…"

"Burrow, *please*," Aria interjected, her voice steady but tight. "Let's not talk about that. I'm sure that Mina doesn't want to dwell on how bad things were."

Burrow looked apologetic before slipping an arm around Aria's shoulders in a casual, familiar way.

"Ah, sorry. I just get excited when things work better than expected. Glad to officially meet you, Mina."

Mina's jaw tightened as she took in the sight of Burrow's arm draped over Aria. Her focus shifted to Aria's face, catching the way her expression stiffened slightly, her eyes darting downward before quickly rising again. It wasn't embarrassment, it was something more complicated. An awareness, perhaps? It occurred to her that there was a weight between Burrow and Aria that she couldn't fully make out, but it was there, like a half-written sentence left hanging in the air.

Mina's lips fell into a faint frown as Burrow gave Aria's shoulder a playful squeeze before releasing her. He turned his attention back to Jaxon, but Mina's remained on Aria. She wanted to lean in and ask who this person was, to her family, to *her*. Before she could, someone called for Aria to take her place for the official ceremony.

Aria turned to her and whispered, "Don't run off." She let her gaze linger for a second too long to be casual.

"I won't," Mina told her, a smile on her face as she watched her walk away toward the front of the room. Whatever history Burrow shared with her, Mina wasn't concerned. It wasn't *him* Aria insisted on staying, and she let that spread through her.

The Governor stood up front with a few other official-looking people and made remarks about how brave Aria was. Mina watched with a smile on her face, and she cheered loudly with the rest of the crowd when the Governor officially named her Captain of Security, putting a sash around her with a medal on it.

Mina felt the air shift, a low hum stirring inside her. She frowned, instinctively bracing herself. Before she could pinpoint the cause, a familiar voice cut through the air.

"Enjoying yourself?" Director Peterman asked, appearing at her side.

Mina stiffened, her unease making sense. "More than I thought I would," she said, cutting her eyes toward him.

He stood in his dress uniform, his sash heavy with medals. He was a presence in everyday clothes, but in full regalia, he was even more so. Mina shifted her gaze back to Aria, hoping he'd move on. But he didn't.

"I'm surprised you're still here, Mina. I thought you would've moved on. You don't strike me as a stationary type of person."

"I'm not, really. But Aria asked me to stay for her ceremony, and I wanted to honor that."

"Yes, she's taken a liking to you. The entire group has. What a difference from the bowels of the prison."

Mina looked at him as he drank a bright blue liquid from his goblet, her instincts swirling.

"I suppose I owe you a bit of gratitude for saving my daughter. But you're free now, don't you think it's best to move on before the winds of fate...*change*?"

There was a hint of a warning in his tone. She looked at him, and he stared at her with hard, bi-colored eyes before smiling, almost as if he wanted to make sure he got his point across.

"I know you don't like my being here," Mina told him.

He nodded, not denying it. "That's accurate. I don't like criminals within my family home. But in all honesty, I want to help you. I think I have some information you might find useful." He looked at her, and she held his stare, curious about what that would be. "Why don't you come by my office tomorrow after breakfast, by yourself? I think we should have a little chat, hmm?"

"Alright," she told him hesitantly, and he smiled.

"Good. Then enjoy yourself tonight, Mina. You've earned the right to rub elbows with the civilized." He lifted his cup to her and drank, and then moved on into the crowd, towards the front where Aria stood.

She watched him go, her internal alarms swirling inside of her. She didn't like him, he wasn't a good person, she felt that keenly. Why would he want to see her alone tomorrow? To arrest her? Throw her back into the prison cell, tell everyone she had left?

Would anyone know? She thought about that, and it seemed plausible.

"You ok?" Chello asked, coming up behind her.

She turned and looked at him, swallowing. "I think so. Let me ask you something, do you trust Jack Peterman?"

His eyes went wide, and he seemed taken aback by the question. She wondered if she was going too far, trusting one of Peterman's own.

"Of course, he's the head of security. What's wrong?"

Mina could see his concern and tried to smile, an attempt to downplay her panic. "He just asked me to meet with him tomorrow, alone."

"Ok," Chello said, still not seeing any reason for distrust. "And?"

"He doesn't like me, that's no secret. He just told me he thought I would be gone by now and that he didn't like criminals in his house. Now he wants to meet with me alone?"

Chello narrowed his eyes and nodded, seeing a bit of what Mina meant.

"Look, I'm not saying anything is going to happen, but if I disappear, if he throws me in a cell again, I…I just wanted someone to know. I didn't run off or leave."

She saw understanding in his expression, and she felt relieved when he put his hand on her shoulder. She put her hand on his as well, and he nodded.

"Ok, ok. I see what you're getting at. I honestly don't think you have anything to worry about."

"Thank you. Don't say anything about this to Aria, I don't want her to know I'm suspicious of her father, and maybe it's just that I'm being overly…crazy. But I wanted someone to know. Just in case I disappear."

"It'll be fine, Mina. I'm sure of it."

She didn't believe him, but squeezed his shoulder and dropped her hand when Marcus walked up.

"You two gonna make out?" Marcus asked, and Chello dropped his hand and threw his elbow into his ribs. "Ouch! I am just fecking around for feck's sake!"

Mina smiled. "Why, you jealous, Marcus?"

"Of him, maybe, but not you," He chided, and they shared a laugh that put Mina more at ease.

Her eyes moved back to Aria, who was at the front of the room receiving congratulations from nearly everyone in attendance. "So, she's the Captain now. Kind of a big deal, eh?"

"Feck, yes. She's the second in command under her father. We all technically report through her. It's a huge deal," Marcus told her, and Mina noticed the way he looked at Aria with admiration.

"I'm glad for her. It seems everyone respects her. So, what happens now that the ceremony is done?" Mina asked.

"Now the night will take entirely too long to come to an end," Marcus told her. "I hate this formal shit. No good music, we can't drink too much, it's a waste of fecking time." He seemed to think about what he said and added, "But I'm happy for Aria. She deserves it."

"Well, your man looks like he has had it. Maybe you should see if Jaxon wants to head back. He looks tired," Chello told him, and the three of them looked over at Jaxon, who was standing next to Greyson with a stoic face.

"Probably bored to death with whatever bullshit Greyson is chirping at him," Marcus joked, and they all chuckled.

Mina looked Greyson up and down and silently wondered if she could escape his clutches should it come to it in the morning. She decided to let the thought go. There was no point in thinking about it, the God would give her what she needed exactly when she needed it. She would trust in that, not herself.

The night lingered, and eventually the crowd thinned, and Mina finally found herself alone with Aria, off to the side away from the few people who were left.

"Some night, Captain," Mina chided her.

Aria laughed. "It was, thank you again for being here. I know I wasn't as available as I wanted to be."

"The boys kept me company. I'm beginning to wonder if Chello is keeping his eyes on me as much as you, though."

Aria let out a small laugh. "He has really taken to you, everyone has."

"Everyone?" Mina asked slyly, her eyebrows raised. She put her hands in her pockets and swayed her hips from side to side, looking at the different colored eyes in front of her.

"Yes, everyone," Aria told her quietly and dropped her gaze.

Her face blushed, and Mina swallowed, trying not to let her head get too dizzy from the sight of it.

"I'm so done with this night," Aria told her. "I wish I could disappear, just slip out and escape from the rest of this."

Mina smiled and looked around at the remaining people, most having conversations and not paying Aria any more attention. "Well, that's a skill of mine, you know."

Aria looked at her with eyebrows raised. "But you prefer to work alone, so I guess I'm stuck here..."

Mina smirked, stepping in close, so close she could see the fresh pigmentation swirling in Aria's pupil. Her voice dropped to a murmur. "If you stay close to me, I think I can make an exception."

The closeness made Aria's heartbeat explode, and she whispered back, "How close?"

Mina smiled, grabbing her hand. "Extremely."

They stood staring at one another, their hands wrapped around each other's. Mina flashed the cocky smile that Aria loved and then led her through the room. She was a child, moving in an overly exaggerated fashion from one side of the room to the other, ducking and dodging servants and people who were looking for their coats to leave.

Aria laughed, letting herself be pulled along, their zigzagging path making little sense but feeling entirely right. By the time they burst through the far exit, laughter spilled from both of them, their hands still clasped together.

"Now that was some impressive maneuvering. What an escape artist you are! I thought for sure we were to be captured by the drink tray," Aria told her.

Mina laughed. "Well, you can never be too careful. Especially with those shifty drink trays."

They stood with smiles on their faces, and Mina looked at their hands, which were still together. She noted the difference in pallor, the softness of Aria's skin, and she wanted to run her fingers up her forearm and feel it completely. She pulled herself from the thought and let go of her hand, embarrassed.

"That was fun, thank you, Mina."

Mina shrugged and tried to seem indifferent. "It wasn't a bad night at all. Congratulations, Captain."

They began walking through the corridors and eventually made it home to Aria's side of the house. Mina felt a pit in her stomach, not wanting the night to end. She had spent the majority of her life alone and was just fine. But now all she wanted was to be near Aria. It was unnerving and exhilarating.

When they got to Mina's room, they paused, neither one really knowing how to end the night.

"So, I guess this is goodnight," Aria told her, and Mina thought she sensed the same apprehension to end the evening.

"I guess so. It's probably late."

"Probably."

"And I'm sure you're exhausted from your big day...and your big...eye...thing."

Aria laughed. "Yes, getting injected with permanent dye was exhausting. I just laid there. I think I almost fell asleep."

"I give you credit. I'm not sure if I could let anyone touch my eyes."

Aria looked as if she were about to say something in defense, but Mina held up both hands and said:

"I know, I know, it's a tradition and an honor. I get it. And I mean it. They don't look as bad as I thought."

"You thought they would look bad?"

"Horrible," Mina said, but smiled to let her know she was joking. "I knew they wouldn't change your look."

"My look?"

"Yeah, you know. That doe-eyed, innocent, helpless beauty thing you have going on."

"Helpless!" Aria gasped, and she pushed Mina by the shoulders into the door with force to show her she was strong enough to handle herself.

"Ok, ok! Maybe not *totally* helpless. You've got a little gusto in you, Richy."

Aria stared at her, and Mina couldn't help but notice that she hadn't lowered her hands; they remained on her shoulders, pressing against her. Mina looked into her eyes, and for a moment, things seemed to slow down; she thought she could see the elements that made up life swirling around her. She swallowed and let her eyes drop to Aria's lips, so close, so inviting.

"You two alright?" the hall guard called out, and Aria pulled away quickly and raised her hand to him.

"Yes, thank you. The door was stuck, but we got it open."

He tipped his hat and turned, going back to his post.

Mina looked at her and smiled. She put her hand behind her on the doorknob and turned it, opening the door a crack.

"Yeah, that did it. Opens right up now," Mina told her, and Aria rolled her eyes.

"I'll see you tomorrow?" she asked, as she always did when they parted, as if Mina would disappear overnight.

Mina thought for a moment, thinking about Jack Peterman and his request to see her alone. "I'll be here," she told her, and didn't want to keep anything from her. "Your father asked to speak with me after breakfast. Should I be worried?"

Aria furrowed her brow a bit and then shook her head. "Of course not. I wonder what for. Perhaps he wants to offer you a place with us."

Mina thought about the way Jack sneered when he said he didn't like criminals in his house, and knew that wasn't the case. She didn't want to speak badly of him to Aria, so she kept it to herself.

"Yeah, maybe," Mina told her, but there was something off in her tone, and Aria heard it.

"He's heard all the incredible things you've done. I'm sure he wants to offer you a place. He just needed to warm up to the idea."

Mina looked at her and knew she believed her words. She couldn't agree with her but didn't want to upset her, either. She smiled and slowly lifted her hand to brush back a loose strand of hair that was dangling in Aria's face.

"I know, Richy," Mina told her, tucking the hair back in place. "Sweet dreams, eh?"

Aria didn't say anything, she only stared after Mina as she slowly backed into her room and closed the door. She felt her insides swirling and considered following her, not letting the night end.

She lifted her hand toward the doorknob and then stopped, second-guessing herself. If Mina wanted her to come in, she would've invited her. She let out a frustrated sigh, wishing she could read Mina's mind and know exactly what she was feeling. Was she just being playful, or was there something more behind their interactions? The way Mina looked at her made her heart beat out of her chest.

She let her hand drop from the doorknob, clenching it into a fist as she forced herself to step back. The last thing she wanted was to misread this, to push too hard and ruin whatever fragile thing was growing between them. But it was getting harder to ignore the pull, the way Mina seemed to take up space in her head even when she wasn't around.

Aria bit her lip, staring at the door as if it might open again, as if Mina might change her mind and pull her inside. When nothing happened, she exhaled sharply and turned away, shaking her head at herself. This was ridiculous. She was ridiculous. But as she slipped into her own room, the ghost of Mina's touch still lingered on her skin.

Chapter 13

Mina was shown into Jack's office by Greyson, who shut the door behind them and stayed in the room. To the left was a wall of windows with a stunning view of the city skyline, and Mina let her eyes briefly take in the panoramic view before settling on Jack, who was sitting behind the polished desk. He sat confidently, his presence filling the room, the weight of his authority pressing into every corner. His gaze was sharp, staring at her as she entered. He had a small smile on his face, but something in the air felt wrong. Tense.

"Sit," Jack told her, and gestured to the chair in front of his desk.

Mina hesitated for just a moment, looking back at Greyson as if she expected him to be lunging at her with cuffs. She sat and swallowed. She didn't see any visions, nothing that was triggering her senses, so she tried to relax.

"Don't worry about Greyson. He already knows what I'm going to tell you. No secrets between us, eh, Grey?"

Greyson smiled and nodded. "No, sir."

Jack focused back on Mina, his different colored eyes sharp. "You've been here for several days now, Mina. Surprising, considering that you're fully healed."

Mina's jaw tightened, but she kept her gaze steady. She knew he didn't like her, didn't want her here, and was prepared for this sort of track. She thought he was going to tell her she had to leave, or she would be put back in her cell.

"I'm healed, yes. And as I said last night, I told Aria I would stay for her ceremony."

Jack leaned back in his chair, his cold eyes narrowing just slightly. "Yes, I understand that. And now her ceremony is over. What are your plans?"

Mina's brow furrowed. She wasn't sure what her plans were. She knew she had to move on, to get back on her journey of vengeance, but wasn't sure where to start, or, if she was being honest, how to leave Aria. For the first time in her life, there was something else she wanted besides her vengeance.

Jack seemed to sense her hesitation. "I know you're searching for someone, and I believe I can help you. I've had some people investigate the information you're after. The man who killed your family, the one you've been chasing all this time."

Mina's pulse quickened, and she looked at him incredulously. How could he know who she was looking for and why?

"How is that even possible?" Mina asked doubtfully, but couldn't deny the hope and excitement that coursed through her at the thought.

"I'm good at what I do because I know how to do it, Mina. Things aren't always as cut and dry, as black and white, as people think. We all have connections; people we share information with from city to city. It might be foreign to you, but it's how civilized societies operate."

Mina felt like the last bit was a jab, but she didn't care. She wanted to know what information he had, regardless of how he came about it. Any tip would be something new, providing the next path for her to take.

Jack took a slow breath, his fingers tapping against the desk in a quiet rhythm. "I think the man you're looking for is named Sanderson. Goes by Moss. Holed up in the far north, just past the Swamy mountains."

"Moss Sanderson," Mina repeated, letting the name roll around in her mind. There was nothing familiar about it, no tick of recognition.

"It's difficult to get any real information from places like that. The further out you go, the more desolate and dangerous it becomes; rumors are spoken more than truths. That's his name now, at least. Who knows what it was before? He's a mercenary, dangerous. So, make sure you know what you're doing, and be certain you want to find him."

Mina narrowed her eyes. "I do. I know exactly what I'm doing." The thought of a lead this strong was hard not to get excited about. She reigned in her excitement and then looked at him curiously. "How do you know who I'm looking for?"

"Do you think I would let you out of that cell, put my daughter's life in your hands, if I didn't know everything about you? Please, Mina."

She nodded but still wondered how he could know such a thing. "The Swamy mountains are littered with those half-human creatures, the Gores. Are you sure this information is reliable?" She thought she saw his eyes flicker with something she couldn't place.

"Of course I'm sure. And I'll be honest with you, Mina. I sought and *bought* this information to help you, but only because I want you out of my city. That's the hard truth," he told her, leaning forward.

Again, she looked back at Greyson, half expecting him to be coming at her. She didn't like Jack, but a small part of her respected his honesty.

"Let me be honest in return," she told him, and he sat up, surprised at her confidant tone.

"I appreciate your honesty in admitting that you don't like me. I know you wanted me gone, or dead, or in that cell again. I'm grateful for the information, truly."

Jack let something like a smirk cross his face and nodded at Greyson. "Greyson will ensure you're set up with any supplies you may need, Mina. You don't want the trail to get cold. You'll want to move fast…if it really matters to you."

Mina's eyes hardened; nothing else mattered more to her. But then she furrowed her brow and thought about Aria, her thoughts jumbling. What would she tell Aria?

As if reading her expression, Jack's voice softened, taking on a tone almost like he was offering her a concession. "And, of course, there's the matter of Aria."

"What about her?" Mina asked, her tone flat.

"Aria has responsibilities now. She's the Captain. Plus, there's the matter between her and Burrow now that she has ascended."

"Burrow?" Mina asked, confused. She suddenly felt hot, as if the room had gotten very small and there wasn't enough air to breathe.

"Our families have been working on their marriage for a long time. It will secure our position in the city, more so than we could have imagined. The possibilities are endless at what our combined strength and power can do."

"Marriage?" Mina whispered out, the word tasting like poison. Her mind flashed to last night, Burrow constantly touching Aria, putting his arm around her. It made sense now, and she felt her chest tighten in despair.

"Yes, that's right. Aria knows what she needs to do and will do what's best for the family. She always does. She's already accepted it."

His words hit her like a punch to the gut, and for a moment, all she could do was stare at him, disbelief written across her face. Aria was going to marry him. Why wouldn't she tell her this? This changed...*everything*. Mina swallowed, trying to process what she was feeling, but Jack didn't give her any time to do so.

"You've overstayed your welcome, Mina. The best thing for you would be to take the information I've given you and move on with your life. There's nothing for you here in the city."

Mina nodded absently, thinking about Aria being married to someone, and she felt sickened by it.

"I'm such an idiot," she murmured to herself and shook her head. What a fool she had been, allowing this thing to distract her from her purpose. Jack was right, she needed to get back on track and do what she needed to do. "Moss Sanderson. Swamy mountains," she confirmed.

Jack nodded, satisfied. "Again, let Greyson know what you need and be off, the sooner, the better."

Mina stood, slightly shaken, and nodded. She walked out the door with Greyson, and when it clicked shut behind her, a finality echoed in her chest.

***

They sat side by side on the low stone wall just outside the north city gates, Chello listening to what Mina was telling him.

"And then what happened?" he asked when she finally paused.

Mina shrugged, bent down, and picked up a dry weed growing at the wall's base. She rolled it in her fingers, examining it.

"I went straight to her quarters. I was hoping Jack made it up to get me out of the city." Mina shifted her weight where she sat. "As soon as I walked in, I blurted it out, asked her if she was going to marry that guy." Mina winced, the reality of it all still raw.

"What did she say?" Chello asked softly.

Mina looked over at him with a downtrodden expression. "She didn't say anything. I saw it on her face, and I knew it was true. She murmured something like '*It's complicated*' and I sort of shut down. I told her I was leaving, Jack had given me a strong lead on who I was looking for."

Chello put his hand on her shoulder and squeezed a bit, feeling bad for her.

Mina shook her head. "She asked me when I was going to leave, and I said right now, there was no point in sticking around."

Mina jumped up off the wall and paced a bit, Chello watching her with weary eyes. He was worried about her and could see the pain and heartache on her face.

"And you know she acted like *I* was doing something wrong for leaving so soon!" Mina told him incredulously. "She said '*please don't leave*' or some shit as if *I* was the one getting married and blindsiding her!"

Mina threw the weed she was holding down with force, but it fluttered to the ground slowly, and she kicked at it when it landed.

She looked up at the sky, wishing Yip were there. She needed him, needed his presence.

"Mina, I'm so sorry," Chello told her, and it was sincere.

She let her eyes drop to him. He wasn't Yip, but he wasn't bad, either. The man who had taken her from her cell had been nothing but kind to her from the moment they'd met.

She walked over and sat next to him, so close that their sides were pressed together, and put her arm around him. She would miss him, all of them, but him specifically. It hurt to think that she thought she fit in here with them, and now she had to leave.

"Thanks for everything, Chell. You're one of the best people I've ever met, and I won't forget you." Her voice was laced with emotion.

"Same, Mina. I wish you would stay," he told her. "I think you belong with us."

Mina winced at the words, wanting very much to believe them. "She's going to marry someone else. I don't think I could take it."

It was as close to an admission of her feelings as she had ever spoken, and the understanding on Chello's face made her feel worse for some reason.

"Even if she wasn't going to marry someone, I need to find the man who killed my family," she said somberly, and she thought about how she hoped that this would be a place she could return to. But she couldn't, not if the person she wanted to come back to was with someone else.

"He might not be there, you know," Chello told her. "A million things could have changed between the time Jack got this intel and now."

"But the one thing that hasn't changed is my vengeance, Chell. It's all I've known my entire life."

He watched as she looked back at the city, a longing in her eyes.

"When it's all said and done, Mina, what then? Who will you be? What will you live for?"

She looked up at him and narrowed her eyes, trying to keep emotion off her face.

"Honestly, what has been done to you is horrible, and the person responsible deserves your vengeance; you are well within your rights to want to seek it. But that doesn't need to be who you are. Pardon the intrusion, but I believe you could have something much more to live for if you stayed."

Mina dropped her head and shook it, not wanting to hear the words. Aria was getting married, she wasn't for her to love.

"I can't listen to this, Chello. She's going to marry someone else."

"Out of duty, not love! If you stayed, if you gave her a reason, I bet she wouldn't marry him. Her father's plans be damned! I know Aria better than anyone. I see the way she looks at you. Stay, Mina. Tell her how you feel."

Mina scowled, hating the possibility of his words. She fought against them, even as her mind teased a life with Aria.

"And what then? Jack would have me thrown into a cell or worse. He made it pretty clear that I wasn't welcome. I need to stay on track. I know what I need to do. And it isn't entertaining rich girls in their daddy's political scheme."

Chello nodded, knowing his words would do little to sway her from her course. But he felt better saying them. "Just wanted to say my piece, is all. Because I think you have a choice."

"A choice?" Mina snapped at him.

He nodded. "Yeah, a choice. Love, or vengeance? If you can only have one, which will you choose? Which one would fill you more?"

Mina scowled and pushed past him, nudging his shoulder hard as she did. She took a few steps down the street and stopped, hanging her head. She liked Chello. Respected him. This wasn't his fault. She dropped her bag and turned back, looking at where he was still standing, and returned to him.

"Thank you, Chello. For everything. I honestly hope our paths cross again. In another world, I would've really liked to have been mates," she told him, clapping his shoulder.

He smiled and nodded.

"Same, Mina. Take care of yourself. And please know I'm happy to be mates in any world, including this one. Think about what I said, ok? I know Aria. It doesn't have to be this way. You can choose love."

"Shut the feck up," she told him, but pulled him into a hug as she said it. "Thanks for everything."

"Be safe," he told her, and as he pulled back, he added: "Come back to us when you're done."

She nodded and turned from him before the tears flooded her eyes. She didn't want to leave this life, these people.

"Take care, Chell." And with those words, she moved down the street, picked up her bag, and left the city proper.

***

Aria stood on her balcony and inhaled the night air, a deep sadness in her chest. Mina was gone, and with her went a piece of her heart. She knew Mina would want to leave eventually, go and seek her vengeance, but this was all too quick, too sudden. She thought they would have more time.

176

The way she had left, so abruptly, so detached, left a hole in her chest that she couldn't stop feeling. It felt like a door slamming shut, and so much should've been said. She closed her eyes, tears she refused to let fall burning behind her lids. The what-ifs gnawed at her, relentless and cruel. What if she had told Mina the truth? That she wasn't concerned with the politics or the marriage or even her father's disapproval. That all she wanted was her. Would it have mattered?

She wrapped her arms around her chest and closed her eyes, pushing back at everything that wanted to be felt. Her mind lingered on the way she felt when Mina smiled that cocky, confident smile of hers, the way she made her feel so *safe*, even in the deadly marshes. Mina was incredible in every sense, and she just let her go without a word.

A sudden thud on the roof jolted her from her thoughts. Her head snapped up as she heard the scrape of something sliding down. She turned, heart hammering, just as a figure tumbled off the roof and landed in a crouch on the balcony.

For a second, her mind couldn't catch up. It had to be a hallucination, some cruel trick of her longing. But then the figure straightened up, tossing her bag to the side with a shrug.

"Who's in charge of security around here? It's total shit," she said casually with the maddening smirk Aria absolutely loved.

Aria stared, frozen. Her breath caught, her hands trembling. "Mina?" Her voice cracked with disbelief, emotion surging to the surface as tears blurred her vision. She couldn't believe it. Mina was here, standing in front of her, her expression unguarded and sincere.

Without thinking, Aria launched herself across the balcony, throwing her arms around her in a hard embrace. She felt Mina hug her back just as tightly, with no hesitation, no distance. It was real. And it was all Aria needed. She pulled back just enough to look at her, her heart pounding with something she couldn't contain. Before she could second-guess herself, she pressed her lips to Mina's, her silent desire finally filled.

At first, it was light, exploratory. But when Mina began kissing her back, it was with greedy passion, and Aria felt her insides ignite. Mina ran her fingers down her back, and when she got to her backside, she lifted her off the ground and slowly spun them in a circle. Aria was certain that her heart would explode.

Mina took a few steps with Aria in her grip, and when they were inside the threshold of the balcony doors, she gently put her down, and they pulled apart, looking into each other's eyes. Aria's heart was pounding, her breath was short. Mina lifted her hand and cupped her cheek, and Aria covered it with her own.

"You came back," Aria whispered with tears in her eyes.

Mina slowly smiled. "Yeah, I guess I did."

Aria let out a small, incredulous laugh, and they threw themselves into each other, all doubt falling away. She clung to Mina as if anchoring herself, her fingers threading into her hair, pulling her impossibly close. Mina's hands traced the curve of her back, slow and reverent, as though she were memorizing something sacred. Their breaths tangled, their bodies molding into one another with an urgency that had nothing to do with haste, only the deep, aching need to feel, to know, to be known.

Their touches were careful yet desperate, full of wonder and certainty. Neither rushed, but neither could stop, drawn forward by the gravity of a love they had never dared to name yet had always been there, waiting. Mina's fingers traced the line of Aria's jaw before tilting her chin up, deepening their kiss with a tenderness that sent a shiver through them both.

They moved as though they had always belonged to each other, like two pieces finally falling into place. Warmth met warmth, breath mingling, hands exploring with devotion rather than demand. Every touch, every sigh, every lingering kiss was a silent promise, a vow sealed not with words, but with the sheer, unshakable certainty that this was where they were meant to be.

***

Aria lay in bed with Mina wrapped around her naked body, her strong arms a protective cocoon. She let out a contented sigh, and she heard Mina chuckle.

"You ok, Richy?"

"Better than, actually." And she truly was. She had never felt such bliss, such fulfillment in her life. She suddenly frowned, wondering what Mina was feeling. "Are you…how are you feeling?"

Mina laughed and placed a kiss on the top of her head. "I'm perfect."

Aria turned her head to look at her, to see her expression and if what had transpired meant to Mina what it did to her. Mina had a soft smile on her face, and it lightened all her features.

"Are you?" Aria asked and turned her body to face her, snuggling into her.

"Did it not feel perfect to you?" Mina asked, eyebrows raised and a smirk on her lips.

"It did, perfectly perfect. I just, I…I know how I feel, but was curious how you felt."

"I think I showed you how I feel," Mina told her, kissing the tip of her nose.

Aria nodded and let her eyes drop, and Mina laughed.

"Ah! I could kiss that face forever when it gets all pouty and reflective!" And she began rapidly planting kisses on Aria's forehead, cheeks, and eventually lips.

Aria giggled. "I am not pouty!"

"But you are!" Mina protested and rolled on top of her so her arms were on either side of her. "Whenever you're not sure what to think, your little bottom lip pouts out, and you look so adorable. The first time I saw it, I could barely contain my thoughts."

Aria blushed but kissed Mina back when she lowered her face down to kiss her and nibbled on her lower lip. Aria wrapped her in an embrace and mumbled:

"I just want to make sure we feel the same. What do you feel?"

Mina pulled back and looked into Aria's eyes, the green one more translucent than her natural blue one. She could see apprehension there, and while she would normally try to put up an act, pretend it all meant very little to her, she didn't want to. She didn't want Aria to think what transpired between them meant anything less to her. Instead, she kissed the tip of her nose and inhaled, closing her eyes.

"I feel as though I am me, truly me, for the first time in my life," Mina said quietly, and she meant it. All the hard toughness was gone; she didn't want it in this space, not with Aria. She wanted her to see the real person she was.

When Aria didn't speak, Mina opened her eyes, and although it had been nearly fifteen years since she had felt loved by anyone or anything, she knew for certain that it was love looking back at her. Aria was staring at her like she was afraid to blink, as if doing so might make Mina disappear. The intensity of it made Mina's insides crack, her heart flutter, and she swallowed a lump in her throat.

"You are so incredibly special, Mina. In every way possible." And Aria kissed her hard and true, and again they lost themselves in each other, the darkness within healing with each kiss.

***

Aria stared at the scars on Mina's back, some healed over, some deep welts that would remain uneven and rigid. She winced, trying not to imagine the horrors she must have lived through to obtain such markings. She frowned, wondering how anyone could endure such a brutal life.

Slowly, she reached out her hand and lightly grazed her fingertips over the marks.

"Each one tells a story," Mina told her quietly, and Aria removed her hand, surprised Mina was awake. "Don't stop. It feels nice."

Aria swallowed, and with emotion in her eyes, brought her hand back up and began lightly running her fingertips over the scars, tracing the outlines of some, being careful of the ones that still held a purple coloring.

"It doesn't hurt?" Aria asked and again had to fight to keep the emotion out of her voice.

"No, the opposite, actually. I don't think anyone has touched my back before. It feels...nice."

"I'm so sorry you went through this," Aria whispered, her voice cracking. "I can't imagine..."

"Most of it was a long time ago, Richy," Mina told her in a muffled voice, her face pressed against the pillow. "Like I said, each one tells a story. A time when I wasn't as careful as I should've been."

Mina went silent for a moment and then said, "I'm not being as careful as I should be right now."

Aria shifted and leaned forward, brushing her lips gently across one of the scars, placing a light kiss upon it. Mina inhaled deeply underneath her but didn't speak. Aria repeated the motion for each scar on Mina's shoulders and back, and when she kissed them all, she told her:

"You won't get a scar from me. I promise you that."

Mina turned over and faced her, and Aria saw emotion in her eyes, something that surprised her. They stared at one another, and it was as if tethers were being attached to each of their hearts.

"Mina...I..." Aria started, a tear leaking from her eye. Mina reached up and wiped it, and then nodded.

"I know, Richy. I know. Me too."

And they lost themselves in each other yet again, forgetting who they were or where they had been. All they were at that moment were each other's, and that was enough for them both.

***

"Is this Velho?" Aria asked, running her finger down Mina's upper arm. The tattoo was of a tower, half appearing above a horizon.

"Yeah, how I remember it, anyway." Mina sat up in the bed and turned her body to the other side, so Aria could see her other arm. "And this arm has the things that matter the most to me, my very heart."

Aria looked and saw four featureless figures shaded in black, side by side. Under them was a bird drawn in intricate detail.

"Your family?" Aria asked, and Mina nodded.

"Yes, my mom and dad, grandmother and grandfather. And this," she said, tapping the bird, "This is Yip."

"Yip? A bird?" Aria asked, letting her finger drift along the tattoo, the black lines bold against the smooth, mocha hue of Mina's skin.

"Yeah, it's how I first met him, so it's how I think of him when he isn't around."

Aria looked at her strangely, wondering what that meant. Yip was dead, she watched him die. Mina saying he just *wasn't around* seemed out of place and wrong.

Mina saw her contemplation and smiled. "So, I'm sure you know about Velho and the people who lived there? Or at least heard the stories."

"Of course. You are supposed to be people of magic, blessed by the God."

"Some of us, I guess," Mina told her, frowning a bit. She thought of the entire city falling and being destroyed. She came back to the present and said, "Yip is a Chimathian."

"Chimathian? I've never heard of that?"

"It's from Velho, a gift from the God. Not everyone had them, and we never really understood why the God assigned them to certain people. But I got one. Yip showed up when I was six years old, as a bird. Landed right in my lap as I was playing outside, which was weird because we were rarely allowed outside. And we never saw birds; most couldn't survive in such a scorched place. My grandmother went nuts, dropping to her knees and thanking the God. I had no idea what was happening, I was just excited that a bird had landed in my lap."

"But what is he?" Aria asked, still confused.

"A Chimathian is a gift from the God, like a chosen guardian who stays with a person for their lifetime. Once the person they are assigned to is dead, they stop being sent back. Every time a Chimathian dies, usually in the service of protecting their person, they come back in a new form. Sometimes Yip is human, sometimes an animal."

"That's incredible!" Aria exclaimed. "And you have no idea why you were assigned one?"

"No. My grandmother used to say it was because I was going to be special, to do something great, and the God knew I would need the help." Mina stared off, seeming to be lost in a different time. "Maybe she was right. Maybe the God knew I would be the only one to survive."

Aria reached out and touched Mina's cheek, caressing it. The pain she must have locked inside made her so sad.

"Anyway," Mina said, trying to shake off the memory. "Yip was a bird, so that's why I got the tattoo of him like that."

"But he came back after? As what?"

"He was killed by a sand viper when I was 9. I snuck outside to see a sandstorm, and Yip was circling above the tower. He saw the thing about to strike me and swooped down and put himself between me and the snake. I cried and cried. My grandfather kept telling me he would be back. And when he came back some months later, it was as a human child. A small little thing with big brown eyes, black curly hair, dark complexion like mine. And he loved to talk," Mina told her, laughing. "It was like he had been a bird so long that he was so happy to be human again, so he could talk. We called him Yip because he yipped and yapped nonstop." Mina thought for a moment and then added somberly, "He was there with me the day they came and destroyed our city. And then it was just him and me making our way across the world, looking for answers."

"How long was he the boy for?" Aria asked, totally engrossed as if she was being told a fairytale.

"Not too long after, once we cleared the desert and tar pits and made it to the border of the two Spheres, things got hard. People tried to take us, forced labor, things like that. I was used to escaping, but like I told you, it comes to me quickly, and I act, I don't think. And it's always easier on my own. Yip knew that. We had talked about how I should go when given the chance, because he would always find me. I had to leave him behind in one of the mining camps that kidnapped us. A while later, he came back to me as a mouse. I couldn't believe that the God would send something so useless, but that Yip turned out to be the *most* useful. I could carry him around in my pocket, he gnawed through ropes and restraints on more than one occasion," Mina laughed, thinking about it. "He was the mouse for a while. Then, a human again, a bird once more, and then, when I was locked up in Greensk, he was a human. And that's who he was until the marshes got him."

"So when will he come back?" Aria asked, and Mina shrugged.

"I guess when the God wants him to. The God sends who we need when we need them, that's what my mother used to say." And she cut her eyes over to Aria, who smiled widely.

"He knew I needed you," Aria told her, and threw her arms around her.

"Well, we'll have to see what your father says about that. He won't be happy I'm back."

"I'll handle him. We'll go to him together, and we should. I want him to hear it from me, so he doesn't find out elsewhere and explode and do something rash."

Mina exhaled and let out a long breath. "He's going to lock me up again. Or worse."

"I can handle him, Mina. I promise."

Mina looked over at her, her eyes conveying the truth she felt. She thought about Jack, the information that he gave her, and frowned.

"What is it?" Aria asked.

"He gave me a pretty solid trail to follow, where to find a man who might be responsible for Velho. I've been searching my whole life, I don't know if I know how to stop."

Mina looked troubled, as if this was yet another decision she'd have to make, and Aria sensed it. She didn't want Mina to leave. Honestly, she couldn't imagine being apart from her for a single moment for the rest of her life. But she also didn't want Mina to feel like she had to choose between being with her and avenging her family. Gently, she reached out and placed her palm on Mina's cheek.

"I know what that means to you, believe me, I do. And if you feel you have to follow that lead, if you feel you can't be whole without searching, then we'll go and search together. I won't ask you not to go, but I don't want to be without you. If it means that much to you, it means that much to me."

Mina looked at her with wide, disbelieving eyes, letting out an incredulous breath.

"I mean it," Aria told her. "We'll go together and find out who did this to you. And when you've had your vengeance, we'll start our life together. Here in Fusia or some other city, if my father can't tolerate us here. I'm with you, either way, Mina. I promise you."

"You would give all of this up? For me?" Mina asked, her voice barely above a whisper, as if she was afraid saying it too loud might shatter the moment. She couldn't believe what she was hearing. No one had ever chosen her before. Her eyes welled with tears, and her heart pounded like it was trying to catch up with everything she was feeling.

Aria pulled herself up and into Mina's lap, straddling her so they were face to face. Mina instinctively wrapped her arms around her waist, still staring at her like she was something out of a dream, too good, too impossible to be real.

"I don't want to be without you, Mina. I love you and I've never been made to feel so loved, without any conditions or stipulations, in my entire life. You want nothing from me, yet I feel your...love." She said it hesitantly, but Mina grabbed her face with both hands, one on each cheek, and pulled her very close.

"I do love you, Aria. For the first time in my life, I *feel* love. And it's you. One hundred percent you. I love you and don't ever want to be away from you."

Mina pulled her into a kiss that felt like freedom, like home. They stayed that way, embraced and lip-locked, tears streaming down their faces, finally feeling like they were whole.

Aria wasn't thinking about the expectations she was born into, and Mina wasn't thinking about vengeance or loss. For once, there was no past, no future. There was only the warmth between them, and the quiet, steady sense of oneness they never thought they'd find.

Chapter 14

Jack Peterman sat at his desk and stared at the drawer of artifacts he still had from his Vanguard Ascension, so many years ago. They were in the locked bottom drawer, a collection of things that were interesting but proved to be less than helpful to the city and its progress. He reached into the drawer and pushed past various baubles and mechanical items to the one he had been thinking of since he heard the criminal was back in his city.

He pulled out the small item wrapped in cloth, taken from his victim moments after he killed him, the thin man with the dark skin and beard. Jack placed it on his desk, shut the drawer, and then carefully unwrapped it. It was an archaic-looking stopwatch, a grey-green weather-washed stone native to the uninhabited Sphere. He ran a finger over it, stopping at the top button. He clicked it, and gold blades sprang out from the sides, still sharp and shimmering in the light. The face opened to show the hands of the clock, frozen, the mechanism not having been wound in nearly fifteen years.

He sat back and sighed, wondering how the last Velhoian in the world could find her way to Fusia. He should have tracked her down and killed her after demolishing that city, but he didn't think the child would have survived. He assumed she would've died from exposure to the elements or any number of other causes. But now, it seemed, she was the thorn in his paw. And he needed that thorn removed for good.

A knock on the door startled him, and he looked up as Greyson came in with Chello.

"Sir, you wanted to see me?" Chello asked as he entered.

"Yes, come in, Chello," Jack told him and rubbed his face with his hands, tired and annoyed. "You escorted Mina out of the city yesterday, did you not?"

Chello walked up to the desk and stood, nodding. "Yes, sir. I took her to the north gates, sir. We walked out of the city and said our goodbyes, and I watched her walk down the path until I couldn't see her anymore. I believe she said she was going toward the Swamy mountains, sir."

Jack stared at him and saw no deceit in his face, it was probable that he didn't even know she had returned. "And have you seen Aria since?"

"No, sir. She has kept to her room and canceled her combat training today." He hesitated and then added: "If I may, sir. I believe she's very upset at her friend leaving the city."

Jack nodded and stood, pushing his chair off to the side in aggravation. He put his hands behind his back, staring out the window.

"Her *friend* indeed. It seems I underestimated her."

"Sir?" Chello asked, confused.

"I believe Mina is back. And if you're unaware, it leads me to believe that she snuck in purposely so no one would know."

"Back? Sir, are you certain?" Chello asked, and Jack turned and leveled him with a stare. "I can find out at once, sir."

"No need. I'll handle this. But I want you to tend to Aria tonight. I don't want her going off or doing anything stupid, do you hear?"

"Of course, sir," Chello told him, wondering what exactly that meant and what he planned to do with Mina.

"Good. That's all."

Chello nodded, and as he did, his eyes dropped to the desk and the pocket watch sitting on the open cloth. It gleamed innocently in the light, yet a sense of dread crept over him like a cold wind as recognition set in. He had never seen it before, of course. But Mina's voice echoed in his mind, recounting its every detail in the marshes, her conviction that it was the key to everything she had lost. The way her voice had wavered with both hope and desperation, the certainty that this small, fragile object held the answers to the chaos of her past.

His stomach twisted. A slow, sinking weight dragged at his chest, squeezing his ribs until his breath came shallow and uneven. His fingers twitched at his sides, the urge to reach for it warring with the dread curling in his gut. This was what she had been searching for. And if it was here, then what did that mean for the answers she had so desperately chased? For the truth she had been searching for.

A sick, cold certainty settled over him. This wasn't the relief of discovery, it was the prelude to something far worse.

"Sir?"

Jack turned around and looked at him.

Chello swallowed. "What an interesting gadget."

"An old relic from my Vanguard Ascension. Hardly useful, unfortunately."

"It has… *a raw sense of beauty*," he said, repeating what Mina had told him, and he looked up as Jack scoffed.

"Useless. Like the people I took it from. You are dismissed."

Chello nodded and turned and left, his insides swirling with disbelief and total despair. He needed to find Aria immediately.

***

Aria and Mina took the back way to her father's office, hoping to avoid anyone who might see them. Aria was determined to be the one to tell him that Mina was here to stay. If he didn't like it, Mina would leave. But only if Aria went with her. She thought she'd be nervous, especially since seeking her father's approval had always been ingrained in her. But she wasn't. She didn't want to disappoint him; a part of her loved him. But she also wanted Mina, and nothing would change that.

"You sure about this?" Mina asked her as they were about to enter the hall from the back staircase.

Aria took hold of her hand. "I've never been more sure about anything in my entire life."

Mina smiled and leaned over and kissed her. Both of their insides swirled, the love they felt for one another swimming through them freely. When they separated, they entered the empty hall, hand in hand, and walked to Jack's office.

Greyson had just stepped out and looked at them. "Aria," he said, surprised, his eyes dropping to their joined hands. "Your father is going to want to speak with you."

"That's why we're here. Can you please let him know I've come, with Mina, to speak with him?"

"Come right in," Greyson told her, and he cut his eyes to Mina in a hard stare. "Sir, your daughter," he announced and held the door for them. He entered after them and shut the door.

As soon as they stepped into the office, Mina's instincts triggered, and she stopped walking, sweat beading on her forehead. She knew this feeling and knew it meant she was in danger. She didn't see any visions of escape, only the image of the spears hanging on the wall flashing before her eyes.

"Are you alright?" Aria whispered, and Mina looked at her, but before she could answer, Jack spoke.

"Well, this is not what I was expecting at all. I can't tell you how disappointed I am, Mina. I thought we had an unspoken agreement."

Mina focused on Jack and swallowed, trying to calm herself. Greyson had moved over to the wall on the right, standing under the spears displayed from some previous battle, the very ones Mina had just seen in her vision. Something was off. She could feel it. There was something in the air, something that was pulling at her.

"Father, if you can listen for a moment," Aria started, but he held up his hand.

"Darling, I appreciate that you were probably seduced by this criminal, but I need you to stay out of it. This is between us."

"Don't call her that!" Aria told him, raising her voice, and Mina looked at her.

"It's ok. He isn't wrong," she told her and squeezed her hand. "I did tell him I was leaving." Mina looked up at Jack from across the desk and said, "I did leave, but then I came back."

"Snuck in, didn't you? Like the criminal you are. Not even the common decency to come in through the front door," Jack told her, and Aria again protested.

"Father! Please! I know it's not what you want, but Mina is here to stay! I need you to understand what she means to me so we can move past this and on with our lives and progress here in Fusia."

"What she *means* to you?" Jack asked and laughed, looking at Greyson, who stood with his arms crossed over his chest. "She can't mean anything to you, darling, because she *isn't* anything." He looked at Mina and told her, "I gave you a chance. You should've taken it and walked away."

"Father, I..."

"Silence, child!" he yelled, and Aria cringed. Jack laughed again and shook his head. "Aria, sweetheart. I love you and I want you to be happy."

"I hope so, father, because Mina makes me happy."

"I know you think that. I truly believe you do. Please, step out and let me have a quick word with Mina alone, will you?"

Mina gripped her hand tightly, and Aria let out a breath and shook her head. She swallowed, about to tell her father no for the first time in her life. Her fingers trembled as Mina's hand tightened around hers, grounding her in a way nothing else ever had. For as long as she could remember, she had never once said no to her father. His demands, his expectations...they had always been the rule she followed without question, the weight of family duty heavier than her own desires. Every choice, every path, had been shaped by his will. She had sacrificed pieces of herself, one at a time, to please him.

But now... now she was about to do the one thing she had never dared to do in her life.

Her heartbeat thundered in her ears, panic threatening to choke her, and for a moment, she thought she might crumble under the pressure. This wasn't just a refusal, it was the breaking of years of silence, of compliance. It felt like a betrayal, like stepping into an abyss with no guarantee of what awaited on the other side.

But then she looked at Mina, and the doubt faded, replaced by something sharper. Something fierce. Mina was worth it. The thought was simple, yet it gave her a strength she'd never known she had. She had given so much of herself to her father, to his expectations, to a life she never chose. And in that moment, she realized she had nothing left to give him. But Mina... Mina was the one person who had never asked her to be anything but herself.

Taking a breath, Aria stood taller, the weight of years of obedience lifting with the exhale. Her grip on Mina's hand tightened, steadying her resolve. This time, she wasn't going to give in. Because Mina was worth it.

"No, Father. What you need to say, you can say in front of us both. If you love me, you will respect this, you will respect *her*," Aria said boldly, and she felt a flicker of pride inside herself.

Jack stared, momentarily stunned, the unexpected refusal hitting him harder than he anticipated. He shook his head in disbelief, bringing a hand up to rub at his eyes as if trying to erase the reality of the situation. This wasn't how he wanted things to unfold. He had hoped it wouldn't come to this. But now, with the air thick with tension, he knew things were about to get very ugly.

***

Chello raced to Aria's room and banged on the door rapidly, hoping the sound would reach the back bedroom if that was in fact where they were.

"Aria! Mina! Please! It's urgent!"

His heart nearly exploded with relief when the door opened, but it wasn't Aria or Mina; it was Gretchen.

"Where is she?" Chello blurted out, and he asked with such intensity that Gretchen took a step back.

"I believe she went to see her father," she told him, eyes wide. "Are you quite alright, sir?"

"Her father? Just now?" Chello asked, wondering how he missed her in the main corridors. "Mina as well?"

"Yes, just a few minutes ago."

Chello thought for a moment, his eyes going big. "Oh no," he whispered, and then slammed his hand on the door jamb and turned to run back up to Jack's office.

***

"I don't want any trouble," Mina told Jack, who looked at her with a hard stare. "You don't want me here, and I understand that. I'll leave if that's what you want."

"But if she leaves, I'm going with her," Aria added.

Jack scoffed. "Go with her? Follow her around from city to city like a savage? You're a Peterman for feck's sake. You have a purpose here, Aria, a future. Your family and your city are both counting on you. Don't you see that?"

Aria winced and dropped her eyes. She didn't want to walk away from her life. She would, for Mina, but she really wanted her father to understand.

"What have I always taught you? Stay focused. Stay clear. Know your purpose and keep at it!" he scolded, and Aria nodded slowly.

Mina had dropped her hand, so she looked over at her with a furrowed brow. Mina stood frozen, her complexion drained, her eyes wide, staring at something on the desk.

"Mina?" Aria asked softly, her voice tinged with worry.

But she didn't respond. Aria followed her gaze to see what she was looking at and drew in a sharp breath. Her chest tightened as her eyes fell on the object: a pocket watch. Rugged and unassuming, yet unmistakably the one Mina had described from Velho.

Aria's breath caught. The air in the room seemed to disappear as a cold, numbing dread washed over her. Her heartbeat pounded in her ears, each beat marking the slow, inevitable collapse of everything she thought she knew.

No. No, it couldn't be. But the pieces were already falling into place, sliding together with sickening clarity. The way her father had bristled whenever Mina was mentioned. His relentless insistence that she was dangerous. The hatred in his voice when he spoke of her and how he wanted her gone.

Aria's eyes lifted to him, searching, pleading, for some sign that this was a mistake. That she was wrong. But as she met his gaze, the blood drained from her face. There was no mistake. It was written on his face, the way he looked back with something close to dark satisfaction.

Mina's voice broke the silence, and there was a trembling in her tone. "Where... where did you get that?"

Jack looked at her, his expression dark and almost amused. He met her gaze with a slow, deliberate sneer, the kind that cut deeper than words ever could.

Mina's throat tightened as the realization hit her, and she felt tears sting her eyes. She had waited her whole life for this moment, for *this man*. She had found the one responsible for the decimation of her family, her people. And it was *Aria's father*.

Mina saw the vision in her mind and knew she had to act, and she never wanted to act on anything more in her life. She glazed over, her mind going somewhere else as she moved with a fierce speed. She picked up one of the chairs in front of the desk by the back and swung it with force into Greyson, who was standing against the wall, not expecting the attack.

The chair smashed into his face, a spray of blood exploding from his broken nose. Mina kicked him in the groin and put her hands together, pounding down on his back, and he fell to the ground in pain, barely conscious. She wasted no time in pulling a spear off the wall, just like in her earlier vision, and leaped over the desk, throwing herself at Jack.

Jack threw up his arms and blocked her lunge, but he fell backward with the force of her body, and they ended up in a heap on the ground. She drove her fist into his face, not once but twice, and he was able to evade the third punch and sent his elbow into her face. She flew backward, blood streaming from her split lip.

Jack tried to stand, but Mina used the dull end of the spear to knock his feet out from under him, and he fell backward. She pulled herself up and, ever so faintly, heard Aria calling her name, but blocked it out. This was the man who killed her family, who destroyed her entire clan of people. Vengeance was here, in front of her, and it was finally going to be hers.

Jack stumbled up and stood, throwing himself at her, but Mina saw it seconds before it happened. She moved to her left, grabbing him by the shirt and throwing him on the desk, the contents scattering everywhere.

She punched him in the face twice more, and then Aria was there trying to hold her arm back. Mina didn't look at her but shrugged her off, pushing her aside and kneeing Jack in the groin, watching as he fell to his knees in front of her. She kicked him in the chest, and he fell backward.

She raised the spear, her knuckles whitening from her fierce grip. An image flashed in her mind; she saw herself piercing it through his chest.

For her mother.

For her father.

For her grandmother and grandfather.

For Velho.

The weight of their memories bore down on her, sharpening her fury. She hoisted the spear higher, her voice breaking with raw emotion.

"For Velho!" she screamed, tears streaming down her face.

But before she could bring her vengeance down on him, Aria cut into her line of sight. She threw herself between them, kneeling in front of her father, a hand on his chest and the other reaching out towards Mina.

"Mina! Mina, please!"

Mina saw her and froze, tears streaming down her face. She looked at her, truly looked at her, and the rage within wavered for the first time.

Her vengeance had always been the loudest thing inside her, but now, as she stared at Aria, something else began to scream louder. Her heart.

"Listen to me, please!" Aria's voice cracked, desperate. "Please don't kill him!"

Tears stung Mina's eyes as she bared her teeth, growling. Her hands trembled as she raised the spear again, fighting against the pull of her heart.

"For Velho!" she shouted out again, trying to drown out the chaos inside her. The love she felt for Aria was battling her vengeance, the dichotomy fierce. She felt as if she was going to crack in half, the opposition inside of her so violent.

"Please! Baby, please!" Aria cried out, her face crumpled in anguish.

The word *baby* pierced through Mina's rage like a hot knife. She blinked, the vision of Velho's destruction wavering in her mind. Instead, she saw Aria, tear-streaked and broken, her voice trembling as she begged for mercy. Mina's heart wrenched, a raw ache blooming where her anger had been. Chello's words echoed in her mind:

Vengeance or love, which will you choose?

The spear trembled in her hands, the weight of it feeling unbearable now. She screamed a guttural, primal sound that tore from her throat.

"Baby, please," Aria whispered again, her voice breaking. "I love you. Don't do this."

The words shattered Mina. She hated herself for hesitating, for wanting something more than this vengeance. Her grip on the spear loosened. She let out another scream, and it ripped through the air, filled with rage, grief, and the bitter taste of defeat. She slammed the spear against the desk beside her, the vibrations jolting through her hands. Again. And again. The wood splintered and cracked, shards flying as the spear exploded under the force of her fury. She stood there, breathless and trembling, staring at the shattered remnants in her hands. Her vengeance, her purpose, her entire life's mission, reduced to splinters.

Her eyes shot up as someone came barreling through the door. It was Chello.

"Mina..." he huffed out, and it jolted her into action.

She flung herself over the desk and across the room, Chello stepping out of her way as she barreled out the door. He looked at the scene before him and ran over to Aria, who was on top of her bloodied father. But he was alive. Mina didn't kill him. Chello sat back on his haunches, looking back at the door in shock. Mina had chosen love over vengeance.

***

Aria stood in front of the fountain in the garden, the evening sky giving way to night. Her mind was a knot, her heart shattered, and she had no idea what to do about any of it.

"Are you alright?" Chello asked, walking up to her.

She didn't turn, only wiped at a tear that was trickling down her face. "No one knows where she went. North gate confirmed she ran out that way, but that's it."

Aria swallowed and couldn't keep it in; she let out a gasp and brought her hands to her face, tears coming out in streams. Chello placed his arm around her, and she turned and let him embrace her.

"I wish I knew what to say," he told her, but was truly at a loss. He wasn't sure what the worst thing that happened today was, and if he felt it keenly, he knew Aria felt it more so.

"How could my father do such a terrible thing? How could it be possible?" Aria whimpered out, and it sounded heartbreaking. She pulled away from him and wiped her face, letting out an angry groan. "I'm so angry!"

Chello watched with sad eyes, wanting to tell her it would be ok, but he felt no such assurance. He wasn't sure how she, *or any of them*, would recover from this. The truth about Jack had already spread through the security teams: Jack had been the one to kill Mina's family. Mina, who wasn't born into them but who everyone felt was very much a part of them. The whispers were everywhere, and no one could believe it. He could already feel the loyalty within the teams beginning to fracture.

"I can't believe she left me," Aria added softly. The thought hit her like a physical blow, and she staggered back, her chest tight with a mix of grief and disbelief. It wasn't just the loss of Mina that tore her apart. It was everything that had come with it. The truth. The betrayal. Her father's actions.

"Maybe she just needs time," Chello said, and he winced at the lie he knew it was.

Aria walked past him and sat on the edge of the bench, the very bench just days before she sat with Mina. Her heart was heavy with the weight of it. How could she face the world now? How could she go on knowing what her father had done? And alone, without Mina?

"She won't be back. I took the one thing she lived for away from her. Her vengeance was there, and she didn't take it because of me." Aria grimaced and let the pain rip through her. "What am I going to do now, Chell? What do we do?"

Chello went and sat next to her, again placing his arm around her and pulling her into him. He was curious about that as well. "I don't know, Aria. I really don't know."

"I can't look at my father the same. I can't look at myself the same." There was silence, and the questions swirling in it were deafening. "I love her. So much. And now she's gone."

Chello squeezed her, and Aria wiped at her face. Everything was ruined. The man who had raised her was a killer. The woman she loved had left her. She was alone in the darkest place she had ever known. Her breath came in ragged sobs, but there were no answers, no comfort to be found. She had never felt so utterly lost. How did things turn so quickly, from utter bliss to total devastation?

Mina was gone.

And her father? He was a murderer.

There was no going back from this. There was no fixing it.

Aria closed her eyes, feeling the wind against her skin. What now?

The answer was nothing. There was nothing left.

Part III.

Vengeance.

Chapter 15

There is beauty in darkness, in forgetting the past. The pain, the regret, the everything of a life left behind. That was the one common thread among the bands of Gores that rumbled through the forests and up the mountains before the Levite mines.

Once, these beings had been people, but no longer. The remnants of their humanity had slipped away, abandoned by choice. They were a collective of broken things, a ragged, disjointed mass that clung together not from need or affection, but from a shared, primal instinct for survival and destruction.

They wandered the lands, twisted and silent, like lost animals haunted by the memory of a past that no longer held meaning. Words were few between them, and conflict flared more often than not. They looked at the world with a strange indifference, as though the burden of existence itself had become too much to carry. In a way, they had chosen this, leaving behind any trace of who they once were.

It was a way to escape the unbearable weight of memory, the unbearable burden of being. It was easier to be a thing than a person. Easier to be cold, mindless, and feral than to feel the sharp pangs of a humanity that had betrayed them.

And to Mina, it was another prison cell. Somewhere to waste away time and life and forget all that once was. She wasn't as far gone as most of those she roamed with, she had only been in the mountains with them for half the year. But she could feel herself letting go, forgetting everything she once knew, everything she once was.

The grey and white wolf-dog sat by her side obediently. She knew, as well as he did, that he was the only reason she hadn't let herself go completely. But it was there, waiting to happen, and each desolate moment added to the possibility.

A feral growl and then a whooping sound alerted her that something was coming, and Mina watched from her perch on the rock face as the Gores below began stirring to life. She knew this dance and hated it, but it was part of who she was now. Someone had come too close to them, travelers who should have known better, and the Gores were going to make them pay.

Mina looked down at the golden eyes looking up at her, they pleaded for her not to go. She offered a quick nod of her head, letting him know she was going. Killing an innocent would never be something she did, but she liked the frenzy of it all. She could lose herself in the swarm and not think about anything or anyone.

She stood and dropped the animal fur she was wrapped in, exposing her bare arms to the frigid cold. Below, the Gores swarmed in a circle, riling themselves up. When they took off through the forest to the worn path that served as a road, she jumped down and followed behind them, trying desperately to forget who she was.

Trailing them, she watched the chaos, heard the strikes and blows, the growling and screaming. She didn't stop it, but she didn't participate in it, either. Instead, she tore her way through tents and belongings, as if looking for something lost or forgotten.

Yip, very much opposed to this new life, stayed in the trees, refusing to enter the frenzy unless Mina needed him. He watched and whined as Mina entered a makeshift tent, the contents being thrown this way and that.

She entered the next tent and was met with the blunt force of a blow to the midsection, and as she fell back in pain, she smiled.

Finally, she thought. *Make me hurt. Make me forget.*

She jumped up and threw a punch, missing the face of the man but connecting with his shoulder, and he fell backward. Mina spun around to pounce on him, to hopefully make him throw more punches at her, and stopped with her fist in the air. She stared down at him, a whisper from the past. His face was now bearded, but his eyes were the same, one green and one blue.

"Mina?" Chello asked in disbelief, recognition clicking, even though her appearance was different.

Two other Gores came barreling in, snarling and growling. When they saw Chello, they immediately moved to attack him, rip his throat out like the animals they had become.

Mina watched as the first Gore lunged and landed on top of him, and her eyes cut to the second, who was about to spring. As he did, she stuck out her hand, grabbing his arm. He growled at her, and she punched him twice in the face, his nose and mouth exploding with a bloody spray. He fell to his knees and looked up at her in shock. She brought her knee to his throat, and he fell back, choking on his blood.

Mina grabbed the Gore Chello was trying to fend off, and threw him to the side. The Gore looked at her, confused.

"Leave him alone. Get the others and go," she said in a very even command. The Gore grunted and growled at her, then she added: "Or you'll all die."

He ran out of the room and tore the tent as he did, ripping it down so Chello and Mina were standing face to face in the dim forest.

All around them, the fight continued. Without another word to each other, they began fighting the Gores until they all ran off, leaving Mina behind.

She looked at the group, some faces stirring a distant memory, and then over at Chello, who was on one knee, staring at her. She felt her eyes burn and took a deep breath, turning and running off into the woods.

***

Mina sat on her rock perch, the other Gores stewing below, looking up at her with hatred. She wasn't afraid; fear had left her a long time ago. They could try to kill her if they wanted, but Yip would make that difficult to do. He wanted her alive more than she wanted to be and kept a tight watch, growling and baring his teeth when someone got too close.

She sat and stared out over the rocks and trees, trying to keep her mind from thinking. She didn't care. Couldn't care. Those people were just a part of another life, a life that was long gone. And it needed to stay buried there. She pulled the fur tighter around herself. For some reason, she was feeling the cold more than usual. Yip lay at her feet, a low whine in his throat. She closed her eyes and refused to feel.

***

Chello stood with a small group of his people and thought that this was the way Mina had gone. He didn't bring everyone from camp, only a handful, in case the Gores found them first. They had business and needed to stay on their course, but he couldn't leave without trying to find her.

He led the small team through the woods to the rocky outcrop, and just when he was about to give the order to turn back, he heard a deep growl from the darkness.

The archers immediately nocked arrows, the others drawing daggers and taser staffs. Chello froze, his heart pounding as two golden eyes emerged from the darkness. A low, menacing growl rumbled in the creature's chest as it crept forward, its massive paws crunching the bracken on the ground.

"Easy, team, easy," Chello said, his voice steady despite the dryness in his throat. "Don't fire unless it attacks. Maybe we just got too close."

The wolf paused, its posture shifting as it heard his voice. Its hackles lowered, and it tilted its head as if trying to understand.

"What the feck is it doing?" someone whispered.

Chello shook his head. "I have no idea, but stay on your guard."

To their surprise, the wolf began wagging its tail. Lowering its head, it crept forward cautiously, each step deliberate, as though trying to show it meant no harm.

"Sir… should I fire?" one of the archers asked nervously when the wolf was within striking distance.

"No," Chello said tightly. "Just hold."

The wolf stopped a few paces away, its head bowed submissively, tail wagging. Chello hesitated, then slowly crouched, extending a hand toward the animal. The wolf barked playfully and leaped forward, startling the group as it began licking Chello's face and rubbing its muzzle against his chin.

"What the…?" someone muttered in disbelief.

"Whoa, easy there, boy!" Chello said, laughing despite himself as the wolf's tail wagged furiously.

"This isn't natural. I don't like it," another voice grumbled.

As if it understood, the wolf turned and trotted back into the woods. It paused to look back at them, barking once, as though inviting them to follow.

All eyes turned to Chello, and he nodded. "Let's go."

***

Mina sat looking out over the horizon and didn't turn when she heard boots crunching on the frosted ground. She already knew who it was.

"Hello, Chello," she said evenly, keeping her eyes forward.

"It is you."

She heard his approach and sat still when he knelt beside her and threw his arms around her, hugging her. She closed her eyes, pushing hard at the onslaught of the past.

Chello realized she wasn't responding to his hug and pulled back, looking at her. "Are you… alright, Mina?"

He took in the sight of her, dirt and blood caked on her face, her hair a snarly mess. Her face was gaunt, her eyes hollow. She looked nothing like the woman who had saved his life a year ago.

But before any more words could be spoken, Yip came bounding up to them, jumping on top of Chello and licking his face.

"Whoa, boy, whoa!" Chello laughed. "You have a friendly dog here."

Mina turned her head slightly in his direction and felt the corners of her lips twitch, threatening a smile. Memories of the past flooded her mind, and she felt like she was slipping. She steeled herself, refusing to give in to the past.

"He remembers you," she told him.

Chello sat up, stroking the head of the wolf. "What do you mean?"

"That's Yip."

"Yip?" he asked, his eyes going wide in disbelief. At the sound of his name, the dog barked and wagged his tail. "But how…"

"It doesn't matter. What are you doing here, Chello? These are dangerous lands, you shouldn't be here."

Chello sat on his backside, crossing his legs under him so he could look at Mina and continue to pet Yip. He eyed her, there was a wildness about her, something feral and dangerous. She wasn't who she used to be; he could see that clearly. Roaming with Gores could only mean one thing: she had given up.

"I'm happy to see you, Mina. I missed …" he started, but she cut him off.

"Go back where you came from."

The rebuke silenced him for a moment, but then he said, "I can't. We're on our way to the Levite mines."

Mina looked over at him for the first time, a glare of disbelief. "That's suicide."

Chello looked at Yip, who was enjoying the attention. "I know. But we have no choice. We need one of the gem crystals from there."

"That's impossible. No one has ever survived the mines, the traps going in, or the creatures inside."

"It's Jaxon's Vanguard Ascension." He waited, but she didn't say anything. "Things are different now, Mina. "The city is… different." His voice went quieter. "We're on the verge of an all-out war with Greensk. The battles are constant. We're losing people. Every day."

He glanced at her, but Mina didn't lift her head. She sat motionless, her face angled toward the ground like she wasn't listening, but he knew better.

"Tech-no managed to develop devices to create a secure perimeter. A laser fence, in theory. But nothing can power it properly. Solar's too weak. We need something stronger. Our only hope left is a Levite gem crystal. They're supposed to be eternal."

Still no reaction. But he saw the slight tilt of her head, the subtle shift that said she was listening after all. He hesitated, then said more quietly, "You should know… Jack is dead."

Her body stiffened, just slightly, but she didn't speak.

"Greyson's in prison. And Jaxon… Jaxon volunteered for this. He knows the stakes, and he knows the city depends on it. Aria…"

"Stop." Her voice cut sharply through the air. "I don't care. Go back where you came from, Chello."

But he heard it, the catch in her throat, the pain she couldn't quite mask. Yip whimpered, nudging him with his snout as if he wanted to hear it. Chello nodded and continued talking to Yip.

"You wanna hear it, Yip?" he asked, and on cue, Yip barked. "Greensk demanded to know who broke in and freed Jaxon. They wanted that person in exchange for peace. Otherwise, they would wage war. The city structure was already in chaos because of the Peterman feud, with most of the security team following Aria and some staying with Jack. There was a big falling out after you…" He stopped and cut his eyes to Mina and decided to move on. "Anyway, no one wanted war, of course, but no one wanted to turn anyone over to Greensk. There was debate over what to do and how to defend the city. Aria's team had their ideas, and Jack had his. No one could agree. Things were already so fragile in the city with the divided loyalties." Chello's jaw tightened as he said, "Then, Jack went behind everyone's back and struck a deal with Greensk for Aria. In exchange for her, they would withdraw their attack. With Aria out of the way, Jack thought he could regain control of the city."

Yip growled, and Chello saw Mina turn slightly in his direction, trying not to listen.

"But Jaxon… Jaxon didn't let it happen. When word of Jack's plan got out, Jaxon confronted him. He volunteered to go back to Greensk himself, to offer his life instead. But…" Chello hesitated, his voice catching. He looked down, unable to continue.

Yip let out a soft whine, his ears flat against his head. Chello nodded faintly, his hand rubbing Yip's coat.

"It didn't end well."

Jack stared at Jaxon, his request to return to Greensk hanging in the air. "Do you believe Greensk would want you back? No one wants you, Jaxon. Not even your former captors. Not this city. Not me. You're worthless. Meaningless. You should've died in that prison. Everyone would've been better off. You've always been a disgrace. Not just to this family, but to the city, to anyone who's ever had the misfortune of laying eyes on you. Weak. Pathetic. Always crying, always feeling. I never wanted a son like you."

"That's enough," Marcus called out from the other side of the room. Jaxon looked up, his face beet-red and tears in his eyes. His chest heaved under the weight of the insults, his nails digging into his palms. He had heard it all before, a lifetime of insults that left scars deeper than he cared to admit.

Jack glared at Marcus. "Get out. Both of you. Go back to your side of the city. The deal is done. They'll come for Aria, and you will let them take her. She's as useless to me as you are. Your softness, your incompetence, it's infected her. I wish neither of you had ever been born."

"So, you admit it, then?" Marcus asked, his eyes narrowing. "You made a deal with Greensk for Aria's life?"

Jack turned his gaze to Marcus, unflinching. "I did what needed to be done. Aria is a tool, nothing more," he sneered, his lips curling.

Jaxon's breath hitched, his fists clenching at his sides. "She's your daughter," he whispered, his voice trembling but rising with each word. "How could you?"

"She's no longer anything to me!" Jack roared, cutting him off. "Just like you!"

Something inside Jaxon snapped. A raw, primal scream tore from his throat as he lunged, every ounce of his anger and pain boiling over. His hands, shaking with fury, found his father's neck. His vision blurred, blood rushing in his ears, the world going red.

Jack's eyes widened, not in fear, but in shock. Jaxon, the weakling, the failure, the one who'd never stood a chance, was finally fighting back.

The struggle was chaos. Jack's fists hammered into Jaxon's face, each punch landing with bone-crushing force, but Jaxon didn't flinch, didn't back down. Years of rage, humiliation, and hopelessness surged through him. Decades of being told he wasn't good enough, that his dreams were foolish, that he was nothing more than a disappointment. The weight of it all pressed down, suffocating him, but also propelling him forward.

It was no longer just about survival. It was about destruction. The self-loathing, the suffocating absence of love, the belief that no one had ever cared about him... it all pulsed within him like a storm, demanding to be released. His hands tightened around Jack's throat, the fury that had been dormant for so long finally roaring to life.

Jack stumbled, a rare misstep, and Jaxon seized his chance. He tackled his father, pinning him to the ground, his fists raining down with unrelenting fury. Jack reached for the blade on his waist and pulled it out, but Jaxon grabbed at it, and a struggle ensued. In the mess of it all, Jaxon ended up with the blade, and as he pulled back his arm to strike, he yelled: "For Aria, and Mina, and Velho!"

"Then he drove the blade into him. But he called out you and Velho before doing it," Chello told them, his voice breaking at the end.

Yip whined, and it turned into a howl. Chello thought he heard Mina let out a gasp, but she didn't speak. Yip continued to howl as he stood up and went over to Mina, rubbing his muzzle into her limp hands. She wrapped her arms around him and hugged him, a deep part of them both affected by the news of Velho being called out, a different sort of vengeance coming full circle. Chello watched them and felt the sting of tears in his eyes.

When Mina let go of Yip, Chello saw her wipe her face, trying to hide the tears. He continued:

"After that, things happened fast. Greensk kept attacking; we spent all our time on the walls defending the city. Tech-no finally created a defensive gate, but it lacked a proper power source. They said a gem crystal from the Levite mine was supposed to be eternal and would work. Jaxon volunteered as his Vanguard Ascension. He knows it's impossible, but I think he feels he has to try. He hasn't said anything, but Marcus thinks what happened with Jack fecked him up, and this is his way of dealing with it."

There was silence, only the sound of the wind hollowing down in the canyon, and finally, Mina spoke.

"Is she alive?" It was barely a whisper, almost involuntarily.

"She is, yes," he told her, and Yip thumped his tail on the ground, showing his approval. "She's…different. Harder now. But she's been through a lot. After you left, she…I don't know…she changed. She refused to answer to Jack, denounced him as her father, and started her own security division. It all got messy quickly. But you were always at the front of her mind. She was obsessed with finding you. She sent out search parties and looked everywhere. She was relentless…"

"Please stop," Mina told him, and she closed her eyes as tightly as she could, pressing against the emotion. "You need to go home, Chello. Take Jaxon and what's left of your party and leave. We're not the only Gores in the area, it's not safe."

"We? A Gore now, Mina?" Chello asked. "Come with us. You don't have to stay here like this, you don't have to…"

"To what? To feel?" she barked at him, and stood up, turning toward him. The quick movement made Yip jump back. "You have no idea what I have and have not to do!"

Chello looked at her and swallowed, recognizing that this wasn't the same person he had gotten so close to so quickly all that time ago. She was different. Like Aria, she hardened herself to protect herself.

"I know you hurt, Mina. I know it's deeper than I can ever understand, and for reasons I never will. But you're the last of your people, those blessed by the God. Is living this way really doing their memory any honor?"

Mina walked to the edge of the drop-off and looked at the dark sky. She hated his words, hated their truth. But she hated herself even more.

"Goodbye, Chello. Heed my advice and go home. There's nothing but death at the Levite mines."

He knew the conversation was over, so he stood, gave one more rub to Yip, and then told her:

"Holding yourself hostage to the things of the past doesn't heal anything, Mina. I miss you. And so does she."

And with that, he walked back to where his people were waiting and disappeared into the darkness.

***

Mina sat still as stone for a long while after he left, staring at nothing, doing her best not to think or feel. It was hard. Seeing Chello was like a breath of air and a punch to the face. What a random thing to happen. But she knew something like this wasn't random.

"There are random things in this world," her father used to tell her, *"But big things that matter are never so. They are from the God, and as people blessed by the God, we owe our obedience."*

She winced as she thought the words, not wanting to have to consider life again, the pain that came along with it. Chello's words rang in her head next to her father's: *"Is living this way really doing their memory any honor?"*

Yip walked up to her and dropped a hare that he had caught at her feet. He whined, and she looked at it, then at him. He tilted his head to the dead fire ring, urging her to light it for warmth and to cook the hare.

"I don't want to eat. You have it," she told him, and he let out a whine. "What's the point? I wish I had never seen his stupid face."

Yip nudged her arm with his snout, and she shrugged away from him. She didn't want to feel, and now all she could think about was Jaxon trying to enter the Levite mines on a suicide mission for their dumb and pointless tradition of the Vanguard Ascension. He wouldn't get up the front-facing cliff alive, of that she was certain.

Her mind shifted to what Chello had said about Jaxon, how he'd killed Jack. His final words had been an ode to Velho, spoken like a vow, a prayer. It made her heart ache in a way she hadn't been prepared for. He did something she couldn't.

The emotion that welled up inside her at the thought was something else entirely, something that stole her breath and made her eyes burn. Gratitude. Pure and unfiltered.

Jaxon had remembered. He had carried her pain with him, honored it, honored her people. He had spoken Velho's name; he hadn't let her memory fade.

She hadn't been there to see Jack fall. She hadn't been the hand that ended him. But someone had stood in her place, not out of duty, not for glory, but because it mattered. Because *she* mattered.

She rubbed her hands over her face, wiping at the tears. She owed Jaxon for that, a debt she wasn't sure how to repay. But as she thought about what he was trying to do, his Vanguard Ascension, she realized there *was* something she could give. Something she could do. She exhaled shakily and shook her head.

"I don't want this. I don't want any of this. I want to cease to exist. Can't you understand that?" she cried, voice rising to the sky.

She let Aria's face into her mind for the first time in what felt like forever, and the pain of it was immediate. More tears flooded her eyes.

"I can't," she whispered, then screamed, "I *fecking* can't!"

She pounded the ground with her fist. Yip barked, startled, taking a step back.

"I'm staying here," she growled, breath ragged. "I'm not getting involved."

Yip whined softly, then let out a low growl and a sharp yip at the end. Even he seemed to know that some things were non-negotiable. If the God needed you to act… you acted.

She looked at him, his ears pricked, tail wagging slowly as if waiting.

Then she looked up into the thick dark of the sky. No, she didn't want any of this. But deep inside, she knew that want had nothing to do with it.

Chapter 16

Mina followed them at a distance, watching them move through the forest and up the mountain, sending Yip to ward off any Gores or creatures who had ideas of attacking. She wasn't sure what she would do, but there was a pull inside of her that compelled her to follow, to watch and see.

She recognized a few faces: Jaxon, Marcus, and Meesh. It was hard, her mind was losing its grip with each moment she observed them, wondering what they were talking about, and how things were back in the city. She tried to stay focused, already knowing she couldn't watch them die.

When they approached the mines, Yip let out a low whine. He, too, was concerned for them. Marcus and Jaxon moved forward, the chosen two to enter and claim a gem crystal.

Yip looked up at her, and she exhaled, feeling her instincts kick into gear. She closed her eyes and offered up a prayer to the God, asking Him to have his hand on her, on them. *And if someone must die, let it be me, not them.* She opened her eyes, and Yip licked her face.

"Go on," she told him, and he licked her hand before scrambling down the hillside. He walked up to their group, Chello smiling when he saw him.

"Yip!" he called out, and Yip let out a friendly bark.

The group was standing in a line, with Jaxon and Marcus up ahead at the edge of the cliff that gaped the front face of the mines. Yip sat obediently next to Chello, who put his hand on his head.

Mina slowly walked out from the tree line, feeling eyes on her as she did. She didn't bother to look at Chello, instead, she walked up to where Marcus and Jaxon were, placing her hand on Marcus's shoulder.

"Feck, Mina! It really is you," he told her, and the happiness in his eyes drove the shell she had put up back a bit.

She squeezed his shoulder and motioned with her head for him to fall back.

"I can't. I have to go with him."

"You'll both die if I don't go. And I can't keep all three of us alive. Let me go with him," she said, and Marcus looked at Jaxon.

Jaxon's eyes teared up as he looked at her, and he pushed past Marcus, grabbed hold of her, and pulled her into a hug. She felt her arm twitch to hug him back, but refrained. Instead, she pulled away and said:

"I make no promises. You will need to do exactly what I say when I say it, no second-guessing or protesting. Our lives will depend on it."

He nodded and put his hand on Marcus's shoulder. "Take care of them," he told him, nodding towards the group.

Marcus swallowed, both relieved and concerned. He turned and went back and stood in the line next to Meesh, who had relief on her face.

"Thank you, Mina," Jaxon told her.

"Don't thank me yet. What do you have there?" she asked him, motioning to the bag Marcus had left.

"Glow balls, two rope anchors, daggers, a…."

"Stop," she told him. "Weapons aren't going to help us in there."

"How are we going to…what …." Jaxon started and stopped when Mina shook her head.

"Remember, do exactly what I tell you when I tell you."

He nodded, and Mina saw the fear in his eyes. He didn't have the nerve for this, but she knew he had to be the one, as their ridiculous Vanguard Ascension dictated.

"Is there any possibility of me talking you out of this?" she asked him, and he silently shook his head. "If something happens to me in there, you get out, ok? You need to stay focused and remember why you're here."

He swallowed and nodded, and then she motioned to the bigger of the rope anchors.

"Fire it across, up on the first ledge there."

He did and then anchored it to the ground where they stood. He looked at her for direction, and she took in a deep breath, trying to see what she felt, which was nothing, no warnings or triggers at all.

"You first," she told him, and he put the bag, which now only held the glow balls and the other anchor rope, over his body.

Jaxon shimmied his way across the rope, and when he was halfway, she started across herself. Yip let out a low whine, but there was no way he could come with her. They maneuvered to the cliff face, and Jaxon began the ascent. When he was at the top, about to pull himself over, Mina felt the trigger inside of her, her eyes glazing over.

"Stop!" she called up, and he froze. "Something's on the other side. She looked around for another way, and to the right was a smaller wall with an even smaller ledge. "There, use the other anchor over there."

"But there is no..." he began, and she cut him off.

"Do it. Now."

Jaxon fired the other anchor where she told him and had nowhere to anchor it on their side, so he wound it around the rope they were hanging from. He carefully maneuvered off the rope onto the smaller one and held his breath when it dipped and sagged. Once it leveled back out, he began moving up it until he reached the ledge, a small outcrop that barely held him. He gave the thumbs up to Mina, and she started her way over.

Jaxon helped Mina up when she reached him, and they both looked at the main ledge. They could see what looked like a bubbly pool, perhaps acid, awaiting anyone who tried to climb over.

"We would've been dead already," he huffed out, and she shimmed past him to lead the way.

"Step where I step, move where I move," she told him, and he nodded and followed her across the small ledge and onto the main entrance platform.

The entrance to the mine was small and dark, and Mina could feel the evil even before entering. Stories told of creatures so vile that they couldn't show themselves in the light of day, their evil compelling them to stay in the depths of the cave. No one ever lived to see one and tell, of course, and Mina could feel her entire body tingling as she looked into the darkness.

She looked at Jaxon and held out her hand, and he put two glow balls into her palm. She squatted down on her haunches and tossed one into the darkness, its blue light blazing once it hit the ground. As it rolled and cast light against the walls, there was a hissing sound and what looked like darts flying across the space. There was a pause, and then more darts flew. Another pause, and then more. Mina counted the seconds, six, between sets of darts. She sat and waited for the glow ball to dim, and when it did, the darts stopped.

"We have six seconds to make it across. When we go, don't stop for anything. You keep moving until I say otherwise," she told him, and he nodded, taking a deep breath. They both stood, and Mina swallowed nervously.

She got in a runner's crouch, Jaxon by her side, and threw the glow ball. She watched it bounce and illuminate, and the first set of darts triggered. They leaped forward, Mina counting in her head while trying to see ahead as well. They ran through the corridor, and when she was at a count of 5, they both fell to the ground, tripping over a raised piece of rock. From her back, she heard the whoosh of the next set of darts, and they were well past them.

"Are you ok?" Jaxon whispered, but Mina didn't answer. She was looking at the ceiling in the fading light of the glow ball. "Mina, are…"

"Shhh," she hissed, slicing the air with her hand. Her gaze snapped to the ceiling and saw movement. Too much movement. Her instincts triggered; they needed to move.

"Go! Now!"

She grabbed Jaxon by the shirt and hauled him up just as the ceiling erupted. Spiders, fat, glistening things the size of pillows, rained down, splattering against the floor with sickening, wet thuds. One hit Jaxon squarely on the shoulder. He staggered with a grunt, the creature clinging with needle-thin legs, green slime oozing from its underbelly.

"Get it off!" he choked, swiping at it.

She lunged, tearing the spider free with a wet *pop* and hurling it aside. "Run!" she barked, already pulling him forward, the floor behind them alive with the skittering of too many legs.

They were past the light from the glow ball, everything was pitch black. But as they ran, Mina's instincts triggered again, and she saw a gap in the ground ahead of them. There was no time to think or stop.

"Jump!" she yelled, and they leaped into the air, soaring across the space without knowing what lay beneath them. They heard it, though, and whatever it was erupted from the water with a roar. What felt like a tentacle slapped against Jaxon as he sailed over, and he cried out.

They landed hard on the other side and scrambled away, both of their hearts beating out of their chest.

"Are you hurt?" Mina asked him frantically and kept her eyes moving in the darkness, but she sensed nothing.

"I don't think so," he huffed, squinting over his shoulder in the darkness. "How did you know what was there?"

Mina took another glow ball and tapped it, keeping this one in her hand. She held it up and saw nothing down the dark corridor.

"If we live, I'll tell you one day. Be careful, something doesn't feel right," she told him, and squinted her eyes in the glowing light.

"None of this is right!" Jaxon huffed out, his voice tight, his panic rising fast.

Mina saw it, too, the way fear was gnawing at the edges of control. She turned to him, swallowed hard, and placed a steady hand on his shoulder.

"Easy, Jax. Just breathe. I'm scared, too. But we can't let it control us. If we do, we're already dead. Stay strong with me, okay?"

He wiped at his eyes and nodded, though she could still see the tremble in his jaw, the fear written plain across his face.

Mina gave his shoulder a firmer squeeze. "You and me," she said. "You can do this. I know you can. That's why I'm here."

He closed his eyes and took a deep breath. When he opened his eyes, he seemed better, more in control. Mina nodded at him and focused her attention on the darkness in front of them.

Something in the air was heavy, *different.* Her insides were thrumming, and it was nothing like she had felt before, a different type of trigger warning.

They were in a small corridor that seemed to abruptly end and veer off to the left. She could sense something ahead, but didn't know what. It was too quiet, too still, she thought, and wondered if they had made it to the main mine.

She squatted and rolled the glow ball down the small incline and watched as it hit the far wall and then rolled to the left, taking the glow of light with it.

After a moment, there was a rattling sound, and she gasped when the glow ball came rolling back into the corridor. It wobbled and rolled back down, the slight incline making it impossible for it to come to rest. Again, a rattling sound, and the ball returned to their area.

"Mina...I don't like this," Jaxon whispered, his voice shaky.

"Follow me and keep quiet. No matter what you see or hear, you keep your eyes on me, do not panic, do not run. Do you understand me?" she asked, and he nodded hesitantly.

She gripped his head with both hands as if she were to kiss him, and repeated: "Do not run or scream or react in any way at all. You will die if you do." She wasn't sure how she knew this, but she was certain. "They feed off fear."

"Who?" he asked in a panicked voice, but she ignored him, grabbing his arm sleeve and tugging him along.

There were stories in Velho, stories of their origins and how they were the people blessed by the God. But there were other stories, too. Stories about *others* who were not blessed but cursed. They were the antimatter to Velho, her grandfather used to tell her. Mina never gave much thought to those stories, but the thrumming in her chest and the fear in her heart made her wonder if she had stumbled across those *others*. Something felt different, and not just because of their situation. She felt it in her core that there was somehow a connection here to who she was, to where she came from.

What is this place? she silently asked the God, but felt nothing in return. She took a deep breath and calmed herself.

They walked slowly to the end of the corridor, and Mina's heart was hammering in her chest. There was a coldness from around the corner, one she felt in her bones. When the glow ball came back out at her feet, she stepped on it, preventing it from sliding back down. She waited, and there was a shuffling sound and then silence. When she let the ball go, it didn't come back.

She steadied herself and closed her eyes, asking the God to give her strength. Whatever was here was meant for her. She knew she wouldn't be in this situation unless it was meant to be. Finding

Chello and coming across these people again wasn't random. She tried to remember that as she took a deep breath.

Mina walked in front of Jaxon, her hand still clutching a fistful of his shirt sleeve. They could hear scrambling noises and tried to keep their eyes sharp in the darkness. They rounded the corner, and it opened into something unexpectedly beautiful; a glow of green light from gem crystals embedded in the floors, the walls, and almost every surface. They illuminated the entire area, and as Mina looked up, she saw that they were in the actual mine, and it went up until she could only see the glow of green.

Soft light sparkled against the dark rocks; the cavern filled with the soft emerald glow. It was mesmerizing, which was its intent. Mina nearly forgot the scrambling noises, and just as she had that thought, a figure jumped in front of them, freezing them in place.

It shot across and out of sight, and they stood still, their eyes darting this way and that. She found it hard not to look at the gems' illuminating light, but when she was able to fix her eyes away from them, she could see black figures crawling all over the walls, closer to them than she realized. Mina swallowed and stood still; part of her wondered why nothing was triggering inside of her, no warnings or visions of escape.

"Let's get one and get out of here," Jaxon nearly cried, and she felt him reach forward. She yanked him back, and he looked at her, confused.

Mina knew they were listening, and somehow knew they understood. She felt it keenly and spoke to him louder than necessary. "We don't take what is not ours."

He looked at her incredulously, and she cut her eyes to him and shook her head ever so slightly. His eyes flickered from hers, and now that he wasn't looking at the glow of the gems, he could see the shadows everywhere, coming to life all around them. He swallowed and tried not to move, closing his eyes and remembering what Mina told him. He couldn't run, couldn't panic.

"What can we offer for one of your gem crystals?" Mina called out, not sure what she was doing. But she was going off feelings and instincts, something that rarely let her down. She thought if they were to be killed right away, she would have seen an escape. Or perhaps it was just her time to die. Either way, she needed to trust who she was.

There was more scrambling, and from behind them, a shadow flashed forward, slicing through the air with a sharp whoosh. The gust stirred around them as she looked over at Jaxon, his eyes squeezed shut, his face twisted in fear.

Another shadow flashed past, and then another. Mina stood her ground, her grip on Jaxon's sleeve so tight that her knuckles were aching. Her heart was pounding in her ears, and she couldn't deny her fear. The shadows were maddening, and she wished they would stop moving or just kill them both, the back and forth driving her insane.

A shadow appeared before them, and in the glow of the emerald light, Mina got her first glimpse of what they were; hunched dark creatures with jagged teeth, dark slits for eyes, and a pointed elongated nose like a beak, no other distinguishable features. It was as if they were actual shadows rather than flesh and bone. It stood in front of them, low to the ground, seeming to inhale their auroras.

Mina wanted to scream, to panic, and run, to do everything she told Jaxon not to. The compulsion was overwhelming.

"You're not one of them," the creature hissed out in a raspy voice and inhaled deeply. "This is something else."

Mina watched in horror as darkness engulfed them and a swarm of shadows surrounded them. She clenched her jaw, waiting for death. She felt their presence all around, their auras humming through the small space. It made her skin itch, and she was glad Jaxon had his eyes closed so tightly. She wanted to scream, to fight her way out of the shadow creature crowd, but that would be deadly.

The creatures seemed to assess them, smelling them, sampling their auras, making sounds that Mina was sure she would never forget; strange tickings, hissings, and salivating. They were so close but not touching them, the hum of their presence everywhere. When she thought she could take no more, they began to thin, and once again it was just one of them before her.

"You are from a lost world. You don't belong here," it hissed at her and snapped its jaws as if it wanted to take a bite. "Your people are gone."

Mina's eyes narrowed, and her mouth fell slack. How could they know such a thing, creatures who have been in the dark for who knows how long?

"Velho has fallen. How have you been left behind?" it asked, and Mina swallowed, not knowing what to say. "It must be true, no one else can make it this far. Why have you come, chosen one?"

Chosen one? Mina thought, and Jaxon also heard it and opened his eyes, looking over at her. He had sweat beading down his face, all color drained from it. Mina looked at him, nodded slightly, and said:

"We've come to ask for a gem crystal. What trade would you accept?" She tried to keep her voice steady, but it was difficult given the fear pulsating through her.

The creature hissed and snapped its jaw open and shut. "The man is trade enough. Leave us the half-breed, take your crystal, and be gone, Velhoian." The creature again snapped its jaws and crouched, preparing to lunge at Jaxon.

Mina stepped in front of him, and he gripped her shoulders, putting his head between her shoulder blades, trembling.

"He is not an option. You can have me. He will leave with the crystal," Mina told the shadow creature, and there was a universal hissing from all over the mine. It echoed through her ears, and her eyes winced, the sound horrific.

The creature hissed, and suddenly, its jaw was in front of Mina's face, saliva dripping from it. It was so close that she could smell it, a putrid mix of death and everlasting life.

"The blood of a Velhoian is not something we are allowed. But he is not pure. He will be ours." The creature snapped its jaws over Mina's shoulder, just outside her ear.

She saw what was about to happen in her mind and reacted. Just as the creature opened its jaws and prepared to lunge at Jaxon, Mina spun and grabbed him, throwing him to the ground. She lay on top of him, shielding him from the attack.

She felt intense pressure and pain, jaws clamping down and biting into her right shoulder, the feel of fangs ripping through her flesh. She cried out in pain, which caused a frenzy to erupt all around. Shadows flew this way and that in hysteria.

"The blood of Velho!" the creature cried, its voice a rasping shriek as it collapsed, writhing in pain.

The air trembled with a strange, electric hum, a surge of sound rising like a wave. From every shadowed crevice of the mine came a collective cry, raw and unearthly, as if a thousand voices screamed in sync. The noise was more than sound. It buzzed in the bones, rang in the teeth, a high, keening wail laced with agony. It echoed off the stone walls in sharp, discordant bursts, turning the mine into a chamber of suffering. They were connected. And they had all felt it.

Mina sat up, put her hand on her shoulder, and felt the blood, the wound open across the top. She winced, both from the pain in her shoulder and at the sound in the mine.

"Give us the man and be on your way!" another creature hissed, sounding as if it were in agony, and again the sound came from everywhere.

Mina stood and looked at the creature that bit her. It was convulsing in pain on the ground, smoke billowing up from it. It looked like it was dying. Another was next to it, swaying back and forth.

She looked down at Jaxon, his face pale and trembling, fear consuming him. She thought about the strength it took for him to survive the Greensk prison, the strength it took to stand up to his father, to *kill* his father. He was courageous and strong, he just needed to believe he was. She reached down and pulled him up, and then looked at the creature, and said:

"This is no ordinary man. This is the vindicator of Velho. He is not a sacrifice or a bartering chip. He is the wrath-bringer who avenged the Velhoian people when I couldn't do it myself. He may not be born from Velho, but his heart burns with its fire."

Jaxon looked at Mina, her words cutting through his fear. They went into his ears and directly to his heart. Her words were an invitation to rise above everything he'd been convinced he was. She saw strength in him, and for the first time, he dared to see it too.

She looked over at him with eyes that seemed to see into him. "I believe in you," she whispered.

Her words awoke something deep inside of him, and he didn't want to be trembling by her side. He wanted to be brave and worthy of what she just said about him. He had never felt like anything to anyone in his entire life. And here in this place, staring at death, Mina made him believe he was something. She spoke life into him, and he wanted to be the person she described, someone who could vindicate, someone strong and bold. He didn't want to be the weak man his father told him he was. He wanted to be more. He *was* more.

Jaxon stood up straight and nodded, letting the fear fall off him. The creatures hissed as they sensed the change, no longer smelling his fear.

Mina felt her blood dripping down her arm and onto the ground, and when it did, the creatures in front of her scampered back.

"Take your gem crystal and be gone, Velhoians. Your blood burns in this place," it told them, and Mina nodded to Jaxon to take a gem crystal.

Before he could step forward, she pulled him back and touched his forehead and neck with the hand that was covered in her blood. She didn't think they would bite him with the blood on him.

He swallowed and nodded, then bravely stepped forward and reached for the nearest green gem, the shadow creatures scampering back as he did. He pried a gem out of the wall, which was much bigger than he expected, most of it being buried in the rock. He needed two hands to pull it out and place it in the bag around his shoulders.

"What will you take from us in return?" he asked, and Mina looked at him, surprised not to hear any fear in his voice.

"A promise to never return. That is the trade, wrath-bringer of Velho."

"Done," he agreed.

Mina nodded at him, and they turned and headed back to where they came.

"Your blood will clear your path out, Velhoians. Fear not. And remember us when the time comes, and your God rebuilds this world."

Mina didn't know what that meant, but she nodded and said, "You have my word."

They turned their backs and left, and part of them both waited for an attack, but it never came. They lit a glow ball once they were in the dark and walked out on a flat, clear path, no sign of a fluid-filled gap with a creature in it, no sign of giant spiders or poisonous darts.

Once they reached the opening of the mine, they both fell to their knees, exhausted from the fear and anxiety. Jaxon pulled Mina into an embrace, holding her shoulder gingerly and gripping the back of her neck.

"I can't believe we're alive!" he cried.

She couldn't help but put her good arm around his neck and hug him back. She would have bet a thousand times that they both would not make it out alive.

"You did good, Jaxon. You should be proud," she told him, and he helped her stand.

He looked at her shoulder and squinted. "That doesn't look good."

"It's fine," she retorted. "Let's get out of here."

"No, I mean it doesn't *look* good. There's something in the wound. Something glowing."

Mina looked at him and saw he was both serious and concerned. She moved her shoulder and felt the pain, but also a strange stinging sensation inside it.

"Let's get down first, then worry about it. We aren't out yet."

Jaxon nodded, and they walked to the rope anchor and worked their way down. The others all gathered as they descended, in disbelief that they were out alive. As soon as they were on solid ground across the chasm, the entire group swarmed around them, and Mina felt Yip licking her face as she collapsed to her knees, hugging him.

"I'm fine, you big oaf," she told him with a smile.

Chello dropped to his knees next to her while the rest of them rallied around Jaxon. He hugged her tightly, his relief evident.

"You're hurt," he told her with concern, and took a cloth from inside his vest pocket and pressed it to her shoulder.

She let out a grimace and nodded. "I was bitten. But Jaxon did his job and got what you came for."

The crowd cheered, and Marcus said, "What the feck happened in there? Your face, Jaxon!"

Jaxon rubbed his hand over his face, Mina's blood smeared all over it. "The blood of Velho," he said with a shrug and a smile.

Mina smiled back at him.

"I thought for sure after the second day, you were both dead. But Yip kept barking every time we tried to decide if we should leave, so we knew you must have been alive," Marcus told them.

Mina slowly stood and looked at Jaxon, who furrowed his brow.

"Second day?" Jaxon asked, and Marcus's face faltered a bit. "How long were we in there?"

"Today's the third day," Marcus told him.

Jaxon looked confused. "Impossible," he said, looking at Mina as if she could confirm they were not gone that long.

Mina looked at Chello, who nodded slowly, and he frowned. As if to confirm, Yip whined and barked at her, licking her hand.

"Three days? It felt…less," she said.

There was a rumbling sound, and they all turned and watched as the rock face where the anchors were attached crumbled, the entire thing falling into the chasm below.

"Let's get moving," Jaxon told them.

The jovial group went somber as they looked at one another, realizing that something wasn't right.

Mina stayed where she was, and while she was eager to get away from the mine, she wasn't sure she could go with them. Yip, who was at Chello's heels, turned back and barked, causing everyone to stop.

"I can't go with you, Chello," she told him and grimaced as she reached back and touched her wound, which was throbbing. "Go and be well."

Chello walked over to her, concern in his eyes. "You can't stay alone, not with that wound. Come with us as far as our satellite camp, we have a medic there. Please, Mina. I can't leave you wounded out here. You're my friend, and I never leave a friend."

Mina had been away for a year, yet her heart still ached for Aria and the life she left behind. These people were a reminder of that. Of everything she had lost. But no matter how she tried, she couldn't fight the pull drawing her back to them. She tipped her head to the sky, closing her eyes as the past pounded at the door, relentlessly.

A soft whine made her look down. Yip watched her, ears twitching, sensing the storm within her. Jaxon stepped forward and gave her a knowing nod, and at that moment, she wasn't sure she had the strength to argue.

They were here. The very people she had once craved were here as if placed in her path by the God Himself. Emotion welled in her eyes, but she turned away before it could spill over. Instead, she nodded, hesitant, but certain enough. Yip nudged his head under her hand, grounding her, and she absently stroked his fur before finally stepping forward. Without another word, she followed Chello into the forest.

***

Mina sat at the edge of the camp, away from the group, who were circled tightly around the fire. She tried to block out the banter, the back and forth that she enjoyed so much when she was a part of them so long ago. It was one of her favorite things, the sense of community and belonging. Now it gnawed at her heart and begged her to give in to a life she knew she couldn't have.

Yip had been sitting next to her, but once the food started to be cooked, he made his way over to Chello, who was happy to give him his share. She watched them, the way Yip was at Chello's feet, having his head scratched. She thought it was comical that even in animal form, the bond between them was still strong.

Next to them, Jaxon was trying to sidestep the tale of what they went through in the mine, and while they pressed for details, they

237

were mostly just happy for him; happy he survived and happy he would be successful in his Vanguard Ascension.

Mina could sense something different about the way Jaxon was holding himself. He wasn't caved in, he was sitting confidently, as if what happened in the mine changed how he looked at himself.

"We won't bite any worse than what already got you," Marcus called out to her. "You afraid to come warm by the fire?"

"Come on now, Mina, come get warm. I'm sure it'll do your shoulder good," Meesh told her, and Yip barked as if he had to have his two cents in on the matter.

She didn't want to offend them, but didn't want to lower herself into a false sense of belonging. They would move on, go back to their city and their lives, and she would still be alone, with no one. She couldn't make that harder on herself.

"I'm good," she told them quietly, and Yip let out a low whine. They fell back into their conversations, no one pressuring her.

After some time, Jaxon stood up and came and sat next to her, handing over a piece of warm bread stuffed with what looked like meat filling.

"You'll need to keep your strength up. Eat this."

"I don't want it," she told him, but he refused to take it back.

He crossed his feet under him and rubbed his hands together, warming them. "It's cold over here."

"It is. So go back by the fire and stay warm," she commanded.

He shook his head. "Nope. I'm fine with you."

"Go on, you idiot," she told him, pushing him, and he let himself fall over in jest.

He sat back up and smiled, and she could tell there was a massive weight lifted off him after succeeding. He only needed to make it home alive with the gem crystal.

"What do you make of us being in the mine for three days?" he asked her in a serious tone.

Mina took a bite of the bread, shaking her head with a shrug.

"I don't understand how that's possible. And you know what else?" he asked, nudging her arm. "The rocks crumbled where our anchors were as soon as we were out. They could have fallen at any time, but why just then? It's like those…things… were controlling it or something."

Mina chewed and listened, thinking about the strangeness of it all. Like the stories she had heard growing up, the anti-matter that guarded the gateway to the underworld. She wondered if maybe the stories were more than stories.

"Yeah, I don't know. I don't know how to make sense of it," she told him, and then frowned. "But whatever they were, they knew Velho. Something tells me there's more to it, a deeper connection than we know."

Jaxon nodded and after a few reflective moments said, "I can't tell you how grateful I am you were with me. I owe you a great deal, Mina. So much that I can't begin to think how to repay it. You've saved my life twice now." He placed his hand on her knee, and she closed her eyes, not wanting to feel his gratitude.

When she was silent, he looked at her and saw her struggle. "I know it hurts, Mina. I know you want to forget. When I was locked up in Greensk, I…I felt the same. I felt like I was going to go crazy, thinking about everyone and everything I had lost and left behind.

Their torture was a distraction. It let me not think about life if that makes sense."

His voice was somber, his thoughts drifting to a place he clearly didn't want to revisit. Mina opened her eyes and looked at him. He was older than her, but not old enough to have lived through all that he had. She knew what Greensk did to people, how they passed the time with cruelty and experiments meant to crush even the strongest spirit.

It was strange, the things they shared in common. And looking at him now, she still couldn't quite reconcile it, the man who had killed his father. The same man who whimpered and squeezed his eyes shut in the mines, yet had somehow survived Greensk. He was a contradiction, all strength and bravery wrapped in fear and softness. Too gentle, too good for the life he'd been forced to live.

"I'm sorry for all you've gone through, Jax. You're too good a man for any of it," she told him.

He looked over at her with tears in his eyes and nodded slightly.

She paused for a moment, trying to reconcile the tangle of thoughts in her head, and then added, "Thank you for what you did, for your words about Velho. Thank you for remembering me and my people during what was a terrible time for you. I won't ever forget that. What you did will bond us for life." She took his hand from her leg and held it, giving it a gentle squeeze.

Jaxon stared at their hands, one dark and one light, and he squeezed back. He thought about his father and how it all happened so quickly.

"It happened so fast. I don't know why it came to me, but you and Velho flooded my mind as it was happening. Almost as if it were a part of me or something." He shrugged and looked at her, unable to explain it any further. "He was such a bad man, Mina. Cruel for sport. What he put us through growing up is nothing compared to the cruelty towards you and your people. I would do anything to undo that for you."

"You've done enough. You did what I wasn't strong enough to do. And I thank you. I will always consider you my Velhoian brother," she told him.

He smiled. "I like that." He thought for a moment and added, "I don't think it was that you weren't strong enough, Mina. I think it was the opposite. You *were* strong enough. Strong enough to choose love. You may not realize it, but what you did was more valiant. Choosing love is always the right answer."

Mina stiffened and dropped his hand, not wanting to think about it. That choice, that love, had been what she worked so hard to try and forget. Before she could end the conversation, he continued, and she couldn't help wanting to hear it, the battle raging inside of her.

"She really fell apart when you left. I'd never seen such despair. I don't think I've ever seen my sister love anything or anyone so deeply."

Mina shifted where she sat and closed her eyes, pushing at the memories of two soft and loving eyes, one green and one blue, looking back at her.

"She had teams look for you all over the place, in the nearest cities and the lands between. She was obsessed, trying to track you down. I thought she was going overboard. But she told me that with you, she felt something she never knew existed, and it filled a part of her soul that had always been empty. She said you were her light, and she would never stop trying to find you." He paused for a moment and wrapped his arms around his knees, pulling them to his chest.

"Then everything with my father got crazy, we all split from him, and she threw herself into leading us. I think you were always on her mind, though. Still are, if I had to guess."

Mina lifted the back of her hand to her eyes and wiped at a rogue tear that had betrayed her and spilled forward. She steadied herself and exhaled slowly, thinking about how much she wanted to go back to Fusia, to Aria, after she left. But she didn't, she was too weak, too scared.

"That was a long time ago," she mumbled in a weak voice.

"It was a long time ago, but I think it was also just moments ago. At least that's how it works for me. No matter how far I push things down, no matter how I try to forget, they always linger. Especially Greensk."

"I guess all memories fade, but never go away," she told him, and he nodded.

They sat in silence for a few moments, each of them chewing on the past. Finally, he asked her:

"So? Ready to come join us by the fire, or should we send you back to the Gores?"

She looked at him, and he smiled, a warm and welcoming grin that she couldn't help responding to. She shoved him and stood, and they went and joined the others.

***

They arrived at the satellite camp a few days later, and she recognized some faces. There were friendly hellos and then raucous applause for Jaxon once word came that he succeeded. Mina couldn't help feeling her heart come to life at the warmth of it; these people truly cared for one another.

Chello took her directly to the medic, a small-framed woman with two brown eyes.

"Cinder, this is Mina. She was bitten on the shoulder and needs attention. Can you help her?"

Mina watched as Chello moved to another group and instructed them to ride ahead and inform Aria that Jaxon was alive, had succeeded, and they were coming home.

She closed her eyes and pushed at the call in her heart, the ache to lay her eyes on Aria. Her entire struggle for the last year was for nothing, as thoughts and memories were at the surface, fighting with her guilt.

"Are you in pain?" Cinder asked, bringing Mina from her thoughts.

"A little." She took off her fur skin to expose the shoulder in question.

Cinder grimaced. "Wow, that's…different. What was it that bit you?" she asked, putting on gloves and eye spectacles.

Chello returned to where they were, eyeing Mina's wound.

"I don't know what it was, exactly. Some sort of creature," Mina told her.

Cinder looked at her with eyebrows raised. "An animal or a Gore?"

"Neither. It was a creature I'd never seen before, inside the Levite mines. I couldn't get a good look at it. Some sort of vampire."

Chello and Cinder stared at her, not sure what to make of it.

Mina shrugged and added, "Jaxon was there. He can confirm. It was a creature with fangs and claws."

Cinder nodded and poured a solution onto a rag. "This is going to sting a bit, but it'll disinfect and hopefully clean it."

Mina nodded and inhaled slowly as she poured the fluid on her shoulder and then rubbed it with the rag. The sting was harsh but bearable.

"What's interesting is that the wound looks like it's trying to keep itself from closing. I've never seen a membrane or a..." Cinder stopped and leaned closer. "What is that?"

Chello stepped closer and looked, nodding. "That's what I noticed when she first came out of the mine. I don't know what it is, but I can tell you there wasn't that much of it when I first saw it. Whatever that is, it's spreading."

"Some sort of venom?" Mina asked, and Cinder shook her head.

"I'm not sure. It's a strange color. I'm going to try to pull it out." She took a pair of long silver tweezers from her pouch, poured disinfectant on them, and looked apologetically at Mina. "This won't feel great, Mina. Tell me if it gets too bad."

Mina nodded and again inhaled slowly, bracing for the pain.

Cinder poked the wound, and Mina flinched, but didn't protest, so she continued. She picked at some debris, removed it, and then went deeper into the strangely colored swirl in the blood and mucus. She couldn't get anything with the tweezers, so she switched to a swab. What came out was a gelatinous mess of blood and emerald-green colored mucus, something the medic had never seen before.

"It removes, but barely. And it's thickening. Look at this, it has a jelly-like consistency."

"It's spreading. There wasn't that much when I first saw it," Chello repeated, and he looked at Mina. "I'm no doctor, but I don't think you want this stuff in your bloodstream, especially if it came from some unidentified creature."

"What are the options?" Mina asked, concerned. "Can you get it out?"

"Not here, not without the proper equipment. I think we can laser-scape it. Remove the entire mass since it's thickening. But I can't do that without the proper tools, and honestly, I'm a field medic. Someone else should do that. But don't worry, we have the resources and tech-no back home."

Mina frowned and shook her head. She couldn't go back there; that wasn't an option.

Chello seemed to read her mind and frowned. "Don't be stupid, Mina. You can't risk your life, or worse. We have no idea what that is."

"I can't go back, Chell," she whispered, and Cinder sensed they wanted privacy and excused herself.

"You have to, Mina. You can't let this go untreated," he told her, running his hand over his hair and looking at Yip, who was lying at her feet. "Look, you want to go back to living with Gores, do it. But I can't in good conscience let you go knowing you have this wound. Please, Mina, come get it taken care of. And then you're free to do whatever you wish."

Mina thought of what that would mean and stood up off the stool she was on and paced past him. Going back to the very place she had tried to forget would open wounds she didn't think even the Gores would be able to make her forget.

"I can't see her. I wouldn't know what to…" Mina felt the pain in her chest and closed her eyes. Yip whined, and she shook her head when she felt Chello's hand on her other shoulder. "You don't understand, Chello. The guilt, the hatred I feel toward myself for leaving her. Going back would make that impossible."

"And walking away now wouldn't? You're already different from the half-Gore who attacked me, Mina."

"I didn't attack you," she told him, shaking her head. She was embarrassed about him seeing her that way. She exhaled and ran her hand over her face. "When I left, I thought I would never forgive myself for not killing him." Her voice was hoarse, thick with the weight of all she had carried. "But in the end, what consumed me more was the guilt of leaving her behind." Her breath hitched. "It wasn't her fault. I should've gone back. I should have..." Her throat closed up. The words burned, but the tears threatened worse, so she swallowed them down and shook her head violently. "I can't."

Chello stepped closer, his face etched with something between sorrow and urgency.

"Do you know that she will never forgive herself for stopping you?" His voice was quiet but firm, cutting through her defenses. "It eats at her every day. She searched for you, Mina. She never stopped. She carries just as much guilt as you do." He hesitated, then added softly, "You both need to release that. You may find a way to forgive each other, but the hardest person to forgive is yourself."

Mina let out a shaky breath, tilting her face toward the sky as if it might hold an answer. It was already too late. Her heart was aching, and this time, she knew... she *knew*... it might never stop.

"You asked me once if it came down to my vengeance or my love, which would I choose?" She exhaled sharply, a bitter laugh escaping before her voice fell to a whisper. "Well, I picked neither. I failed at both." She turned to him then, her hazel eyes shadowed with something raw, something unspoken. "I wasn't strong enough to stay with her. I wasn't strong enough to go back." A tremor ran through her, and she looked away. "The only love I ever knew, and I was too weak to stand up for it."

He removed his hand, and she heard him sit on the stool, not leaving her. She wanted to go, run away, and not have to think about this, but she knew she was already in too deep.

"Look, just come get it taken care of, ok? If you don't want to see anyone, you don't have to. But I think you owe yourself a little grace here, Mina."

Cinder came back with a pouch and held it in the air. "I'm going to properly dress that for you, Mina. I'm shocked it isn't infected. I fear something is keeping it from healing and infecting."

Mina nodded, moving back to the stool, and Chello stood and walked away, leaving her with her thoughts.

As Cinder patched her up, Mina thought of Aria, of the love she had abandoned, the warmth she had thrown away for the sake of a vengeance that had crumbled to dust in her hands. Aria had been so full of love, so open, offering them a world they barely had time to imagine before Mina shattered it. In so little time, they had created something rare, something Mina had never known before. And she left it. She left *her*.

How could she ever go back? How could she stand before Aria, look into those eyes that truly saw her, and admit that she had run? That when it mattered most, she had been a coward instead of the person Aria deserved, someone who would fight for their love, not flee from it?

A sharp ache pressed against her ribs, her breath uneven as she bit her bottom lip. What did Aria think of her now? Did she hate her? Had she moved on? Mina dropped her gaze, and a single tear gathered at the corner of her eye, threatening to fall.

Yip was there in an instant. He let out a soft whine, his ears folding back as he watched her. Then, as if sensing the weight pressing down on her, he lifted his paws onto her lap, propping himself up to lick her face. The warmth of his touch broke something in her. Mina exhaled shakily, her fingers threading into his fur as she held on, grounding herself in the only constant she ever had.

"Thank the God for you, Yip-o," she told him, and he whined and made a noise deep in his throat. "I know you want to go back, but it's not that easy. You weren't there. You didn't see it. It was perfect, Yip. Fecking perfect. We fit like two perfect puzzle pieces."

Yip licked her once more before hopping down, settling beside her with a heavy sigh, his tail thumping against the ground. She exhaled, steadying herself. He was right, she needed to get her shoulder taken care of. That was all. Then she could leave. She didn't have to stay. She didn't have to see *her.*

But even as the thought crossed her mind, it felt hollow. A lie she wanted to believe. Mina tipped her head back, staring up at the vast, indifferent sky. She let out a slow, shaky breath and closed her eyes. She called out to the God, a silent plea to put her on the path intended for her. She opened her eyes and looked at Yip, considering that she might already be on it. She nodded and prayed for strength. Strength to stay, or to walk away. Strength to keep the past buried where it belonged. Or maybe, just maybe, the strength to face Aria again.

Chapter 17

Fusia came into view, and Mina felt her emotions swirl, a combination of longing and fear. So much was coursing through her, memories of every kind. She put her hand on Yip's head for comfort and asked:

"Remember when we first saw this place? Coming in from the other side?" she murmured. Yip huffed softly and licked her hand. "I know. We were amazed at the size of it and said we could stay lost in this city for a long time if we wanted."

She remembered the moment like it was carved into her memory. She had never seen a city stretch so far across the horizon. Fusia was enormous, a place where stone met steel, and the old world had collided head-on with something newer, sharper, and louder.

The buildings had taken her breath away: not just two or three stories high, but stacked with winding balconies, gear-lined lifts, and glass-paneled atriums that glittered like cut crystal beneath the twin suns. The streets were alive with clatter and clang. Lanterns fueled by gaslight and crystal cores hung from every corner, bathing the city in a golden glow that never truly dimmed, even at night.

Compared to the dusty villages and fractured towns she'd passed through on her way from the other Sphere, Fusia had felt like a different world altogether, unreachable, almost unreal. And somehow, even now, it still did.

She thought about the first time she saw Aria, sitting in the meeting room, looking uppity and self-important. She assumed that she was a spoiled rich brat, but Aria surprised her by bringing them the apples. She thought about sneaking back into the Peterman house, the night she came back after Chello escorted her out of the city; the night that changed everything.

"Stay focused," she whispered to herself, and Yip placed his head on her lap, sensing her struggle. "It's going to be ok," she told him and herself, and swallowed as she took in the scene ahead of her.

It wasn't exactly how she remembered. Now, guard stations and blockades stood in front of the gates, a sign of heightened security due to the conflict with Greensk. It was sad to see the remnants of lives once in motion, now reduced to silence and ash. She hadn't anticipated the impact would be so profound, but it was; the shattered homes and empty windows spoke of what was lost, stirring within her a deep, aching grief for the past.

"Greensk focuses their attacks on the other side, mostly. But they tried to circle the city a few times," Chello told her from the seat across from her.

"What are those big metal pillars set up around the walls?" Mina asked him.

"Those are what will hopefully save us. Tech-no devised a shield system for when we're attacked. When we get it up and running, electro pulses will run from pillar to pillar, and anything that comes close gets electrocuted or lasered, or whatever they call it. That's what the gem crystal is going to power."

Mina looked at the pillars in awe, wondering how such a thing could even be thought of, let alone constructed. It was impressive.

"Have you pursued them, the Greensk? Surely, Fusia's army is stronger and has more devices that could defeat them?"

Chello nodded. "Well, I'm sure you remember from your time there that they have a few tech tricks of their own. Their tech isn't what ours is, but it's still advanced. We did try to run them back, but we can only make it as far as the marshes. They seal off the main road, so it's difficult to do. And we're not looking to attack and take over their city, we just want peace."

Mina nodded and exhaled slowly, realizing she was entering a different city than she left. She let her eyes scan the familiar streets as they entered, and her heartbeat increased when they arrived at the government circle. She looked to the left, to where the Peterman compound was, and swallowed hard. It was time to go back to what she left behind.

***

Chello and Jaxon sprang out of the hover as it stopped, both wanting to get to Aria before Aria came out to them. They had discussed how she might react to Mina being back, and while Jaxon thought she would be thrilled, Chello thought it would be best to give her a warning, not to spring it on her.

They rushed over to where she stood awaiting their party, under the arch which led to the Peterman side of the circle.

"Thank the God! Thank the God!" she exclaimed when she saw them, a relieved smile on her face. Jaxon grabbed her into a hug, squeezing her tightly. "I'm so happy to see you, Jax. Gem crystals be damned," she whispered.

"I'm so glad to be home," he told her, and then Chello was there, and Aria went to embrace him as well.

"Are you ok? Hurt?" she asked him as she pulled him into a hug.

"A few bumps and bruises, but I'll live," he told her and began gently pushing her backward into the arcade, behind the large pillar.

"What are you doing?" Aria asked, looking at him, confused. She pulled away and looked at his face, which was apprehensive. "What's wrong?"

Jaxon stood next to them, his tall frame blocking any view Aria might have of the hovers or the people coming out of them. He shifted uncomfortably, glancing between Chello and Aria with an uneasy smile.

"Nothing is wrong, exactly," Chello told her carefully, placing both hands on her shoulders. "We just... wanted to tell you something privately before you saw for yourself."

"Saw what? What's going on?" Aria demanded, her voice sharper than intended. "Just get to the point."

"Mina is with us!" Jaxon blurted out, his words rushing over each other.

Chello closed his eyes, wishing Jaxon had used a little more tact. "Yes, Mina. We found her in the mountains. She helped us, saved us. She's hurt, so we brought her back for treatment."

Aria froze, Chello's words tumbling through her brain. "Mina," she repeated, her voice barely above a whisper.

The name felt so foreign after so long. Her eyes darted to Jaxon, who had crossed his arms defensively, one hand now covering his mouth as if he'd said too much. She tried to look past him, and he shifted to the side so she could see.

And then she saw her.

Aria's breath caught, a sharp gasp escaping her lips as her hand slowly reached out to grab hold of Chello's arm for balance. The world around her faded to a muffled hum, her vision narrowing until all she could see was Mina. Her heart pounded, her breath catching as she took in the figure before her. For a fleeting moment, before the weight of the past could settle in, all she felt was warmth, *love*. Mina was here. *Alive*.

Mina stood in the center of the courtyard, her long hair wild and tangled. She was draped in the tattered fur of some animal. She looked nothing like the poised, confident woman Aria remembered, but there was no mistaking her. The way she moved, the subtle tilt of her head as she spoke to the massive dog at her feet, it was her.

Aria's heart hammered, a flood of joy and pain crashing over her. She took a half step forward, then stopped, shrinking back. She didn't know what to do or how to feel as she watched Mina look around at the buildings with familiarity. The past came crashing back to her, the feel of Mina's warm embrace, the feel of her love. Aria swallowed as other memories followed, the broken and shattered expression she last saw on Mina's face as she ran away.

She had dreamed of this moment, of seeing Mina again, but now that she was here, Aria wasn't sure if she had the strength to face what came next. What did Mina think of her? Did she hate her? Would she even care to see her after what she had done?

Mina's eyes looked her way, and Aria jumped back, hiding behind the pillar, pressing her back against its cool surface as if to ground herself. Her chest heaved with shallow breaths, her mind racing. How could this be real?

"Are you... okay?" Chello asked, his voice soft but urgent, cutting through the fog in her mind.

Aria shook her head numbly, unsure of what she was. Part of her wanted to run to Mina, and another part wanted to run in the opposite direction, the weight of their history too much to get past. She looked at Chello and Jaxon, the concern in their eyes reminding her too much of the time when she was broken after Mina left. It made her stiffen, she refused to be that person again. She was the Commander of the city now. She needed to act like it.

"I'm so glad you're back and safe, Jax," she told him in a monotone voice and put her hand on his cheek. "I'm so proud of you." She looked at Chello and touched him gently on his shoulder. "You too, Chell. Have everyone get checked by the med team. I'll call a debriefing meeting for later today, once you have all had time to rest. I thank the God you're both safe."

She walked past them, into the building, and Chello and Jaxon stared at each other in disbelief.

"Is she ok?" Jaxon asked with concern. "I don't think she's ok?"

Chello swallowed, knowing that Mina being back would open old wounds, unseal memories that Aria had tried so hard to forget.

"I think she needs time, Jax," Chello told him and clapped his shoulder. "Come on, we still have work to do."

***

Chello walked into the medical room, saw Mina in one of the surgical prep tubes, and smiled. The grimace on her face made him laugh for some reason. Yip thumped his tail from across the room, where he was lying with his head on his front paws.

"Hope you didn't put up too much of a fight getting in that thing," he told her, and she groggily opened her eyes, the sedative starting to work.

"Worse than your shitty prison," she mumbled, and he chuckled.

"From what they tell me, you won't feel or remember much of anything."

"Feck you, Chello," she slurred, and he couldn't help laughing.

"Have a good rest, ok? I'll come back when they have you out of the tube and in a proper bed."

She didn't respond, only closed her eyes and rolled her head to the side, fighting to hang on to consciousness.

"How long will it take?" he asked the medic in the room.

"A few hours. She's severely dehydrated so she has an IV going. Once she takes that and the sedative is fully functioning, we'll start the removal process and then the cleaning process. It will take her a few hours to wake up after that. I can have word sent when that happens?"

"That would be good, thank you," Chello told him and left to rest himself.

***

Aria stood frozen in the med clinic, staring through the observation window at Mina's still form, her chest rising and falling in the slow, steady rhythm of unconsciousness. The sight of her sent a sharp ache through Aria's chest. She had fought with herself about whether to come, knowing it would unearth feelings she wasn't ready to confront. But when Chello assured her that Mina wouldn't be awake, the choice had been made for her. She had to see her. She had to lay eyes on her, to prove that she was actually here, and it wasn't a dream.

Tears welled in her eyes, blurring the image of the woman who had, against all odds, managed to slip past every wall she had built.

The med tech had asked if she wanted to go inside, but she had declined, her voice barely above a whisper. She didn't trust herself. If she crossed that threshold, if she stepped into that room and stood beside Mina, she wasn't sure she'd be able to hold herself together.

She covered her mouth with her hand and closed her eyes, the emotion spilling over and running down her face. How could Mina be so close yet feel so far away? How much she wanted her when everything fell apart with her father, someone to be with her and guide her.

Aria let out a shaky breath, the weight of the moment pressing down on her chest. She didn't know how to feel. The guilt gnawed at her, stopping Mina from pursuing her vengeance, knowing that it was everything she had lived for. That decision sat like a heavy stone in her soul, suffocating her with the reminder of how much she had taken from her. And worse still, the fact that her father had decimated Mina's family and her people... how could she ever atone for something like that? The thought felt impossible, a mountain too steep to climb.

Would Mina even care to see her? The question hovered, bitter and unresolved. Aria's eyes traced Mina's still form, and a pang of sorrow shot through her. But Mina had saved Jaxon *again*. She had saved her family *again*. She had helped them achieve the Vanguard Accession *again*. Over and over, Mina had given so much to her.

Her gaze lingered on her, and a horrible realization gnawed at her insides. *Mina might hate me. Mina might not want to see me at all.* The thought was a sharp, raw ache that tightened her chest. If that were the case, if Mina still wanted nothing to do with her, Aria wasn't sure how she could survive it. To have Mina in her life again, only to be rejected... *that* would be a wound too deep to bear.

Even now, despite the ache in her heart, despite the part of her that still longed to be near Mina, she knew she would have to guard that love. Mina still couldn't feel the same. Not after everything. Not after what she had done, after what her father had done. The lies. The destruction. How could she?

Yes, she told herself. *That's what she would do.* She would lock away everything she was feeling, push it down, bury it deep. She would be indifferent to this entire situation. She had to. It was the only way to move forward and protect herself.

But as she turned away, something inside her splintered. As if maybe it was a mistake to lock away the love she had yearned for all this time. She didn't let it show. But she felt it. The weight of what she was losing all over again. She wiped her eyes and turned to do what she felt was impossible: pretend like she didn't care.

***

Mina sat in the recovery room, her shoulder wrapped up and IVs connected to her. Yip was at the side of the bed, his head resting on it, Mina petting him. The med team told her it took tech-no to remove whatever was inside of her shoulder and that they couldn't get it out themselves. The membrane was trying to attach itself to her, embed in her cells, but something in her blood was preventing it from doing so. Still, it continued to expand and grow. Tech-no removed it all and then attached an IV of solution that would cleanse her. She didn't like the sound of that, but was grateful that whatever was in her from the bite was out of her.

She felt okay. When she first woke up, she was groggy, but her head had cleared from that, and now she sat in the sterile white room, her mind a jumble for another reason. Aria. It was all she could think about. Somewhere in the labyrinth of connected corridors and tunnels was Aria. What would happen when they saw each other?

Mina let out a sigh, and Yip licked her hand, trying to offer comfort. She looked at him, his golden eyes wide and observant.

"What's crazy is, now I *want* to see her. I went from dreading it to it almost being a necessity," she told him, and he thumped his tail at the statement.

But what would Aria do when she saw her? That was Mina's only fear: how Aria would react. But the more she thought about it, the more she realized she didn't care. She knew Aria couldn't feel the same about her anymore, not after all that had happened. Yet, she couldn't leave without at least seeing her, telling her how sorry she was. The rest could fall where it wanted. She needed that much. To tell her she was sorry.

"Here you are," the med tech said, coming in with a tray. "Another bowl of ice cream."

Mina smiled, and Yip wagged his tail. If nothing else, the ice cream was still good.

***

Aria sat at the head of the rectangular table in the meeting room, the same meeting room where she first saw Mina over a year ago. She listened to what each person said, each account of their journey, from those they lost in the Gore attack to the absolute terror in the Levite mines. It played out like a performance in her mind, the team seeming to share every moment in vivid detail.

"And then she agreed to come back with us, to get her shoulder taken care of," Marcus finished. "Nothing happened on the way back, just a lot of talk and excitement about Jaxon."

"No Gores or bandits or anything of the sort on that final ride?" Ciro, the stenographer, asked, he was taking notes furiously next to her.

"No," Marcus confirmed. "Every time we heard something or felt something out of place, Yip jumped out and roamed the woods to keep us clear."

"And let me make sure I've got this right. The dog…" Ciro started, but Chello interrupted.

"Wolf. He's a wolf."

"Right. The wolf…named Yip. This animal is feral, but belongs to Mina?"

Marcus looked at Aria, who shook her head slightly. She didn't think it was relevant to include that the wolf was a man reincarnated. No one would believe it, anyway.

"Sort of, I guess," Marcus told him and moved on. "Then we got back, a miracle in itself."

Aria stared at the table, its glossy finish loosely reflecting the images of everyone who sat at it. Chello had told her about Yip, and it somehow made her feel a stronger pull towards wanting to see Mina. She recalled when Mina told her about what Yip was, when they were in each other's arms in her bed, something that felt like another time, another world.

"And the gem crystal is already with the tech-no team," Chello told them. "Commander, they will send word once they understand how to use it to power the defenses." When she didn't respond or even look at him, he said: "Aria?"

She blinked and looked up at him, and then let her eyes scan the others in the room.

"Excellent. I am so very proud of each one of you. This was what one might consider to be the most dangerous Vanguard Ascension mission in the history of our city, and you all played a part in its success. You will all be honored properly at a special ceremony once the tech-no team has the defenses up and running," she told them, and they all smiled, enjoying the praise.

"Mina was the difference maker. Both with the Gores and in the mines," Jaxon told her, and Aria felt her face falter a bit. "She deserves a bit of thanks as well."

"Of course. As soon as she's recovered, she will be given such," Aria told him in a steady voice that took entirely too much effort to maintain.

"I have a question," Marcus called out, half raising his hand.

Aria raised her eyebrows at him, silently hoping it had nothing to do with Mina. She wasn't sure she could talk about her and not let her façade slip.

"I know tensions are high, and the city defense is far from stable, but will we be allowed to celebrate Jaxon and his accomplishment?"

The room came to life then, all murmuring and hoping that they would be allowed to have the party, which was a tradition for the teams. Aria let a small smile touch her lips, memories of her team celebration flashing in her mind. She looked at Ciro and said:

"You can go. We're done with business."

He nodded and packed up his things, looking back before he left, almost as if he wished he were a part of them.

"We could use it, truth be told," Meesh said, and Aria nodded, understanding what they had been through.

"The city has been through a tremendous ordeal, and you all have been at the forefront. We will have Jaxon's official ceremony, and yes, you will have your team celebration."

The room erupted into applause.

"I want you to know that I appreciate each one of you, and Jaxon, I am so very proud of you. Plan your celebration and celebrate well. Dismissed."

The liveliness in the room was loud, and it made Aria smile. She wasn't sure a meeting was ever held with such a happy ending. It was important to her, though, to ensure they knew how much they meant to her and the city. She was determined to lead in contrast to her father, who used fear as his main driver.

"You certainly know how to make a crowd happy," Chello told her as he stood.

She nodded. "It's important."

"I know. And it's appreciated. I'm sure that Marcus will have the entirety of it planned before his head hits the pillow tonight."

Aria smiled, knowing he was probably right. "He does love a celebration."

Chello huffed a laugh and then asked, "How are you doing?"

Aria swallowed and put on a forced smile, not meeting his eyes. "Fine. Busy, of course, but that's the job."

Her words were rushed and sounded forced, and Chello nodded, seeing the act for what it was. "Do you want to talk about..." he started, but she cut him off sharply.

"No. I don't." Aria tried to smile, realizing she snapped at him. "I just need to keep it shoved away, Chell. I hope she's well. I do. But I don't want to...I can't..."

She trailed off, closing her eyes, and Chello put his hand on her shoulder.

"When you're ready, Aria."

She forced a smile and gathered her things, but then stopped. She looked at him from the corner of her eye, keeping her head down.

"Did she...ask to come back to Fusia? Did she *want* to?"

Chello swallowed and looked at his hands, wishing he could tell her something other than the truth.

"No, she didn't. I had to convince her, to insist, actually."

Aria flinched as if struck. She turned away, staring blindly at the far wall as the words sank in. Mina hadn't wanted to return. Not even to recover. Not even to see her. She would've stayed gone, vanished into whatever place had become her refuge, if not for the wound that forced her back.

Aria knew it was because she'd broken something vital between them the moment she denied her vengeance. That must have shattered Mina. But hearing it confirmed that Mina hadn't wanted to come back at all, twisted the knife. Chello's words were a harsh reminder of that truth. Mina hated her. Didn't want to see her or come back to the city at all.

Aria felt that pain, the pain she locked away, that she insisted she wouldn't feel any longer. When she was thrust into the leadership role, pitted against her father, she told herself that she couldn't be broken, she couldn't be pining for someone lost. She had told herself the nights of crying herself asleep, days of wandering the city looking for Mina's face in the crowd were over. Her teams needed her. The city needed her.

But here it was again. That same raw, familiar ache pounding at the door of her chest. Demanding to be felt. To be acknowledged.

She couldn't let it in. Not now. Not when her people needed her. Not when her city was still recovering, still fragile. She had no room to unravel.

Mina didn't want her. That had to be enough. Indifference would be her shield, her only armor against the truth. Because the only thing worse than missing Mina… was knowing Mina didn't miss her back.

Aria blinked back the tears in her eyes and nodded slowly, forcing a half smile but not looking at Chello.

"Good night, Chell. I'm so glad you're back."

He nodded and watched her go, a slow, silent despair radiating off her. He wasn't sure if he should push it, so he let it go. He exhaled, wondering how this was going to play out. He rubbed a hand down his face, hoping the God knew better than he did.

***

Mina followed Marcus and Chello into the guest room they had prepared for her on Jaxon's side of the compound. It was a fine room, very similar to what she had stayed in before, but part of her was trying to get past the disappointment that this wasn't Aria's guest room.

"Meesh got you a bunch of clothes, most of them just normal and stuff," Marcus told her, pointing to the closet. "She said you would probably rip the sleeves off, so she didn't want to get anything too fancy. But Gretchen brought over some things, too, once she heard you were here." He pointed to the pile of folded clothes on the set of drawers and shrugged. "Most of it looks pretty girly, not your style, but who knows?"

"Thanks, guys. You shouldn't have gone to so much trouble," Mina told them, stroking Yip's fur as he trotted past her to the big, oversized pillow in the corner in front of the windows.

"And that's for you, Yip!" Chello said happily. "Figured you would appreciate a little comfort yourself, old friend." Yip barked and wagged his tail, thanking Chello for thinking of him. "You'll be good, right?" he asked Mina.

She smiled and nodded. "Of course. I truly appreciate this," she told them, and her tone was off, not sad but a bit distant.

"You can stay as long as you want," Marcus told her. "Our celebration for Jaxon is tonight, which you have to go to, of course, and the official ceremony is tomorrow, which you have to go to."

She smiled and nodded. "Wouldn't miss it, guys."

"Then we can fight over what you want to do," Marcus told her with a smile. "But fair warning, Jaxon doesn't want to let you go. He is two doors down on the left, by the way."

Mina nodded and walked to the window, looking out over the courtyard drive. It was different from the view on Aria's side, which showed the gardens. She thought about Aria, how for the two days in recovery, she hadn't come at all.

"Does she know I'm here?" Mina asked quietly, her gaze steady out the window. She watched two birds teeter on the rain gutter, their balance and grace on display. There was a deafening silence behind her, neither one of them speaking right away. She turned her head slightly. "Chell?"

He glanced at Marcus, who stood just as uneasily, his arms crossed tightly.

"Yeah, Mina," Chello said at last. "She knows. I told her your procedure went well, and about Jaxon insisting that you stay for the ceremony. She knows."

The words sank into her chest like stones, each syllable heavier than the last. So, Aria knew she was here, and still, she'd chosen to stay away. Mina inhaled deeply, pushing at the heaviness she felt. Aria must really hate her. But she couldn't blame her. She had abandoned her, left her alone in the chaos.

"Okay," her voice was calm but distant. She turned to them with a small smile that didn't reach her eyes. "Thanks again, guys. This is really generous."

"We're just glad you're here," Chello told her.

"It feels better when you're around, truth be told," Marcus added with a grin. "Now rest up because tonight..." He wiggled his eyebrows. "We paaaaarty!"

They all laughed, and Mina truly felt grateful for them.

When she was alone, she sat on the edge of the plush bed and stared at the windows, the afternoon sun shining through. She let the pain of Chello's words work their way through her, wanting to be rid of the sadness they were dripping with. Aria didn't want to see her, and could she blame her? She shook her head and exhaled loudly, leaning back on the bed.

Yip whined from his spot on his pillow, feeling Mina's emotions.

"Doesn't matter, does it? If she doesn't want to see me, she doesn't want to see me," she told him and covered her face with her hands.

There was a swish of air, and then the bed wobbled, and Mina dropped her hands and opened her eyes, a giant wolf snout in her face. Yip gave her a wet lick across the cheek.

"You have your own bed, you realize that, don't you?" she told him, and he whined. "I'm not sure these fancy people want you on their fancy bed, Yip."

He hung his head and put his ears back, looking at her with pleading eyes. She kicked off her shoes, pulled herself onto the bed, and lifted her arm so he could lie next to her.

"Feck if I care. Come on, Yip-o." And they fell into the most comfortable sleep either of them could remember in a very long time.

Chapter 18

The tavern was alive with energy, the air thick with laughter and music. The room was packed, illuminated by strings of multicolored lanterns that cast a warm, pulsing glow over everything. Jaxon stood at the center of it all, surrounded by his team, who cheered and toasted him every chance they got. Marcus had blue tubes of alcohol passed around in steady intervals, and although Mina tried to keep her head about her, the bright blue liquid made it difficult.

She sat at a corner table with a drink in hand and did her best to blend into the chaos and let the upbeat atmosphere dull the ache in her chest. Her mind kept going to the last time she was here, celebrating a Vanguard Ascension, with Aria. Her eyes were constantly checking the room, wondering if she would show up.

"Nice jacket," Meesh told her, sitting next to her, and then added, "I'm surprised you didn't cut the sleeves off."

Mina smiled and grabbed the front of the blazer-style jacket and pulled it back, exposing her well-defined shoulders, the sleeves of the shirt underneath missing.

"I fecking knew it!" Meesh laughed, and Mina noticed her eyes were on Marcus, as usual.

"You ever think about telling him how you feel?" Mina asked, taking a sip of her drink, hoping she wasn't overstepping.

Meesh looked at her with a smirk and leaned back, placing her elbows on the table behind her. "He knows how I feel. And I know how he feels."

Mina looked at her with surprise. "I don't get it. Why aren't you guys a thing, then?"

"Not allowed. I'm on his team. I report to him," Meesh said matter-of-factly, as if this was something she hated but had gotten used to over the years.

"Why don't you transfer to another team?"

Meesh shrugged and leaned forward, her eyes watching Marcus's attempt at dancing in the middle of the crowd. She smiled at the sight.

"I don't want to be on another team. I love these guys. We've been together since the academy. If I move, I want to move up, not over. Be a Praector. Nothing else is worth it to me." She paused and then added, "At least I get to see him every day. We get to spend time together."

Mina frowned. It didn't make sense to her, and she thought they both must be very strong people to be able to not act on their feelings out of respect for their jobs.

"If only there were one more Peterman," Meesh added and then shrugged. "I could go for a Praector role and get to stay with the same people. I used to get down about it, but I don't dwell on it anymore. There are worse ways to live," she told her and smiled as Marcus and Chello came over, sweat on their flushed faces from dancing.

"When are you going to show off those sick dance moves?" Marcus exclaimed as he sat next to them. "You've been holding out on us all night."

"He must be talking to you," Mina told Meesh, and they all laughed.

"Ok, one more shot, and then we all go out there and make fools of ourselves together, deal?" Marcus asked, and they all nodded.

Mina chuckled, happy to be a part of them again, even if just for the night. She missed their closeness with one another and their banter, both making her yearn for such a life. She took another sip of her drink, her gaze wandering across the room. And that's when she saw her.

Aria.

Standing just inside the doorway, framed by the golden glow of the lights. She wore a sleek black outfit that fit her perfectly, the kind of tailored elegance that whispered power and intention. Her posture was as poised as ever, but there was something different now. A new weight in the way she held herself, as if the world had pressed in on her shoulders and she'd learned to carry it anyway.

Her eyes were scanning the room, sharp, composed, until they landed on Mina. And in that moment, Mina saw something pass across her face. A flicker of recognition. And then, just for a second, something painful, sorrow, perhaps. Maybe even something else.

Mina's heart gave a small, traitorous thud. A year had passed. A whole year. And yet, somehow, Aria looked both exactly the same and entirely different. Older. Stronger. More closed off. But still undeniably her.

Their eyes locked, and Mina swallowed hard, her whole body reacting. Her hand tightened around her glass, her breath caught, and her heart lurched in her chest as if it had been struck. For a moment, the noise of the tavern faded, leaving only the sound of her pulse pounding in her ears.

She had convinced herself that seeing Aria would be torture. But standing there, framed in warm light, Aria looked just as she did in the memories Mina had tried to bury. Beautiful. Untouchable. The ache in her chest tightened, and months of longing and regret were pressing against her ribs like a vice.

She should look away, should steel herself, but she couldn't. Not when Aria's gaze lingered, not when the distance between them felt dangerously thin. The longing she had spent a year suffocating clawed its way to the surface, raw and unyielding. And worst of all, despite everything, despite the certainty that she had lost Aria for good, hope flickered to life in the hollow spaces where it had no right to be. It was dangerous to allow herself to feel, but she couldn't help it.

She forgot all about her doubts and fears. Aria was here. And there was no way she could keep herself away. She stood, absently placing her glass on the table, and weaved through the crowd towards her, a tentative smile on her lips.

Aria stared at her, her face unreadable, and as she got closer, she looked away, her gaze moving elsewhere.

Back with the others, Chello stood nervously, watching.

"Aria," Mina said when she reached her, her voice low and uncertain. She was never so nervous about any interaction in her life. She had to hold herself back, keep herself from wrapping her arms around her and pulling her close. "You came."

Aria nodded, her expression carefully composed, her eyes not meeting Mina's.

"Hello, Mina. Of course, I came. It's an important night for Jaxon."

The sound of her name from Aria's lips sent a shiver down her spine, familiar and foreign all at once.

"Yeah, it is," Mina replied, searching Aria's face for a hint of warmth but seeing nothing of the sort. "It's... really good to see you."

"Likewise," Aria said flatly, her tone polite but distant, her eyes looking everywhere *but* at Mina.

The formality stung, and Mina hesitated before trying again.

"I was hoping we could..."

"Excuse me," Aria interrupted, her gaze looking out over the crowd. "I should go say hi to Jaxon. Enjoy the party."

Mina stood frozen, her thoughts swirling. Aria's words hung in the air like a cold wind. Her indifferent, polite dismissal stung, as if they had no history, no love at all. She watched helplessly as Aria walked away from her, weaving into the crowd, her focus already shifting to others.

The ache in Mina's chest spread, sharp and unrelenting, as if her ribs were collapsing inward. She fought to keep her composure, to seem unaffected, but she was deeply. She expected some awkwardness, but not such coldness, such indifference.

She must truly hate me, Mina thought, and tried to swallow the pain. What did she expect? After what she did to Aria, after the way she abandoned her, did she really think she would be happy to see her?

She turned back toward her table, her movements stiff and deliberate. Every step felt heavier than the last as if she were sinking in the coldness that rippled off Aria.

The others were waiting for her with looks of concern on their faces. Their vibe had changed completely; the three of them now worried about her. This couldn't ruin the night. Tonight wasn't about her, it was about Jaxon. She couldn't let her pain interfere with that.

She forced a smile and grabbed one of the tubes Marcus was holding and held it up.

"To Jaxon," she said through her thin smile. "And the best fecking team in the world."

They all smiled and lifted their tubes, but Mina could see the concern baked on Chello's face. She threw the alcohol down her throat and closed her eyes, willing herself to push past her pain. She had to. For *them*. For these people who had always been so good to her from the moment they met her.

"Come on," she said, her smile a little too big, an obvious shield against the crack in her heart. "Let's go show them what terrible dancing is all about."

Marcus smiled, pulled all of them together into a bear hug, and plowed a path onto the dance floor, pushing and moving people as he went. They began dancing, laughing, and shouting, and Mina closed her eyes and jumped around, trying desperately to forget who was in the room with her. The music was loud in her ears, although not as loud as the pain in her heart. She swayed and tried her best to blend into the group, and when they were done, she moved to the bar with Meesh, ordering more drinks, her only defense against feeling.

Marcus and Chello went over to where Aria and Jaxon were, and Mina sat across the room on top of a table, her feet on the bench below. She watched Aria smile and laugh with them, seeming so happy and genuine. It was devastating.

"Wanna get out of here? We can hit up one of the public pubs out in the city. It's frowned upon, but feck it, let's do it," Meesh suggested.

Mina smiled, her head leaning back on the wall. She appreciated that Meesh would do that for her. "I appreciate that, but no chance. This is Jaxon's night. We need to be here for him."

"Spoken like a true Fusian," Meesh told her and held up her glass.

Mina forced a smile and clinked it with her own, and as she took a sip, her eyes slid back to Aria, who, to her surprise, was looking back at her. As soon as their eyes locked, Aria looked away, and Mina took a slow breath. She closed her eyes and tried to center herself.

When the person you love is far away and you can't see them, it's heartbreaking. But when the person you love is in the same room, breathing the same air, and wants nothing to do with you, that's something else entirely. That's torture. She would've taken anything... *anything*... other than this unbearable cold. A warm embrace would've wrecked her, sure. Even a sharp retort, a furious *feck off*, would've been better. At least that would've meant Aria still felt something. But this? This polite distance, this practiced indifference. It hollowed her out. The sound of her name from Aria's lips sent a shiver through her, not because it stirred warmth, but because it was empty. Stripped of affection. Casual, like it never meant anything at all.

She had told herself she could handle it. But she was wrong.

The pain she thought she'd buried, every sleepless night, every unanswered question, every quiet moment where she whispered

Aria's name into nothing, rose like a tide inside her. She felt it cresting behind her ribs, sharp and relentless.

Mina kept a fragile smile plastered on her face as people came and went, but the pain in her chest was constant. Aria smiled and blended in with the others as if Mina were invisible, someone who didn't matter at all.

Mina couldn't take it anymore. She stood up while everyone was engaged and headed toward the door. She had just made it out when Chello came barreling out after her, his flushed face and glossy eyes both indicators of the amount of drink he had taken in.

"Leaving?" he asked, putting his hand out to the wall to steady himself.

"Yeah, Chell, I'm going to head back and get to bed," she told him with a forced smile.

He nodded and looked like he wanted to say something, but didn't know how in his current state.

"Tell Jaxon I'll see him tomorrow. And be careful, will you?" She clapped his shoulder and smiled, then turned and headed down the corridor.

"Mina!" he called out.

She stopped and closed her eyes, not turning. *Don't say it*, she thought. *Don't mention her, please.*

"She's really fecked up about it, too," Chello slurred.

Mina swallowed and couldn't make herself turn to look at him. She slowly lifted her hand in a half-wave and continued down the corridor.

When she got to her room, Yip was waiting, tail wagging, and she collapsed on the floor next to him and let it all go. The tears flowed out of her as if on a mission, and Yip curled up next to her and whined, occasionally licking her face. He knew her pain, and although his purpose in life was to watch out for her, he knew this wasn't a pain he could protect her from. So, he let her feel it. He let her break. Let her sob. And he stayed by her side so she wouldn't have to feel it alone.

***

The first light of dawn spilled into the room and found Aria sitting on the edge of her bed, unmoving, her arms wrapped tightly around herself as if sheer pressure might keep her from falling apart.

She hadn't slept. Her mind wouldn't let her.

It had been looping the same memory, over and over—the moment Mina approached her. Quiet. Composed. Real. Like she wasn't haunted. Like it didn't cost her everything just to look at Aria again. It had knocked the air from her lungs. She hadn't expected it, not after all this time, after all the silence.

She had convinced herself that Mina despised her. That she couldn't even *think* of her without bitterness. And really, how could she not?

Aria had taken the one thing Mina lived for. Vengeance. Justice. Closure. And she had ripped it from her hands. She had broken her. And for what? A father who never loved her, never saw her. She chose that over Mina.

Of course, Mina hated her.

But now… now she was sitting here, wrecked by a glance. Haunted by a smile. Torn open by the memory of Mina looking at her like maybe, *just maybe*, she didn't hate her after all.

And Aria didn't know what to do with that.

Because hope like that? It was poison wrapped in silk. It felt soft, almost comforting. Until it slipped beneath your skin and made everything worse. She didn't want to hope. She couldn't afford to.

Because if she let herself believe there was still something there, if she let herself believe that Mina might still care, then she would want more. And if she reached for it and found nothing there? She wouldn't survive the fall.

So, she'd clung to her indifference like armor. Even when her chest ached at the sound of Mina's voice. Even when her knees almost gave out just from being in the same room.

She told herself it meant nothing.

But it meant *everything*.

And as light crept further into the room, chasing shadows from the corners, Aria felt the weight of it settle. Heavy. Inevitable.

She wasn't indifferent. Not even close.

Maybe she never had been. Maybe the pretending was what had been breaking her this whole time. But what choice did she have?

Because loving someone who might not love you anymore, who might never forgive you for what you did?

That kind of hope didn't just hurt.

It ruined.

Tears slipped quietly from her eyes and soaked into her pillow as she eased herself back, lying stiffly on top of the blankets, arms still locked around her middle like a last defense.

"You made the right choice," she whispered aloud to the stillness, to the ache inside her.

But the words were brittle. Hollow. As false as the indifference she wore like skin.

She closed her eyes, praying for sleep. Or forgiveness. Or some small crack of peace in the war inside her chest.

But she knew deep down neither would come easily.

Not tonight.

Maybe not ever.

Chapter 19

Aria could feel Mina's gaze from across the room, a pull so tangible it took all her willpower not to look back. Instead, she forced a smile for the diplomats and high-ranking officials gathered around her, people who had come to honor her brother. Her brother, who, much to her chagrin, was currently enjoying Mina's company. How she wished she could be there with them, laughing at whatever jest was being shared as if it were old times.

Aria nodded at something someone said, her practiced smile never faltering, and allowed her eyes to flicker toward Mina, just for a moment. Mina was smiling at something Marcus had said to Jaxon, but the smile didn't quite reach her eyes. Aria's breath hitched as Mina's gaze shifted to her. She quickly looked away, her cheeks flushing.

Mina looked like she was trying to appear happy, but it didn't seem authentic. Aria sipped her drink and cut her eyes over to them again, and this time, Mina was staring back, a look of sadness on her face.

Aria didn't drop her eyes, not right away. She looked back at Mina, those sad hazel eyes splintering something inside of her. There was no hate or disdain in those eyes. It was something else Aria saw, something deep and real.

The energy in that stare was magnetic, and Aria felt the pull, the familiar feelings of wanting and longing. She couldn't drop her eyes, and she realized that she didn't want to. Her façade was slipping, and her chest went tight with not just the *want* to go to her, but the *need*. It had always been there, lurking beneath her restraint, beneath her pride, beneath her fear. But now, she didn't want to pretend anymore. She didn't think she could.

"It's just about time, Commander," an aide told her, startling her from her gaze.

Aria looked at him and forced a smile, putting her hand to her forehead. She blinked rapidly, her mind swirling from her thoughts.

"Are you alright, ma'am?" he asked.

She nodded, putting herself back into character, and let him lead her to the front of the room to start the official ceremony for Jaxon.

The Governor's speech was longer than it needed to be, but no one enjoyed hearing him talk more than himself. Aria didn't mind too much, however, as the smile plastered on Jaxon's face was a beautiful sight. His face beamed, his new eyes shining bright, one blue and now one green, just like hers.

The Governor put a sash around him with the Medal of Honor attached to it, and Jaxon looked over at her, tears in his eyes. After a few more remarks, the Governor passed the spotlight to Aria.

She walked to the center next to Jaxon, her Commander's uniform donning the same sash with a few more medals on it. When she stood next to him, she saw the absolute joy on his face, and although not part of the script, she pulled him into an embrace.

"I'm so very proud of you," she whispered, and he squeezed her tight.

Aria stepped back and took a deep breath, looking around the room, trying very hard not to look in Mina's direction.

"As Commander of City Security, and, if I may add, as a proud sister, I officially declare Jaxon Peterman's Vanguard Ascension a success and instruct that his name be written in the city Book of Heroes. What he has accomplished has not only moved our city forward but has also ensured its protection. Thank you, Jaxon, for your service and bravery."

The crowd cheered, and Aria heard Marcus above everyone. It made her smile, and she looked at Jaxon and nodded, indicating he could say his few words of thanks as protocol dictated.

"I thank you, Governor, Commander, and everyone here tonight. Especially my brave team. I'm so very proud to be of service to the great city of Fusia."

It was supposed to stop there. A small moment of thanks to the city and team, and then it should have ended. But it didn't. Jaxon paused, took a deep breath, and then continued.

"I also just want to say that I couldn't have done it without my Praector, Marcus. But also, not without my good friend, and someone I consider an honorary Fusian, Mina. Can you guys come up here, please? I feel it's only right that you be recognized, too."

The Governor looked at Aria, who froze as Mina walked up and stood almost next to her. Jaxon was clapping for them, and this in turn made the entire room erupt into applause.

The Governor smiled and waved, as if it were for him, and then moved forward and shook Marcus's hand, and then Mina's. He turned and looked at Aria expectantly, and she forced a smile and moved to do the same.

"I'm so grateful and proud of you, Marcus. Thank you," she told him and shook his hand as he smiled at her with tears in his bi-colored eyes.

Aria stepped carefully toward where Mina stood, and the crowd deflated into a buzz in her ears, everything moving in slow motion. Her hand extended slowly toward her, and as Mina gripped it, Aria raised her gaze to meet hers for the first time in what felt like ages. A jolt ran through her, an electric current from the past as their skin touched, and she looked into the hazel eyes from her dreams.

"Thank you, Mina. For everything," Aria all but whispered, and she couldn't help but squeeze her hand, almost desperately.

Mina swallowed and nodded, her eyes staring intensely into Aria's. "Thank you, Commander."

The crowd cheered behind them. Aria threw herself back into character and forced a smile, releasing Mina's hand. Just as their hands separated and Aria began to turn away from her, Mina grabbed hold of her hand again. Aria looked back at her in surprise.

"The pleasure was all mine, *Richy*," Mina whispered in a barely audible voice.

Aria stared at her with raw emotion on her face, unable to speak or even react.

Mina winked at her, and then she was gone. Marcus and Jaxon grabbed her and pulled her away, and the three of them hugged.

Aria stood dumbfounded, her vision momentarily blurred, and it took her a moment to understand that it was the tears in her eyes that were causing it. She spun in a circle, not sure where to go, her senses and mind a swirling mess of emotions. Chello was there, then, as he always was when she needed him the most.

"Just walk with me, Aria. Come on, smile and walk with me," he whispered in her ear.

She plastered a smile on her face and focused on putting one foot in front of the other until they were away from the crowd, off to the side of the room.

"Are you ok?" he asked, trying to assess her.

She wiped at her eyes and tried to steady herself, embarrassed at her lost composure. She nodded but couldn't speak yet. She was completely undone; in her head, she heard Mina's smooth, low voice calling her the name she simultaneously loved and hated.

Richy.

Chello handed her a glass, and she sipped at it, her mind focusing when she tasted the wine.

"I know that was difficult. I'm not sure why Jaxon went off script," Chello told her.

Aria looked at him then, and he seemed relieved.

"There you are."

"Thank you, Chell. I'm not sure what happened. It was just...I..." Aria couldn't finish, she closed her eyes and shook her head, trying to clear it. "What an idiot I must have looked like."

"Hardly. I think the only people who were watching you were me, of course, and Mina, of course," he told her.

Aria nodded, relieved. "Of course. Good. Good."

"Are you ok? We can probably leave, I think..."

"No, I'm fine. It was a momentary slip. I'll be perfectly fine," she told him and pushed herself back into character. As she did, a group of others came up to them and began talking about senseless things.

Aria forced herself to engage in conversation, her eyes drifting to Mina whenever she could get away with it. She wasn't sure how much longer she could pretend to be indifferent, because she wasn't. Not even close. The hum of Mina's voice pulsed through her, and all she wanted was to go to her, to demand to know what she was thinking, what she was feeling.

She took a deep breath and nodded at something the woman in front of her said, clutching onto Chello for support.

The night dragged on in the same excruciating rhythm, Aria pretending to stay engaged in conversation, laughter sounding hollow in her ears, while across the room, Mina kept looking at her. Or maybe it just felt like she was. Either way, Aria couldn't stop checking.

As the crowd finally began to thin, Aria caught sight of Mina saying her goodbyes. Her breath caught painfully in her throat. She should go over. Say something. Anything. But what? What could possibly be enough?

She bit the inside of her cheek, anxiety swirling in her chest, as she watched Chello pull Mina into a hug. Her heart hammered against her ribs, every instinct screaming at her to move, to act, to not let this moment slip away.

And then Mina turned.

She was walking straight toward her.

Aria's pulse spiked violently, her whole body locking up. Panic fluttered through her like a trapped bird, and her mind raced ahead, fumbling through half-formed apologies and desperate explanations she hadn't even put into words yet. She could barely breathe. This was it. This was her chance. Mina was coming toward her.

Closer. Closer.

Her lips parted. Her body leaned forward instinctively...

But Mina didn't stop.

Without even a glance, she moved right past her, her shoulder brushing the air between them, like Aria wasn't even there.

Any words or explanations died on her tongue, the surge of hope collapsing in on itself so fast it left her dizzy. She stood there, frozen, the weight of everything she hadn't said crashing down around her.

She clenched her hands into fists at her sides, willing herself not to crumble, not to call out after her like a fool. It was too late. Mina was already gone.

And Aria was left standing alone, swallowing the ache that threatened to tear her apart.

Chello walked up to her, apprehension on his face. "She's leaving you, know."

"I know. I just saw her go. What's wrong with me? I just stood there and watched her leave. Why didn't I do something?"

"No, Aria. I mean, she's *leaving*. For good. She told Jaxon earlier. I thought you might want to know."

Aria heard the words, and they were poison to her soul, seeping in and souring everything they touched. Mina was here and now was leaving. She had wasted her opportunity.

"Are you…ok?" Chello asked, and his brow was furrowed as if he wasn't sure he should have told her.

"When?" Aria huffed out.

"Tomorrow afternoon, I believe. Not sure where she intends to head, but we're going to have breakfast with her in the morning. Maybe you'd like to join us?"

"No. I don't think so," Aria told him. She had a sudden headache and needed to leave, to be alone. "I'll retire for the evening, Chello. Please let Jaxon know, will you?"

"Of course," he told her and didn't bother to ask again if she was ok. She clearly wasn't.

He watched her go, ignoring those who were trying to get her attention. Once she was through the door, he closed his eyes and shook his head, wishing things were different.

Chapter 20

Aria slowly made her way down the path that led to the fountain in her garden, the late morning sun glistening. She saw Mina sitting on the bench and inhaled slowly. She wasn't going to walk away this time. Mina was leaving, and this would be her only opportunity. She walked slowly, hands in her pockets, trying to appear casual. Inside her heart was hammering.

"I see you've infiltrated my special spot," she said cooly, and Mina's head shot up, her eyes wide. Aria tried not to blush, finally being alone with her, and swallowed, controlling her breathing the best she could.

"Aria," Mina responded, standing, her momentary shock giving way. "I guess I did. You can have it back, but you'll have to fight me for it," she joked.

Aria let out a small chuckle and approached where Mina was.

"I doubt that's a fight I'll win, so maybe we can just share the space for a while if you don't mind?"

Mina's surprise was evident on her face, and it made Aria feel worse that she'd been avoiding her. She didn't deserve it, regardless of how necessary she thought it was.

"Of course not," Mina told her, looking slightly uneasy.

Aria smiled and sat on the other end of the bench.

"I asked Chello if I could come sit here for a while," Mina told her, as if she needed justification for being there.

"I know. I asked him where I could find you, and he told me," Aria admitted, and from the side of her eye, she saw Mina look over at her, surprised. "I hear you've decided to leave."

Mina leaned forward, put her elbows on her knees, and nodded. She kept her eyes on the fountain, even though she was dying to turn and look at Aria.

"Yeah, I think it's probably best."

"I thought for sure Jaxon or Chello would have convinced you to stay."

Mina sat back and folded her arms across her chest, her gaze still fixed on the trickling water. After a long pause, she spoke, her voice low and steady. "They tried, and I considered it. But I don't think the Commander wants me here."

The words struck like a blow, sharp and unrelenting, and Aria flinched inwardly at the truth of them. She hadn't realized just how deeply her distance had cut until she heard it spoken aloud. Shame crept up her throat, tightening it, and she dropped her gaze to her hands resting uselessly in her lap. She swallowed hard against the lump forming there, the weight of her own silence pressing down on her. Mina had every reason to feel unwanted, and it was her fault.

"That isn't true," Aria told her weakly.

Mina laughed a little. "Isn't it? Kind of feels like it."

"Mina...I..." Aria started and then stopped, struggling to find words to explain.

"Hey, don't worry about it. A lot's happened. I get it," Mina told her, and there was an inflection at the end of her voice that was full of sorrow.

Aria stood and walked the few steps to the fountain, wishing things didn't have to be so complicated. Why couldn't she just tell Mina what she felt? There was a time when she thought Mina was the only person she *could* tell her feelings to. Why did it have to be so difficult now?

"I'm sorry that I've been...distant. I guess I wasn't sure what you were thinking or...feeling."

"Yeah, I guess my long and inappropriate stares weren't obvious enough."

Aria caught herself smiling and quickly hardened her face. "That mouth of yours is still the same, whatever else has changed," Aria told her, and she turned to look over her shoulder, and Mina was staring at her intensely.

"I'm not sure anything else has changed," Mina told her quietly.

Aria turned from her again, closing her eyes. She could feel herself wanting to give in and was still fighting it. "Don't be ridiculous. Everything has changed."

"Has it?" Mina asked, leaning forward, arms on her knees.

Aria felt something in the air, a hint of the past. When she opened her eyes, tears were pooling, ready to leak over. There was a tightness in her chest as she realized that she would never see Mina again after this, and she deserved the truth if nothing else.

"I'm sorry I've been so cold these last few days. I didn't know how to face you. I still don't," Aria admitted, her voice raw. "I didn't know what to say... how to say I'm sorry."

She looked at her through a sheen of tears, ashamed of her weakness, but too broken to care. "How do you apologize for something that shattered a person's life?" she whispered. "Something so cruel... so unforgivable?"

Her hands trembled as she wiped at her eyes, hating the mess she was, wishing she could be stronger for this. But Mina had already endured too much silence. Aria couldn't stay silent any longer.

"I'm sorry, Mina. For what my father did to you. And I'm sorry that I stopped you from doing what you had every right to do. I should have..." Her voice cracked, and she broke, folding in on herself as sobs tore through her. She covered her face, barely able to breathe. "I should have chosen you. Not him. You. And I'm so sorry I didn't."

Mina was already crying, her chest aching from the sheer weight of it all. The sight of Aria in tears, broken and sobbing, was too much to bear. She crossed the space between them without thinking, her hand reaching for Aria's shoulder, needing to ground her, to hold her together. But the second her hand made contact, Aria jerked away.

"No!" Aria choked out. "I don't deserve your comfort, not after what I did. I don't deserve anything from you."

Mina stood frozen, her heart splintering at the sight of Aria unraveling. "Aria..." she whispered.

"I don't expect forgiveness," Aria continued, voice barely above a whisper. "And I'm sorry it took me this long to say any of this. But I stopped you from doing what mattered most to you, from the justice you fought for, lived for. I got in the way, and I can't ever undo that." She shook her head, tears streaming down her cheeks. "I carry it every day. The guilt. The shame. You have every right to hate me."

They stood there, breathless, the space between them thick with grief, with a year's worth of silence. For a long time, neither spoke. And then, quietly, painfully, Mina did.

"No," she said. "You don't get to carry this alone."

Aria looked up slowly, wiping at her eyes.

"I left you," Mina told her, voice trembling. "I didn't come back when you needed me most. I didn't fight. I didn't stay. I didn't think I could handle it all, your father, the pain of my failure." She swiped angrily at her tears. "You were left alone to deal with a mess that was never yours. And I... I disappeared. I should have come back, Aria. To you. To us."

Her eyes lifted to the sky, as if searching for strength from the God. "I'm sorry, Aria. I am so, so sorry."

Aria was silent, her breath catching in her throat. Mina's words unraveled the guilt she had wrapped around herself like armor. There was no blame. No venom. Just sorrow.

"What your father did isn't your fault," Mina continued, softer now. "You're not responsible for his sins. I never blamed you. I only blamed myself."

Her voice cracked again as she said the thing that scared her most. "I never stopped thinking about you."

Aria blinked, sure she'd misheard. Those words... she'd imagined them being true a thousand times, whispered them to herself in the dead of night like a prayer she didn't believe would ever be answered. But Mina had just said it. She had thought of her. All this time.

Aria felt something in her chest break open, soft and trembling. Maybe she hadn't been so alone after all. Maybe they had both been drowning in the same ocean, just on different shores.

"You... you did?" Aria asked, as if the words were only in her mind, another cruel trick of her imagination.

Mina huffed out a small, broken laugh and turned away, pacing to the bench. "Every damn day. You flowed through my veins, Aria.

I tried to forget. I begged the God to help me forget. But you were *everywhere*. In my memories, in my dreams. You haunted me."

Aria let out a soft, surprised sound, half a breath, half a cry, and stepped forward. She sat beside Mina on the bench, closer than before, their shoulders almost touching.

"I searched for you," Aria said quietly. "For a long time. Every street corner, every crowd. I kept wishing I'd see you. Even after I stopped believing I would, I still looked."

Mina glanced at her and, for the first time in a long time, smiled through her tears.

"I talked to you," Mina confessed, eyes shining. "Out loud, like a crazy person. I imagined what I'd say if I ever saw you again. Actual conversations with your memory."

Aria gave a quiet laugh that was more grief than humor. "I had whole conversations in my head with you, too. Things I'd say if I could go back, if you'd just... appear."

Their smiles faded, but the silence that followed wasn't empty; it was full. Of grief, of healing, of fragile hope. They sat in it together, shoulder to shoulder, the ache of the past pressing against them but no longer separating them. For the first time in a long while, they weren't alone in their sorrow.

They absorbed the silence, each thinking about the other and the fact that while it was painful, they both missed each other profoundly. There was no hate or bitterness towards the other, only towards themselves.

"Where will you go?" Aria finally asked. "Back to the Gores?"

Mina leaned back with a grimace that turned into an unsteady smile. Aria couldn't help but laugh a little, thinking of how horrified she was when Chello told her.

"By the God, no. That was…a defense. I…" Mina ran her hand over her head. "I wanted to forget. I just didn't want to feel anymore."

Aria looked at her and nodded, understanding the notion. She felt the same when she threw herself into her work, never letting a moment lapse without something to occupy her mind.

"When I saw Chello, it was a slap back to reality."

"Yes, he said he was quite surprised when you attacked him…"

"I didn't attack him! He threw the first punch at me!" Mina defended, but her face shifted into a smile when she saw Aria's grin. "He's such a little liar," Mina finished.

Aria laughed. "It's so strange how it came full circle. Of all the mountains, of all the packs of Gores…"

Mina let out a huff. "That's the God, no other way to explain it."

Aria nodded, wanting so much to believe that the God wanted to bring Mina back to her.

Mina grunted a laugh. "I tried to fight it, but when Chell told me what Jaxon was going to try to do, I knew the God put me in their path for a reason. Plus," Mina said, thinking of Chello's words, "What honor was I doing Velho rotting away with a pack of Gores?"

They sat in reflective silence, and then Mina told her in a very deliberate tone, "You should be proud of what you've done here, Commander. Your teams are incredible, and your leadership is just. I felt it the moment I arrived, how the vibe has shifted. No one serves in fear anymore. You've done an amazing job."

Aria smiled, the compliment from Mina meaning more to her than from any other. It was the exact change she was trying so hard to make within her teams.

"Thank you. We have some work to do to bring peace and protection, but we're well on our way. Thanks to you." She paused for a moment, and then she said it. She voiced her hidden desire as if it were a dangerous confession. "I wish you would stay, Mina."

Mina closed her eyes and inhaled the words, wishing it could be that easy. *Stay.* As if it were simple. As if she hadn't spent every day since leaving trying to teach herself how not to want this, how not to want *her.*

Her chest tightened. The longing was there, and she did want it. By the God, she *wanted* it. The sound of Aria's voice, raw with hope, cracked something in her that she'd tried so hard to bury.

For a moment, just a flicker, she saw it: the version of her that stayed. The version that let herself be loved. And it hurt, *achingly so,* because she had spent so long convincing herself that she didn't deserve that kind of peace. The words echoed in her like a promise she wanted to believe but didn't dare reach for. *I wish you would stay.* She felt it settle somewhere deep, warm, and aching.

And it wasn't just about Aria. That was the part she could barely admit aloud. It was Chello, Meesh, Marcus, Jaxon, all of them. They had already become her people without asking for anything in return. They welcomed her without suspicion, trusted her without hesitation. She wasn't an outsider here. Not in their eyes. And somehow, without meaning to, they had made her feel like she was home. Like she belonged.

"I've never felt such a sense of belonging as I do when I'm here, with your people," Mina told her. "They're all so good, such good fecking people. It's like this place...all of you...it's the only safe haven I've known. I really hate to leave it."

"Then don't," Aria told her with a bit too much eagerness, and Mina let her eyes flicker over to her. "There's a place for you here, Mina. Everyone wants you here. They all love and respect you so much."

Mina smiled a wry smile and lifted her eyebrows. "Everyone?"

Aria swallowed and dropped her eyes, afraid to admit what she felt. The conversation had flowed, even with such terrible things acknowledged, and she thought they could make it work, make it beyond the past. Even if Mina didn't feel the same as she once did, they could be friends, at least.

"Yes, you idiot. Everyone," she told her, and looked up at her so she knew she meant it. "I don't want you to go. And I'm sorry for how I've acted. It was a mistake, a dumb defense."

Mina looked at her, saw there was something there, a fleck of the past, and wanted to believe that there was still something deeper between them. She let her eyes drift off, down into the garden, the lush landscape a picture of beauty. She saw Yip jumping around, trying to catch a butterfly in his mouth, and she exhaled loudly.

"I guess you're right," Mina told her. "Everything has changed."

Aria stiffened next to her, the fingers of rejection reaching her insides with coldness.

"Oh," Aria whispered, disappointment dripping off the word.

Mina leaned back and looked at her with a smirk. "I mean, Yip's a dog now. That's a big change," Mina told her and bit back a smile. She felt Aria look at her, and she couldn't hold it; her smile broke through. "That's the only thing that's changed with me, Aria."

Aria stared at her, looking into the hazel eyes that she had dreamed about for the last year. Her gaze dropped to Mina's arm, where the bird tattoo of Yip peeked out from beneath the torn fabric of her sleeve.

"I was so glad when Chello told me Yip was back with you," she said softly, reaching out to lightly touch the bird tattoo.

Mina sucked in her breath, Aria's touch leaving a trail of warmth on her skin.

Aria's fingers lingered on the intricate artwork, moving up her arm and trailing over the four figures that represented Mina's family, just above the bird. But then her hand froze as her eyes caught something unfamiliar above them. She didn't recall anything else being there. Slowly, almost hesitantly, she pushed Mina's sleeve higher. Her breath caught in her throat as she saw the new tattoo.

A pair of eyes, one green, one blue, stared back at her, etched into Mina's skin just above her family.

"What… this…" Aria's voice faltered as confusion and emotion swirled within her. She felt Mina tense beneath her touch. "But this is the arm of your heart, the things that matter the most to you," she whispered, struggling to make sense of what it meant.

Mina turned her head, swallowing hard, tears in her eyes. "Still the most beautiful eyes I've ever seen."

Aria exhaled, her breath shaky, tears in her eyes. Mina had put her eyes on her arm, on her heart. It was a declaration more profound than words, more intimate than anything she could have imagined. The flood of emotion was overwhelming, and her chest tightened with the weight of it. Unable to hold it back, she closed her eyes and leaned her forehead against Mina's arm, tears streaming down her cheeks.

Mina's jaw tightened as she felt Aria lean against her. The place where their skin was touching felt hot, like it was burning with all the emotion inside of them. The urge to pull her into an embrace was almost unbearable, but she remained still. She blinked rapidly, fighting her tears, before letting her truth spill forth, no longer willing to keep it buried.

"I've never stopped loving you, Richy," she whispered. The words escaped her lips like a prayer, a confession, a long-awaited release. She didn't care if Aria said it back; she just needed her to know.

Aria lifted her head, her tear-soaked eyes locking onto Mina's. Disbelief and hope stirred within them. After everything, all the pain and guilt that had stood between them, could there still be the love that they once shared?

She wanted to respond with grace, with some confession of her own, but the weight of the moment shattered her composure. She burst into tears and threw her arms around Mina's neck. She needed her, needed to feel the safety that was Mina.

Mina didn't hesitate. She wrapped Aria in her arms, and Aria moved closer, Mina pulling her into her lap. They clung to each other, tears flowing freely, the pain of the past dissolving in the tightness of their embrace. Guilt, sorrow, and hurt fell away, replaced by a love that had been waiting to be rediscovered, to be acknowledged and fed so it could be free to grow.

"I love you, Mina. I never stopped," Aria sobbed.

Mina hugged her tighter, every broken piece of her mending at the words. She buried her face in Aria's hair, breathing her in, grounding herself in the reality that this wasn't a dream. This was real. Aria was in her arms, not slipping away, not lost to time or regret.

Aria trembled against her, her fingers curling into the fabric of Mina's shirt as if letting go would shatter everything.

"I was so afraid," she whispered. "Afraid I'd lost you forever."

Mina pulled back just enough to cradle Aria's face in her hands, brushing away the tears that streaked her cheeks.

"You never lost me," Mina murmured. "You never could."

A choked laugh broke through Aria's sobs, a fragile, beautiful sound. Mina smiled through her tears, pressing their foreheads together, letting the warmth between them fill the spaces that had once been hollow.

Mina kissed Aria's forehead, a quiet promise of all that was to come. They had been lost, broken, but love, it seemed, had its own vengeance planned—unyielding, patient, waiting for its moment to strike. And they sat together, wrapped in the quiet triumph of it, reveling in the vengeance of their love.

Five Months Later

Yip lay on the side wall of the stage, where the sun cut through the buildings and left a warm swath. His fur absorbed the golden heat as he stretched luxuriously, his tail thumping lazily against the stone.

From his vantage point, he could see the gathered crowd, a sea of faces brimming with joy and hope. Today, the people of the city came together to celebrate the activation of the city defense perimeter and the truce with Greensk. It was a happy day, and Yip felt happy, too. Mostly, though, it was because of his new collar. The green collar came with a shiny tag that glinted in the sunlight, proudly bearing his name. It made him feel like he belonged, and he loved that.

The blare of trumpets startled him from his thoughts, and the crowd erupted into cheers. Rows of guards in green and gold dress uniforms streamed onto the stage, their polished boots glinting as they took their places. Yip lifted his head, his ears pricking as the Governor stepped forward to begin his speech.

The Governor's voice boomed across the square, but Yip only half-listened. A fly buzzed too close to his head, and he snapped at it with a sharp click of his teeth, missing it entirely. He huffed in mild irritation but quickly forgot about the fly when the Governor's tone shifted. He was introducing the key members of the city's security force. Yip's tail thumped against the stone as he stood, ears forward, ready to see his humans.

"Please welcome the people responsible for the safety of the city! The Commander of City Security, Aria Peterman, and her Praector, Chello!"

The crowd roared, and Yip let out a bark of excitement, his tail wagging furiously. Chello, standing proudly beside Aria, glanced over at him and smiled. Yip's bark turned into a happy yip, and he wagged even harder.

"Please welcome the Head of Security Engineering, Jaxon Peterman, along with his Praector, Marcus!"

Yip whined softly in approval, his eyes scanning the crowd to see if anyone was noticing his shiny new collar. He sat up straighter, puffing out his chest slightly. Surely, someone had to notice how important he looked today.

"And now, please welcome the Head of Strategic Defense, Mina Peterman, and her Praector, Meesh!"

This time, Yip couldn't contain himself. He let out a raucous bark that quickly turned into a joyous howl. Mina heard him and turned her head, smiling at him radiantly. Yip looked back at her and saw the happiness in her eyes. They were shining bright, one green and one hazel. Yip's tail whipped back and forth like a banner in the wind, and he hopped up and down on his front paws, his collar and tag jingling their own happy tune.

At that moment, Yip felt it all, and he howled up his thanks to the God. He felt so proud of Mina, and he felt such gratitude for the safety of the city. Most of all, Yip felt an overwhelming sense of belonging. This was his pack, his family, and his city. And with his name shining brightly on his tag, he knew he was precisely where he was meant to be.

Five months prior

The med and tech-no team finished the surgery, closing the shoulder of the woman with the strange bite. On the cart next to them sat a jar with the odd mucus membrane, a bright green of something they had never seen before. It was remarkable that they were able to remove it, the way the dense, phlegmy substance seemed to be trying to attach itself to the patient.

"All set from a med perspective. I think she will heal now that it's out of her," the doctor told the tech-no aide. "Not sure if you want this crap," he said, picking up the jar.

The tech-no aide shrugged and took the jar in his hand, holding it up to eye level.

"I don't want this anywhere near me. This isn't tech, this is something else. But I'll run it by Raven to see if she wants to examine it."

The tech-no aide left the med center and walked into the tech-no lab, looking for Raven, the head of Innovation and Experimentation. She was hunched over a microscope, her dark, graying hair pulled back in a bun on her head.

"Raven, I have something here that we pulled out of a patient just back from the Vanguard Ascension in the Levite mines. Do you want to see it, or should I incinerate it?" he asked, and Raven sat up and spun around on her stool.

"The Levite mines?" she asked incredulously, and her wrinkled face furrowed. "Impossible."

"Well, the lady we pulled it from said she was bitten by some creature in there. And the med team and I just pulled it out of her shoulder. It's some sort of membrane that tried to embed in her tissue, but her blood prevented it. Very strange."

Raven came over and took the jar from him, examining the strange substance. It was unheard of that anything went into the mines and lived, and while she wasn't a proponent of human experimentation, this was something she couldn't pass up.

"Get this down to Prison Tech-no Operations. Tell them to *carefully* inject this into one of the prisoners, one who seems the most likely to survive whatever mutation this is. Someone strong, not some waif who's already half dead."

"Sure thing, I'll take it down right now," he told her, and she nodded.

The aide brought the jar to the bowels of the prison basement, to the Tech-no Ops team, and relayed the message.

"Will do. I have just the prisoner. Tell her it will be prisoner 1SM820. Greyson Murlock. I'll get it injected into him right away and put him in an observation cell."

The aide nodded and left, not liking the smell at the bottom of the prison. It was disgusting, a combination of sweat, blood and stale piss. He scurried off, hoping never to return.

The End...

Acknowledgments

Writing a novel is never a solitary journey, no matter how many late nights it takes. I owe a debt of gratitude to the people and places that helped bring *The Vengeance of Love* to life.

To the **Stockholm Writers Festival**—thank you for creating a space where creativity is nurtured and courage is born. Attending your festival gave me the spark of belief I didn't know I needed, and the push to move from dreaming to doing. You truly are the friendliest festival in the world.

To every **friend and family member** who liked, shared, commented, and supported me in big ways and small—thank you. Your encouragement carried me through every step. I may have written this book alone, but I never felt alone doing it.

To the **city of Oslo, Norway**—thank you for being an unexpected wellspring of creativity. I can't quite explain it, but something about your atmosphere made the words flow more freely. That time and space left their mark on this story in ways I'll always be grateful for.

I wouldn't have found the strength to publish this story without all of you cheering me on. This book is as much yours as it is mine.

I am forever grateful.

LoriO

About The Author

LoriO grew up on the East Coast and now lives in the Midwest. She writes emotionally driven stories with sharp edges, stories woven with strong bonds, grace, and the kind of love that sneaks up on you. Often sapphic, emotional, and spiritual, she believes in the power of story to heal, challenge, and reveal.

She is also most likely judging your coffee order.

For updates and info, visit www.lorioauthor.com or @lorio_author on Instagram.

Coming Soon
Book Two of *The Blood of Velho* Series
The Fall of Velho

Before vengeance shaped her. Before loss hardened her.

Mina lived in Velho, a city blessed by the God.

The Fall of Velho returns to that scorched corner of the Sphere,
a place of secret power, quiet abilities, and a peaceful people.

See the city where Mina grew up.

Where secrets festered.

Where choices were made that would tear everything apart.

Mina. Yip. Jack Peterman.

Their connection began long before Fusia.

The truth lies buried in ash.

And the fall changes everything.